PRAISE FOR *JAY'S GAY AGENDA*

"Jason June, please feel free to check 'conquering my heart' off your agenda, because I'm so in love with this book, it's ridiculous. *Jay's Gay Agenda* is funny, sincerely romantic, and infused with love from start to finish, starring a vividly drawn cast of characters who don't even try to play it cool. I'm beyond charmed."

—**BECKY ALBERTALLI,** *New York Times* bestselling
author of *Simon vs. the Homo Sapiens Agenda*

"Jay's journey to finding his place in the world warmed my small-town heart."

—**MASON DEAVER,** award-winning author of *The
Ghosts We Keep* and *I Wish You All the Best*

"Brave, hopeful, and absolutely packed with joy, *Jay's Gay Agenda* crosses every item off my list. I can't wait for readers to fall in love with this powerful and heartwarming coming-of-age story."

—**PHIL STAMPER,** bestselling author of *The
Gravity of Us* and *As Far As You'll Take Me*

"Fantastically hilarious and profoundly sincere, *Jay's Gay Agenda* is a can't-miss debut. Jason June pens a flawless letter to queer teens, a reminder that they are worthy of messy friendships, clumsy firsts, complicated feelings, and cinematic happy endings like anyone else. This book sparkles from start to finish."

—**JULIAN WINTERS,** award-winning author of *Running with Lions*

"*Jay's Gay Agenda* is exactly the kind of funny, upbeat, queer coming-of-age story readers crave. Full of laughs, heartbreak, fun, and tenderness, this story is an ode to first loves, friendships, and learning to embrace yourself exactly as you are because as Jay comes to understand, who you are is exactly enough."

—**KALYNN BAYRON,** bestselling author of *Cinderella Is Dead*

"*Jay's Gay Agenda* is the literal definition of a romp: It's funny, sexy, sweet, and swoony in all the best ways and somehow still manages to capture the delicious, disastrous, and overwhelming chaos and delight of suddenly getting caught up in a world of possibilities when there were none before. Honest and hilarious, this book should be on everyone's to-read list."

—**L. C. ROSEN,** author of *Camp* and *Jack of Hearts (and Other Parts)*

"*Jay's Gay Agenda* is the charming, funny, sex-positive book I wish I had read growing up. Jason June does an incredible job of exploring messy teen relationships through Jay, a charming and deeply flawed protagonist. Painfully relatable and laugh-out-loud funny, *Jay's Gay Agenda* is the teen rom-com of your dreams."

—**AIDEN THOMAS,** author of the *New York Times* bestseller *Cemetery Boys*

"*Jay's Gay Agenda* is a delightful and emotional exploration of what it means to focus so much on checking things off a list that you forget yourself along the way. Every character is complicated, messy, and lovable, and it should be on EVERYONE'S agenda to grab a copy of this wonderful book!"

—**RONNI DAVIS,** author of *When the Stars Lead to You*

"What an absolute delight of a debut! Relatable, hilarious, messy, earnest, and heartfelt, just the way the best coming-of-age stories are. *Jay's Gay Agenda* tackles friendship, first love, and ~feelings~ so masterfully that readers will come back to read it time and time again."

—**EMMA LORD,** author of *Tweet Cute*

Jason June

An Imprint of HarperCollinsPublishers

HarperTeen is an imprint of HarperCollins Publishers.

Jay's Gay Agenda
Copyright © 2021 by Jason June
All rights reserved. Printed in the United States of America.
No part of this book may be used or reproduced in any
manner whatsoever without written permission except in
the case of brief quotations embodied in critical articles and
reviews. For information address HarperCollins Children's
Books, a division of HarperCollins Publishers,
195 Broadway, New York, NY 10007.
www.epicreads.com

ISBN 978-0-06-301515-9

Typography by
21 22 23 24 25   PC/LSCH   10 9 8 7 6 5 4 3 2 1

First Edition

To Jerry, for making me a part of your
agenda, and being a part of mine.

0.
✔ Start a Gay Agenda

I'm not exactly sure what the stats are on people realizing they're gay because of pop stars, but for me it was 100 percent. It was the summer before ninth grade, when my best friend Lu's aunt Carol took us to a Shawn Mendes concert in Portland. Seeing Shawn gyrating onstage with a light blue guitar strapped across his shoulder did something to my heart and my . . . *down there* . . . that couldn't be denied. It was like a superpowered magnet was pulling me toward Shawn and nowhere else. I was surrounded by literally thousands of girls, and not a single one of them would have been able to grab my attention. Not even Lu. I finally knew what Shawn meant about being in stitches without someone's kisses, and I screamed just as loud as anyone else in that stadium for kisses from another boy.

I mean, there had been moments before when I'd wondered. Like when I got that twist in my gut every time Derrick, the cute cashier at the Riverton Diner, smiled at me, or when my nether regions twitched when Dad and I watched football players line up in seriously tight pants during *Monday Night Football*. I should have known *way* sooner that I was gay considering I still have no idea how football actually works. But for whatever reason, it was at that concert, looking at Shawn, that something in me unlocked, and I *for sure* for sure knew. It was the most clarity I'd ever had on something in my entire life.

That night during the car ride home, I couldn't stop thinking about what it would be like for Shawn to throw that guitar from his body and wrap me in his arms.

When we crossed the border from Oregon back into Washington, my pop-star-fantasy-filled silence was finally noticed.

"You okay, Jay?" Lu asked. "You're really quiet."

"Yeah, no, I'm totally okay," I said. My heart raced. I was about to say something out loud that I'd never said before. "I like boys."

"Who wouldn't after a show like that?" Aunt Carol said, the glitter on her homemade concert shirt catching my eye in the rearview mirror.

"No, I mean." I cleared my throat. "I'm gay."

Lu squeezed my hand from her spot next to me in the back seat. "We knew what you meant. We love you, whether you like boys, girls, or any other human."

"I love you too," I whispered, a little stunned at coming

out, a little shocked at how quickly the convo turned to me going on the next girls' shopping trip, and immensely relieved that there wasn't any backlash over my sexuality.

The whole thing was very anticlimactic.

Soon after, I made a list—my preferred method of organization—of everybody else I needed to come out to.

COME OUT TO CREW

1. Mom (will take it the easiest and probably buy rainbow shirts for the whole family)

2. Grandma and Grandpa (Gpa might not get it, but Gma will insist she just wants me to be happy)

3. The entire school (could result in pitchfork-wielding protests in front of our log cabin)

4. Dad (huge unknown—can't tell if his strong silent type is toxically masculine or open and accepting)

Mom and my grandparents went exactly as expected, while nobody at Riverton High seemed surprised. They were like, "He loves to talk about the makeup artistry of the contestants on *RuPaul's Drag Race*; *of course* he's gay." It felt weird that my classmates boxed me into a stereotype, but their assessment was correct, technically. At least they were cool with me, even though our school was in a farming community and about half the kids were Mormon, another 45 percent some type of ProteBaptatholic (short for Protestant, Baptist, and Catholic; there are so many church groups at Riverton, it's hard to keep up), and the remaining 5 percent of us were just like, *Um, hi, I don't know what makes this world tick, but I don't think it's a magical being in the sky.*

There *was* this one instance when Greg Ratford came up to me at my locker and said, "I don't believe in your lifestyle, and I just wanted you to know." I told Lu, and she instantly shrugged it off, saying, "The Rat is an asshole," and everyone working in the journalism lab with her agreed. So we were all on the same page that the Rat was a jerk and I could go on being me. That was the biggest extent of any school drama. I mean, we'd all been going to Riverton since kindergarten and had gotten to know each other pretty well since we were only a class of seventy-seven students. Even if nobody threw a Pride parade in my honor, I guess my classmates felt like I was part of the family, and coming out didn't change that.

The most nerve-racking part was telling Dad. We were in the living room of our tiny log cabin, Dad watching *Monday Night Football* while I went through the most recent pictures posted on Instagram under #instagay. Normally that would keep me very *at attention* due to all the muscly guys in Speedos or posting gym selfies. But I wasn't paying attention to what I was liking. Instead, I was going back and forth about when the best time to come out to Dad would be. Was it better to tell him during a commercial break? No, that's when he went to the bathroom. Yelling this news through the door while Dad sat on the toilet didn't feel like the right moment for revealing my sexuality. Maybe I could tell him during halftime, but would he really be paying attention if he was as distracted by cheerleaders as I was by football players in tight pants?

Even though I had already told so many other people, I was worried about Dad the most. He's the most stereotypical "guy": he loves football, he fixes cars for a living, he even built our home with his own bare hands. I didn't want to be the kind of person who assumed the worst, but I'd read so many horror stories online about kids getting dumped by their hypermasculine fathers. Even though I was pretty sure Dad wouldn't do that to me, there was still a tiny seed of doubt.

Without thinking, I let out a huge sigh. Dad turned down the volume on the game and asked, "Something wrong, Jay?"

That had to be a sign from some deity (or Michelle Obama or whoever brings all of humanity together) and as good a lead-in as any to spill the rainbow-colored beans. "I was just stressing about how to tell you that . . . I'm gay."

Dad didn't skip a beat. "I knew it." He said it with such matter-of-fact certainty that I was a little offended he hadn't brought it up earlier. "Now's a good time to talk about safe sex. Just because you can't get a girl pregnant doesn't mean you can't get an STD."

I buried my face in one of Mom's hideous floral throw pillows. "Ew, Dad, gross!"

"Gross is chlamydia. Which is entirely preventable." He got up, grabbed a banana, and proceeded to walk me through how to put on a condom.

So, it turns out I really had nothing at all to worry about in my coming-out journey. Except for the fact that

I was all alone. Well, I was surrounded by people, but they were all straight. I got a lot of attention for being *the* gay kid, but pointing out how I was different just made me feel that much more lonely. Not one other person at RHS, in *all four grades*, came out after I did freshman year. At first, I thought that maybe my coming out would give other people the courage to do so too. I was certain in no time I would be the president of the GSA and have the perfect boyfriend. We'd have movie marathons on the weekends where he'd wrap me up in his arms, which were larger than average due to all the time he spent playing football.

After a whole semester of freshman year with nobody else coming out and my poster of KJ Apa being the closest thing I had to a boyfriend, I googled statistics about the queer community. I found out that 75 percent of queer youth say their communities accept them, and the US Census Bureau named Provincetown, Massachusetts, the gayest city in America. But since I don't live in Massachusetts, what grabbed my attention was a Gallup poll that said 4.1 percent of the adult population identified as LGBTQ. While we weren't quite adults yet, that would mean that out of the seventy-seven students in my class, at least three of us should be queer. But I was the only one.

I figured I would just have to let it go, but *then* another study said 8 percent of all high school students in America identified as LGBTQ. WTFrack? (Growing up in a heavily religious community has given me a habit of avoiding the word *fuck* that I can't shake.) That meant that *at least* six kids in my grade alone should be siblings in pride, and that in our whole school of 260 kids, twenty should be waving a rainbow flag with me (and that's rounding down from 20.8, because how can you have .8 of a person? Maybe Greg Ratford is .8 of a person because he doesn't have a heart). Statistically speaking, *twenty* kids should be queer in school, and I was the only out one?

The odds weren't ever in my favor.

There's an LGBTQ group in Spokane, the closest city to Riverton, Washington, but it's an hour-and-a-half drive away, and the logistics of working out how to get back and forth with no car were too much. There wasn't even anyone out at our rival high school, Deer Park, which was just thirty minutes away. So I was left as the sole out gay boy in a hundred-mile radius. I spent a lot of time bingeing queer culture like *RuPaul's Drag Race* and *Real Housewives* and talking about it with other gays online, but all the episodes of *Catfish* I watched warned me against trying to meet them IRL. I will admit, I downloaded the Grindr app once and lied about my age just to see if anyone around was secretly out on the internet. The only person I found was someone who looked suspiciously like Jebediah Smith. He ran the only gas station in Riverton and I swear was always eating fried gizzards when I went in to grab a Diet Dr Pepper. There was no way I could ever kiss a guy with gizzard breath, let alone one who was forty years older than me.

It blew my mind that I had never, not once come into contact with another out gay guy. Or a lesbian. Or someone bisexual, or trans, or on the queer spectrum at all. Where were all the people who allegedly identified as LGBTQ?

In trying to keep up the hope that I would organically meet another gay someday, I became a little obsessed with statistics and weird facts about things that happened against all odds. I kept a running list of my favorites, like a lady who's been struck by lightning four times, or a man who got stranded at sea twice in one day, rescued both times, but lost his camera in the second attempt only to have it wash ashore with his pictures intact *four years later*. These things should never, ever have happened. The deeper I dug, the more I was convinced if all this other stuff could happen, I'd have to meet a gay guy, statistically speaking.

All that time researching stats online about the queer community led me to a lot of sites explaining the history of the gay rights movement. A ton of articles talked about the Gay Agenda—a slogan people against the queer community reference, as if all nonheterosexuals have some master plan to take over the world. As I waited and waited for somebody else to come out, and all my straight friends had relationship milestones like losing their virginity one by one, I made an ongoing list of all the stuff I wanted to do once I finally came into contact with another gay. *My Gay Agenda.*

JAY'S GAY AGENDA

1. Meet another gay kid. Somewhere, anywhere . . . please!

2. Go on a date with a boy and hold hands within the first ninety minutes.

3. Go to a dance with a boy and have my first kiss slow dancing to Shawn Mendes.

4. Have a boyfriend, one who likes to wrap me up in his arms and let me be little spoon.

5. Fall in love with a boy, but wait for him to say it first so I don't seem too desperate.

6. Make out, with tongue, and hard enough that I'd get a little burn from his stubble.

7. See another penis besides my own, IRL, and do fun things with it!

8. Lose. My. Virginity!

As you can see, the first items were from my sweet, innocent freshman mind: hand-holding, going on a date, maybe even—GASP!—a first kiss during a slow dance. But then my hormones became a hurricane raging inside me, and everyone else in my class became a permanent resident of SexTown. There was constant talk from the girls about stubble rashes and when to say the L-word or how to give blow jobs without teeth, so the ideas for what could happen when I met this fantasy gay became a little more . . . intimate.

Heading into my senior year, not a single item had been crossed off that list. Almost eighteen whole years on this planet, and I'd never even had a first kiss.

But my odds were about to change.

1.
✓ Get Insulted by Your BFF

Burger grease isn't exactly an exceptionally inspiring smell, but it would have to do. Riverton Diner was the only place to meet in my little country hometown, and Lu had just gotten off her shift. Besides, fast-food smell was the least of my problems: I needed to find someone who I could actually date so I wouldn't be the Forever Third Wheel to Lu and her ever-present tumor—I mean boyfriend—Chip. They both sat across from me in our red-and-white booth while we chewed cheeseburgers and guessed gays.

"What about Ian Rukowski?" Lu asked. "Clara says he told her he's going to sign up to audition for the fall play. He's *never* been in a play before. Why the sudden interest?"

"You can't be serious," I said. "Just because somebody likes theater doesn't make them gay."

I'd had this conversation a lot in Riverton. Just because a preponderance of gay people like things like theater or *Real Housewives* doesn't mean every single gay person is a fan of them. But, because I watched all those things so I could be a part of the queer community online, my point usually got brushed away.

"Well, *he* likes theater and *he's* gay," Chip said, stabbing a french fry in my direction with each *he* for emphasis.

"*He* is sitting right here," I said. That's the problem with the phrase *third wheel*. It's not like you're all three equally noticed and needed and rolling along on the ground, like a tricycle. Third Wheels are really Spare Tires. Only pulled out of some forgotten compartment in the trunk of your car when another tire decides you get to see the light of day.

"Jay is totally right." Silver stars flashed on top of neon-green nails as Lu threw up her manicured hands. "I'm just grasping at straws and fell back on a tired trope."

"Why is it tired?" Chip asked. "All I'm saying is sometimes there's truth to a stereotype. It doesn't make it *bad*; it just makes it a statement of fact."

I face-palmed, my hand hitting my forehead with just enough impact to make my swooped bangs whoosh with dramatic yet cute effect. Too bad my signature move was entirely wasted on oblivious Chip.

"Okay, look." I pumped the straw in my Diet Dr Pepper. The same *eee er eee er* sound would probably be made if I pumped it through Chip's ear and into his brainless head. "Sure, sometimes stereotypes can have a tiny bit of truth. Do I have a ton of Miley Cyrus in my *Drown Out the Bus* playlist? Yes. Have I listened to a lot more Miley than most straight members of the football team? Judging by their bonfire playlists, also yes. But gay people are just as varied as straight people. There are straight guys who love Miley Cyrus and gay guys who love . . ."

Crap. Think, Jay, think. Selena? No. Demi? No. Britney? Dammit!

Chip's lips pinched into a satisfied smirk. "You can't think of any singer who's not a former Disney star, can you?"

I shook my head, cursing Chip's smug grin while he waved his french fry like a magic wand.

"All I'm saying is," Chip continued, "maybe wave that gaydar over Ryan and see if anything beeps."

"Ian," Lu and I said together.

Lu grabbed Chip's hand and laced their fingers. Her ivory skin made his perfect golden tan stand out, giving me yet another reason to curse him. My whole body ached with lobster-red sunburn. I was failing in my summer goal to turn my white, vampire-worthy paleness into a bronze beach body.

"Hey, baby," Lu crooned to Chip, and I instantly cringed. Isn't the whole point of dating getting to use your very unbabyish bodies in super-not-G-rated activities? "I know you're just trying to help, but I think we got this covered."

I still didn't understand how my best friend could date somebody so . . . well, ignorant. Especially when she couldn't stand the outdated chatter of some of the old ladies who visit Tough as Nails (or TAN for short), the nail salon where her aunt works. Lu always talked about how Esther Anderson said her granddaughter was *finally* getting married just before she turned into an "old maid" at twenty-four, or how Ruth Mortimer thinks it's "uncouth" for women to wear tank tops. Lu, meanwhile, uncovered the gender pay gap for our district's bus drivers in an article for the school paper. And she volunteered to help get the first female president elected to our school board. Yet here she was, dating Chip, who said things like "wave that gaydar" and probably couldn't spell *feminism* if he tried.

I tried not to blame Lu. Everybody in our grade paired up with someone for the summer, and the matches weren't always expected. I knew as well as anybody you can't help who you're attracted to. I just wished I could find somebody who was attracted to *me* so I wouldn't have to be the Forever Spare Tire.

"Anyway," I said, "while I do appreciate a good theatrical performance, I don't want to be onstage or anything. Besides, I'm only one data point of gays who like theater. And Mr. Frederickson always says you can't establish a trend with just one data point."

Lu rolled her eyes. "Do not go all statistics on us."

"But it's true!" I said. "If you could tell me the sexuality of the majority of the guys in every theater production ever put on by a high school drama department, *then* we'd have enough data for a trend. You don't know a lot of guys in theater, do you, Chip? But I know that Bruce Miller, Dalton Preston, Johnny Hayes, and Shawn Shapiro are all in drama, and they're straight. And I know the most important detail: who's auditioning for the lead role in *Annie Get Your Gun*."

"Who?" Lu asked. She drummed her nails against the table. She always does that when someone has information she doesn't know but really wants. It's her tell—the way I know she's interested even if she sometimes acts above high school gossip since Chip goes to Spokane Community College.

"Alicia Thomas," I said. "You know Ian's had a crush on her since sixth grade. Clearly he's trying to get closer to her by auditioning for the show."

I could read Lu like a book. Her oval face was so expressive, her flaming-red hair practically changed shades with her emotions, and she always displayed her moods with new nail art. Normally, it was something I loved most about her, how transparent she was. But this time, when her whole body slumped, it felt wrong. She shouldn't have this dramatic of a reaction to Ian pining after Alicia.

"Well, this is just great," Lu said. "Where are we going to find you a date for the Blue Bluff Hoedown now?"

"What do you mean?" I asked. "We always go to the hoedown together."

"Yeah," Lu mumbled. Her nail clacking picked right back up. *Clickclickclickclickclick. Clickclickclickclickclick.* She also does that when she's anxious.

Chip chomped on his last bite of cheeseburger, his eyes darting between us. He was normally so cool, calm, and smugly collected. Now the nervousness radiating off him was so thick, I could chew on it like he did to that Belly Buster.

"I think I'll let you two handle this alone," Chip said. "Talk to you later, babe." He pecked Lu on the cheek, his mouth still full, and got out of there faster than you can say *awkward moment*.

"Lu?"

Lu wouldn't take her eyes off the greasy basket of fries between us. "It's just that Chip wants to take me to the hoedown this year, and I . . ." No matter how hard I tried I couldn't get her to look me in the eye. "I want to go with him too." *Clickclickclickclickclick.*

Images of our past epic hoedown costumes flashed before my eyes.

HOEDOWN HIGHLIGHTS

1. An electrical outlet and phone charger for the Power Couples theme. (Complete with a Lite-Brite thunderbolt that would light up any time Lu plugged into me.)

2. Netflix and Chill for Perfect Pairs. (I wore a cardboard computer screen with a scene of the Netflix homepage while Lu went as that ice princess from Frozen. She could even step into my costume and would spontaneously burst into "Let It Go.")

3. Peanut butter and jelly for Inseparable. (In which we wore giant foam toast costumes that people could spread brown and purple paint all over.)

In Riverton, the Blue Bluff Hoedown and couples' costume contest is bigger than Halloween, homecoming, prom, and all other holidays combined. People go all out, dressing their best, downing Blue Bluff Orchard's world-famous apple cider, and dancing to twangy yet catchy country music all night long. Lu and I had won the award for Best Costume—and the thousand-dollar cash prize that came with it—three years in a row. The theme for this year's hoedown would be announced just after school started, and then we were going to plan the frack out of our outfits to make sure our winning streak went unbroken. I already had a page decked out in my notebook labeled *COMPLETE COSTUME DOMINATION* for upcoming ideas to list.

I should have seen this coming. Lu'd fallen for Chip hard and fast, canceling so many of our summer traditions just to have *alone time* with her boyfriend. We hadn't once gone to Silverwood Theme Park in Idaho to ride roller coasters like we had every summer; she made Pig Out in the Park a date night with Chip, leaving me to wander the hundreds of food vendors alone; and she bailed on Hoop-fest, where we ogled athletes, so she could see Chip play guitar at the same café he played in three times a week. The hoedown was the one tradition I thought she wouldn't mess with for a guy she'd known for only a month and a half. It was *our* thing.

"It's our senior year." I could barely choke out the words. "We're supposed to finish out high school with one more couples' costume. The one to rule them all."

"Just because I'm obsessed with the movies doesn't mean a *Lord of the Rings* reference is going to change my mind." Lu knew me too well. "You're just making this harder." *Clickclickclickclickclick.* "I'm going with Chip. Now that college—"

"Community college," I snapped.

"Don't be a jerk." Lu wagged a fry at me just like Chip had. Gawd, they were *that* couple who adopted each other's mannerisms. "Now that *college* has started back up for Chip, I hardly get to see him anymore. With classes and studying he can't drive out here as much as he did before, and you know I can't drive to him because"—her voice dropped, and she looked over her shoulder to make sure no one was listening—"because Carol sold our car."

I sucked in a breath. Here's a sad stat: half of all people in Riverton lived below the poverty line, and Lu was one of them. A new nail salon opened up in Deer Park last year that was modern, always had available chairs and technicians, and offered champagne or espresso with their services. All the RHS kids went there. Aunt Carol tried to get the TAN owner, Leslie Lovett, to update, but she was in her seventies and wasn't up for the challenge. This left the old ladies at Riverton Trailer Community as the salon's main clientele. As morbid as it sounds, they were getting older and dying, bringing Tough as Nails closer to death with them. The past year was especially slow, and Leslie had cut the store hours by half, meaning Aunt Carol's wages were cut in half too. She'd had to sell their car just the week before to pay rent on their single-wide trailer.

Whenever Lu brought it up it made my gut bubble with worry, but she refused to let me ask how she was doing.

"It's really important to me that Chip is my date to the hoedown," Lu said. "I know having him around has switched up our routine, but Chip has helped take my mind off all the shit that's going down for Aunt Carol and me. Honestly, that prize money for the costume contest could help us out. But just because Chip is going doesn't mean that you and I can't still plan a costume together that will kick ass. It's just that Chip and I will be wearing it. If the rules allowed for a three-person costume, you know I would be all for that, but they don't. Plus, since I was the one with all the romance this summer, maybe my love luck will rub off and I'll be able to find you a date. That way, when I want to do-si-do with Chip, you're not left out."

The bubbles in my gut went from worried to pissed in .2 seconds. Lu wasn't just Spare Tire–ing me. She was slamming the trunk so hard I'd never be found again. And shoving it in my face that she'd had all these relationship milestones while I hadn't. Who did she think she was, say-ing that *she* would find me a date?

"Oh, because you finding your first boyfriend six weeks ago makes you some kind of expert?" Although, TBH, she kind of was an expert. Chip was technically her first boyfriend, but Lu had dated a lot of people and had her first kiss when we were in sixth grade. But that didn't mean she got to imply the reason I had never been with another guy was my fault. "I can find a date on my own, thank you very much."

Lu's eyes went so wide I could see the harsh fluorescent lights reflected in them. "No, Jay, I didn't mean it like that."

"You know what?" I stood up so fast I got light-headed, spots creeping in at the corners of my vision. "You and Chip have a nice time."

I burst out of the diner. In that moment, I understood why so many people stormed off set during reality TV reunion specials.

It felt good.

2.

✓ Win the Gay Lottery

My phone buzzed with texts from Lu as soon as I got home.

OF COURSE you can find a man on your own.

I didn't mean it like that.

Really, I'm so sorry.

Meet me at the salon? I've got a pedicure with your

name on it.

I could practically hear her nails drumming against the TAN front desk. Leslie gives Lu and Aunt Carol a 50 percent friends-and-family discount, and Lu knows how much I love a good pedicure with my nails shined and buffed. But I wasn't in the mood to let her off so easily (and even though I was pissed, I wouldn't let her pay for my own pedicure when money was so tight). I needed time to adjust to the idea that we weren't going to the hoedown together. I could still go, but even if I did end up finding a date against all odds, why would Chip even want to go to the hoedown to begin with? It didn't make any sense. He always thought he was too cool for school, never laughing at any of our jokes or appreciating anything that remotely smelled of fitting in. He only ever wore black, he only ever watched documentary films, and he constantly berated me for drinking Diet Dr Pepper.

I let out a sigh so huge my bangs moved.

"Something you need to tell me?" Dad asked.

"What the frack!" I jumped hard enough to send my backpack flying from my shoulder.

"Didn't mean to scare you. But last time you sighed that big, you came out." Dad got up from his recliner in the living room and walked the two steps into the kitchen to grab a beer from the refrigerator. Dad built our tiny log home, and he's "got the calluses to prove it," as he always tells anyone who asks. He's such a hands-on kind of guy. His dream was always to live in a log home in the country because "nothing can clean the mind better than clean air." It is pretty out here, but the uninterrupted sea of trees out our living room window has turned from pretty to depressing. I recently learned that trees can flourish on six out of seven continents (sorry, Antarctica), yet not even one other boy who likes to kiss boys can grow anywhere on this side of the state.

"What are you doing home?" I asked. It was only three fifteen. Dad usually didn't get off work from Riverton

Motor Repair until five thirty.

Dad cracked open his Bud Light. "I quit my job today." He took a few gulps, then went back to his recliner and nonchalantly pulled the handle so the footrest sprang up. Then he turned on *SportsCenter*, continuing to act like he hadn't just dropped a huge bomb. Was this what a midlife crisis looked like? He seemed pretty content for a guy who no longer had a job.

"Are—are you okay?" I sat down on the love seat, the only other piece of furniture that could fit in the tiny living room besides the recliner.

"Yup." Dad could be a man of infuriatingly few words.

"Are you having a nervous breakdown? You're not about to go streaking through the woods like Larry Gottlieb did on his alpaca farm, are you?"

Dad just gave me his pointed look that said, *What do you think?*

I threw my hands up. "What? You're not telling me anything, so I can only assume the worst."

Dad took another swallow of beer. His Adam's apple bobbed up and down as he glued his eyes to the TV. And his eyelids didn't budge one bit as he avoided my gaze.

I grabbed the remote and hit Mute. "What is it? What aren't you telling me?"

"Son, if you don't want to be grounded for the rest of senior year, you'll give me that remote back right now." Dad held out his hand, palm up.

"Fine." I caved and gave back the remote. "But what's going on?"

"Your mother will tell you when she gets home, Jay-bird. Quit chirping."

"You know, I wouldn't have to be *chirping* so much if you would just answer my question."

Dad turned up the volume on the TV, the sportscasters' voices blaring through the cabin. "Everything is all right. Let me enjoy my early retirement."

My fingers itched to text Lu and tell her my dad was officially losing it. But I didn't want to forgive her just yet. And it would only make me even more mad at her if I called and she didn't pick up because she was busy with that friend-stealing douche. It only hit home the fact that I was alone. I didn't have a boyfriend to rely on, or a best friend to share all my worries with, because she was spending time with *her* boyfriend.

All I could do was march the four steps down the hall into my room and try to fool around on our outrageously slow country internet. But I couldn't focus on my laptop with how angry I was at Lu, how confused I was by Dad, and how annoyed I was by the sounds of ESPN. Dad may have built our house, but he left little pockets in between the logs, so you could hear everything happening in any part of the house at all times. It meant I had to watch every PornTube clip with no sound, so while I can imagine sex clearly, I'm still not sure what kind of noises you're supposed to make.

While Dad sat back and enjoyed football, I spent three torturous hours obsessing over what could possibly be going on.

DAD'S BREAKDOWN BEGAN BECAUSE . . .

1. He got fired and is too hurt or manly or something to admit it.

2. He is having a stroke and I should immediately call 9-1-1.

3. Body-snatchers are real and Dad has been replaced by some alien villain.

4. We won the lottery, so Dad doesn't need to work anymore, but he doesn't want to tell me so that I don't become some entitled trust-fund kid.

5. Oh gawd, Mom and Dad are getting divorced and Dad is slowly slipping into beer-soaked despair.

I finally heard Mom come in through the front door, so I raced into the living room. She had a rotisserie chicken and potato salad in her hands from the Fresh Savings grocery store she managed in Deer Park. This was totally normal seeing as how rotisserie chicken was the five-dollar deal on Thursdays. She was also holding a bottle of champagne. Totally not normal. And it wasn't just any champagne: it was Veuve Clicquot. I may technically be a country boy by location, but I'm not a country boy at heart. I know from all the bottles I've seen popped on VH1 that Veuve Clicquot is pretty fancy, not like the bottles of Barefoot Bubbly Mom usually brought home for her book clubs. Fancy champagne could only mean we were about to celebrate. So no job firings, no strokes, no alien invaders, and no divorce. That only left the lottery. Were we about to become millionaires?

I grabbed the bottle from Mom's hand. "Okay, what's going on? Nobody's getting any champagne until somebody talks."

Mom set down the chicken and potato salad so she could cross her arms and glare at Dad. "Rick, you didn't tell him?"

"I wanted to wait until you were home." Dad got out of his recliner and wrapped Mom in a big hug. "Congratulations," he said, then dipped and kissed her in that overly dramatic movie way that involves way-too-long lip-to-lip contact and side-to-side face motion. It looked like he was trying to unscrew Mom's head from her neck using only his mouth.

"Gross." To distract myself, I attempted opening my very first bottle of champagne. I unwrapped the foil at the top of the bottle, twisted off the wire basket thingy underneath, and the cork immediately shot out. Even the thunk of the cork hitting the ceiling didn't make my parents stop kissing. They were so disgustingly in love with each other. I mean, it's great, but there's only so much one kid can handle.

What did grab their attention was the golden bubbly that fizzed out of the bottle and onto their shoes.

"Frack!" I yelped, and lunged for the paper towel roll.

"What do you think you're doing?" Dad snatched the bottle, which was now less than half full, from my hand. Champagne should come with instructions. "You know there's no drinking until you're twenty-one!" He was always such a stickler for the rules.

"It's only fair," I said. "How else am I supposed to stomach watching you suck Mom's face off?"

Mom whacked the back of my head. "Don't be disgusting."

"I'm the disgusting one? I'm not the one dripping in someone else's saliva right now."

Dad grabbed two wineglasses out of the cabinet and filled them with champagne. Perfectly, I might add, with the fizz just barely touching the rim of the glass before gently bubbling back down in a luxurious golden haze. It's so embarrassing when your mechanic dad is fancier than you are. He handed a glass to Mom, then turned to me and said, "I think you're just jealous."

"Ew."

Now Mom whacked Dad. "You two are derailing the celebration. I've been promoted!"

Mom's worked at Fresh Savings since before I was born, climbing the grocery store ladder from cashier to head of the meat department to general manager.

"Mom!" I wrapped my arms around her, not caring that a little bit of champagne sloshed out of her glass and landed on my favorite jean jacket. "That's amazing!"

"I'm so proud of you, Tami," Dad said, engulfing us both in a family group hug. Sometimes I got included in their disgusting lovey-dovey-ness. I would never tell them that I actually kind of like it. Doubly so since I'd been left out over the summer while everybody—even Lu—went into Heterosexual Hookup Mode.

Dad let go and grabbed the second glass of champagne.

He toasted Mom, rudely leaving me with no drink and a ton of questions. "But wait," I said. "What position is higher than general manager? President?"

Mom swallowed her champagne and gave Dad a look. One of those looks that's meaningful and significant and holds entire conversations without a single word being spoken. That's great for them and all, but it completely left me in the dark. I was even a Spare Tire to my parents.

"What is it?!" I yelled.

Dad walked into the living room and leaned back in his recliner while Mom grabbed my hand and led me to the love seat. It was impossible to sit on that thing with another person without your knees cramming together. The discomfort of Mom's surprisingly knobby knee jamming into mine almost matched the discomfort at how long she was taking to give me some answers.

"Here's the thing," Mom said. "I've been promoted from general manager to district manager. I'll be overseeing all the Fresh Savings locations in Washington and Oregon, and my office is going to be located in Seattle, which means—"

"We're moving," I interrupted. My heart stopped.

Words gushed out of Mom. "Yes, and I'm so, so sorry that you have to move in your senior year. I didn't want to tell you before now in case the promotion didn't pan out and I got you worked up for no reason. But I got the job today, and this is a really big opportunity for us. I'll be making three times what I'm making now. I know it's such a hard thing to leave your friends and classmates behind that you've been with since kindergarten, and if this opportunity would be waiting in a year, you know I would put it off. But I figured since you're going to college next year anyway, this might not be so bad, right?"

I was stunned. I didn't know what to say. My initial reaction was to run to my room and grab the Gay Agenda so I could start adding more Seattle-specific references to each item. Things like, *Get caught in a torrential downpour and dramatically kiss a boy* or *See if date with cute guy is offered as part of Amazon Prime seeing as how Amazon is based there.*

We sat in silence, Mom and Dad totally oblivious to the Pride parade running through my mind. They kept giving each other worried glances.

"Jay," Dad finally said, his forehead sweaty. "Are you all right?"

"EEEEEEEEEE!" I squealed louder than I had at that Shawn Mendes concert. "Are you kidding?" I jumped up and pulled Mom with me. "I'll get to meet gays! Like, actual living, breathing guys who are interested in other living, breathing guys. I'll get to know what holding someone's hand is like, or that infuriatingly long movie make-out you two do way too much!"

No more being the sole gay boy in a school full of sex-crazed students. No more awkwardly fidgeting my thumbs and having nothing to contribute while my friends—especially Lu—talked about their relationship milestones. I was finally going to the big city where I'd get to have milestones of my own. It wouldn't matter that I didn't have a car, because public transportation in Seattle is epic, and I could take myself to any LGBTQ gathering I wanted. In the very immediate future, I'd be meeting the person who owned the first set of lips that would ever be pressed against mine who wasn't my grandma. I could finally have a boyfriend. I'd have items crossed off my Gay Agenda in no time!

"Ohmigawd, number eight could be off the list!"

Mom cocked her head to the side. "What?"

"Nothing, sorry." This was not the right time to discuss my virginity with Mom. It would never be the right time to discuss my virginity with Mom.

"THIS IS THE BEST NEWS!" I screamed.

Dad wiped his forehead. "Phew! I didn't want to talk about it without your mother here because I thought you'd freak out."

I lunged toward Dad and hugged him. "I *am* freaking out!" I lunged back toward Mom. "Thank you, thank you, thank you! When do we leave?"

"I start in three weeks, just after Labor Day," Mom said. "We have to pack everything up here as soon as we can, rent a U-Haul, and move into a new place over there. It's a lot in so little time."

"I've got the to-do list covered," I said.

JAY'S NEW GAY LIFE PACK AND PREP LIST

1. Pack all your clothes and prioritize the jeans that make your butt look the best.

2. Load up all hair products to keep bangs swooshy and swoon-worthy.

3. DO NOT forget your AJ Kapa poster.

"I'm so relieved you're excited," Mom said. "I was sure you'd hate the timing of this with your eighteenth birthday coming up. Not getting to spend it with Lu."

She looked at me tentatively, like maybe the reminder of leaving my best friend behind would ruin the moment and I'd collapse in a heap of drama. But it's not like I'd had a huge celebration planned anyway. Lu and I would have taken Dad's truck into Spokane to go to the county fair like we usually did. But this year, I was sure I would have had to stomach a side of Chip with my elephant ears and chili dogs. Being their Spare Tire would only have made my eighteenth birthday the worst one yet.

"Don't worry about it," I said, squeezing Mom's shoulder for emphasis. "This is the best birthday gift ever."

I'd gone nearly eighteen years in an LGBTQuarantine, despite the stats throwing it in my face that there should be someone else around who identified as queer. But in just a few weeks, I'd be moving to a metropolitan mecca of gays, where I'd be virtually surrounded by people like me.

The odds of winning the lottery are one in fourteen million. Even though my suspicions were wrong and we hadn't won the money, I still felt like I'd won the gay jackpot.

3.

✓ Say Goodbye to Your Old Life

Statisticians talk all the time about how data can be deceptive. You need all relevant information before you can draw conclusions from any set of numbers, or you can read the data wrong. Turns out, I hadn't had all the info. I never once factored in Mom's job and the possibility that we might move into how I'd eventually meet another gay guy. And I never factored it into when or how I'd eventually leave Lu. When I walked into Tough as Nails the following morning, my heart sank so fracking far I could feel its sad *thu-thump* in my feet. Even though our conversation about the hoedown still stung, it finally hit me that I wasn't going to see my best friend every day for another year like I had initially planned. No Saturday sleepovers, no more pedicures joking with her and Aunt Carol, no diner dates over Diet Dr Pepper and french fries.

Lu was already waiting for me at the front desk. I hadn't called ahead or anything; she just knew I would show up. It was another slap in the face. A new school meant no one who would have my back like she did. No one who would know how or even necessarily want to fix things if we got into a fight. Sure, we'd spent less time together this summer than I wanted so she could be with Chip, but that didn't erase the fact we'd known each other for twelve years. It didn't wipe away the lists and lists of memories we had together, or that she always showed up when it really mattered. Like today.

When Lu saw me, she brought her hands up to either side of her face. S-O-R-R-Y was painted on the nails of each hand, a gold letter over white nail polish glittering from each finger.

"I'm so sorry," we said at the same time.

"I didn't mean to say you couldn't find a date on your own," Lu explained. "Or that I was somehow better at finding a boyfriend than you *at all*. You're a catch, Jay, and I never meant to make it seem like that's not the case."

"Thanks," I said. "I just . . ." Lu had hit a nerve. Being the only gay kid meant I had to see people holding hands, making out, talking about having sex in hushed whispers in class *every single day*. I hadn't done any of those things, not a damn item crossed off my Gay Agenda. It didn't help that my best friend was getting to do all those things I dreamed of doing while I got left behind. Before the summer, Lu never seemed to care about having a relationship.

She'd make out with a guy here and there, but it was fun and no strings attached. It didn't feel quite so bad that I wasn't crossing things off the Gay Agenda because her interactions with boys were never about commitment. But then, suddenly, things changed. She met Chip on our first summer trip to Spokane, eyeing him as he played guitar when we grabbed coffees downtown, and that was that. It hurt. Then she was off with an agenda of her own, just like everyone else. It made me feel like a prepubescent prudish dweeb in a school full of sex maniacs. I really wanted to *be* one of those sex maniacs, but there was never anything I could do about it.

"I think feeling so alone after all this time has been finally getting to me. Well, I mean, I'm not alone; I know I have you, but you've had Chip this whole summer and—"

"I know what you mean." Lu yanked me into a hug. The familiar feel of her nails pressed against my back simultaneously put me at ease and made what I had to say so much harder.

When we pulled apart, tears slid down my cheeks.

"It's okay, Jay, honest," Lu said, grabbing a tissue. "Wipe those away. We're good."

"It's not that." I took the tissue and focused on it so I wouldn't have to see her face fall. "We're moving."

Lu fell into the reception chair, rolling backward in shock. "What?"

Her cheeks were red and splotchy, the telltale sign she was holding back tears. Lu hated to cry and would avoid it at all costs.

"Mom got a promotion," I explained. "She found out yesterday. We're moving to Seattle."

"When?"

"A couple weeks." I could just barely squeeze the words past the lump in my throat.

Lu leaped from the chair and flung her arms around me again, her hold on her tears finally breaking. The familiar scent of Strawberry Shortcake shampoo and the Kim Kardashian perfume I got Lu last Christmas washed over me. I completely lost it. I hated knowing that I'd only have a couple more weeks to smell her. Sure, that was creepy, but she has the most soothing scent in the world. I'd had it in my mind that during the school year we'd get to make up for all the times she canceled on me over the summer. She'd be too busy with the newspaper and homework and shifts at the diner to spend as much time with Chip as she had before. The Summer of Chip had changed things between us, but I knew deep down Lu and I were each other's OTP. Our last year together was supposed to remind her of that. But since I was moving, I was the one taking that opportunity away from us.

Tears and snot poured so hard from our faces that it was hard to tell whose was whose. So many memories flashed through my mind: all our LOTR marathons; planning our award-winning hoedown costumes; cracking up over impressions Lu did of the most overly optimistic teacher ever, Mr. Hebermeyer. All of that was over now.

Lu pulled away, running a hand under her nose to

catch a stray snot strand. "It's a good thing this place is empty all the time. That way no one can see I'm really a softie."

I took in the three empty pedicure chairs, then the sad manicure table. White and gold polish sat on top of it, left over from Lu painting her apology nails. But the small rings of dust around the customer chair told me no one had sat there in a while.

"This is just a rough patch, right?" I said. "There's got to be something that will get people through that door."

As if on cue, the bell over the front door jingled, and Chip walked in. He took in the empty salon and me and Lu bawling all over each other. "Uh . . . Is something the matter?"

Talk about the understatement of the century.

"What would possibly make you think that?" I took the tissue balled up in my hands and dramatically blew my nose.

Chip ran his hands threw his hair, searching for something to say. It was actually pretty cute. For the first time I saw a glimpse of what Lu might see in him. "You seem . . . distressed," he said.

Lu and I cracked up, tears running down our faces all over again. Chip laughed uncertainly, and I pulled him in for a hug. Sure, he'd been glued to Lu throughout the summer, but at least he'd still be glued to her when I left. I was a Spare Tire, but Lu had shown over the summer she didn't need a spare. She'd be okay while I was gone.

Chip was Lu's everything now, and I needed him to help her get through the rough times she and Aunt Carol had ahead of them.

"Thanks, Chip," I said. "Your timing was perfect."

———

Over the next couple weeks, while we packed up the house and loaded the U-Haul, Lu and I made a game plan for what the next year would look like. Lu would Skype me as often as she could, which would be whenever she wasn't in school or taking a shift at the diner. Saturday sleepovers were still going to be a thing. We'd Skype to watch trashy reality TV that I streamed from my laptop and she watched on Aunt Carol's phone. I was positive the internet would be good enough in our new place in the city that I could actually stream something at a normal speed (which was going to make watching porn that much more enjoyable). Plus, I promised that I would come back to make sure Lu and Chip's hoedown costume was perfect, and that *technically* our winning streak would be unbroken (and Lu could take home the cash prize). We agreed that we'd double date for the dance—I'd find the perfect guy from the slew of gays I was sure to meet in Seattle. I wasn't exactly sure how all that would go down since I'd never interacted with a real-life gay boy, but whatever.

Before I knew it, it was time to say goodbye to our tiny log cabin. It sold surprisingly fast, which broke Dad's heart a little bit, but personally, I couldn't get out of there quick enough. I'd like to say that when we drove out of Riverton, I looked on the teeny town where I'd spent my whole life with nostalgia. Or that I waved a heartfelt goodbye when we passed the three bland beige buildings that held the Riverton elementary, middle, and high schools. Or that I teared up when we passed the little strip mall that housed all the businesses within the town's limits: The Stop-N-Go gas station and minimart with the garage where Dad worked, the Riverton Diner (which had the best huckleberry milkshakes, especially when served by Derrick), and Tough as Nails, with its Rosie the Riveter flashing a bright red manicure logo.

But I can't say that. Minus a small tug when passing TAN, the place had never quite felt right to me, never felt like home. Even as a kid, I'd always felt an inexplicable loneliness there. When I came out, it only became more confusing, because I felt lonely, but I stood out like a rainbow-colored sore thumb all at the same time. Not to mention the fact that I always held a grudge because the place calls itself Riverton without ever having a river in it. There is a large creek, but really that doesn't count.

So, as soon as the strip mall was out of sight, Riverton was out of mind. I was too caught up planning my new gay life.

I pulled out my custom purple Moleskine notebook. Lu gave it to me for my birthday last year, and even had my name embossed on it in gold letters. I flipped to the Gay Agenda, which I had updated over the past couple weeks with some Seattle flair. The words flashed at me in their purple ink (when I'm given a color scheme, I stick to it) as if they were itching as much as I was to finally cross some items off the list.

JAY'S GAY AGENDA

1. Meet another ~~gay~~ kid. ~~Somewhere, anywhere . . . please!~~ **in Seattle in, like, days!**

2. Go on a date with a boy **at the Space Needle** and hold hands within the first ninety minutes.

3. ~~Go to a d~~Dance with a boy and have my first kiss slow dancing to Shawn Mendes **while getting caught in a surprise Seattle downpour.**

4. Have a boyfriend, one who likes to wrap me up in his arms and let me be little spoon, **and maybe smells like coffee from all the cafés he goes to.**

5. Fall in love with a boy, but wait for him to say it first so I don't seem too desperate, **and maybe he says it for the first time at Pike Place Market or in the first Starbucks.**

6. Make out, with tongue, and hard enough that I'd get a little burn from his stubble.

7. See another penis besides my own, IRL, and do fun things with it!

8. Lose. My. Virginity!

In order for me to get started on the plan to find a date for the hoedown, I'd have to focus on those first two G-rated items. Those last three—which were now extra bold thanks to all the time I spent without Lu this summer filled with titillating internet searches including the words *doggy* and *style* (and I wasn't looking up canine fashion)—could wait until later. But while picking which items I wanted to cross off first was easy, I didn't really know how to go about it. After I met another gay guy, did I simply ask him out? Or did I wait for him to ask me out? I didn't know yet if I was that confident, forward kind of guy when confronted with someone I liked, or—not to sound old-fashioned—if I wanted to be pursued. Courted. Wooed. And where specifically was I going to meet guys? Just randomly in the halls or on the street? Figuring this out was going to take a lot of work.

We were in the final stretch of the six-hour drive to Seattle, heading up Snoqualmie Pass. The dusty barren parts of the middle of Washington were behind us, turning into the deep green of Western Washington that resulted from all the rain that poured on this side of the mountains. We hit the last rest stop on I-90 before Seattle. As I was standing at a urinal where someone had scratched *GOOGLE ME BITCH* onto the wall under a Sharpie rendering of *YOU'RE MOM*, everything clicked.

Google had been my trusty sidekick the past three years getting gay stats. I couldn't believe I hadn't thought of it before now. When Lu and I learned I'd be going to Capitol Hill High School, we tried finding cute guys on Instagram and Facebook using the school as a geotag. That ended up feeling way too stalkerish, and I decided just to leave whatever meetings I had up to the Gay Gods. But the answer of where to find the gays had been at my fingertips all along.

I pulled out my phone in the back seat of the truck while Mom pulled us back onto the freeway. I searched *Capitol Hill High School*, and my new school's website was the first thing to pop up. An angry-looking thunderbolt took up my screen when I entered the site, and *Home of the Thunderbolts* scrolled across the banner. Just beneath that were all the usual menu items: Home, About, Campus— and the one I was most hoping for—Clubs & Activities. I immediately scrolled to the Gs.

"What the hell?" I blurted.

"What's up?" Mom asked, while Dad said, "Language."

"Oh, it's uh, nothing." And that was the problem. There was a Gaming Club, for frack's sake, but no GSA.

I scrolled to the Ls, thinking maybe there was an LGBTQ group. Nothing again.

I had to be missing something. I went up to A and pored over the alphabetical items. Astronomy Club, Culinary Club, even Fandom Freaks. My heart was about to drop out my butt when I finally got to Q and saw the QSA: Queer-Straight Alliance.

I'd been so focused on getting some boy-on-boy action, I completely overlooked the fact that I had the opportunity to meet all kinds of queer kids. I would no longer be *the* gay kid, I would just be one gay in a whole alphabet soup of LGBTQ realness. No more fielding conversations alone from well-meaning but totally misguided classmates like, "But if you're both dudes, who pays for the date?" or "If you've never been with a girl, how do you know you're gay?" What my new school offered me wasn't just the chance to make out with guys for the first time, but to meet and commiserate with and learn from others who share a queer bond. People who could help me when I went about the Gay Agenda, who could share in the ups and downs as I had different relationship milestones, who knew what it was like to feel and be different from so many other people around you. I wouldn't be alone. I could make a whole new friend-family.

It was time to add an item to my agenda.

JAY'S GAY AGENDA

1. Meet another ~~gay~~ kid. ~~Somewhere, anywhere . . . please!~~ in Seattle in, like, days!

2. Go on a date with a boy at the Space Needle and hold hands within the first ninety minutes.

3. ~~Go to a d~~Dance with a boy and have my first kiss slow dancing to Shawn Mendes while getting caught in a surprise Seattle downpour.

4. Have a boyfriend, one who likes to wrap me up in his arms and let me be little spoon, and maybe smells like coffee from all the cafés he goes to.

5. Fall in love with a boy, but wait for him to say it first so I don't seem too desperate, and maybe he says it for the first time at Pike Place Market or in the first Starbucks.

6. Make out, with tongue, and hard enough that I'd get a little burn from his stubble.

7. See another penis besides my own, IRL, and do fun things with it!

8. Lose. My. Virginity!

9. Become part of a super-queer, super-tight framily.

The QSA could be the answer to crossing off all the items on my list, including the new one. Finding it would be step number one on the first day of school. But once I found it, that still didn't answer the question of how to ask someone on a date if that opportunity ever (please, Andy Cohen, Hayley Kiyoko, Billy Porter, any Gay God!) came up. Fortunately, the Urinal of Destiny's other inscription of YOU'RE MOM, grammatically incorrect or not, sparked an idea.

"I know the two of you met at Dad's shop," I said, loud enough to be heard over Dad shouting along to Shania Twain, "but, like, how exactly did you start dating?"

Dad cut short his off-key shouts to grunt knowingly in the passenger's seat. "Your mother played up the damsel-in-distress trope."

I face-palmed. "Ew, gross, Mom. What about feminism?" Mom was the manager everyone looked up to, the one who had worked her way to the top. She was regularly on the phone with her employees making sure everyone got enough hours or that shifts were covered when someone's kid got sick. To hear that she'd pretended she was anything but the kickass boss she is was . . . cringey.

Mom whapped Dad in the back of his head without taking her eyes off the road. That was more like the woman I knew. "I did not," she said. "My brakes were *legitimately* squeaking when I came into your shop."

"So you're saying it was just a coincidence that your left blinker, then your brake lights, then your right headlight, then *your right blinker* all went out within that same month?" Dad asked. "And it turned out they all were just a little loose and easily screwed back in?"

Mom grinned. "What? It's not my fault it took you so long to get the hint and ask me on a date."

"You're right, Tam," Dad said. He grabbed Mom's hand and kissed it. "But I'm glad this slow guy finally figured it out."

Not only did their cuteness make me want to barf, but their story was no help whatsoever. "Due to the strict rules of a couple totalitarians I know, I don't even have a car, so flirting with a guy over a broken brake light is out of the question."

"I thought all you kids found love online anyway," Dad said. "Swiping left and right and whammo! Soul mates!"

"Don't rush it, sweetheart." Mom looked at me in the rearview mirror, her eyes crinkled with a knowing smile loaded with sympathy. It made me feel super pathetic that my parents had so much game when I'd never even been able to start playing the game. "Love will show up when you least expect it. Look at your dad and me. I didn't expect to meet my husband at the mechanic, but the stars aligned, and here we are."

I looked up at the sky as we drove through the mountain pass. My obsession with stats and probability made it nearly impossible for me to believe that those far-off suns had anything to do with finding a soul mate. Or even someone to fool around with, for that matter. But on the off chance Mom was right, I wished the stars were lining up perfectly to bring two gay boys together.

Me being one of them, just to be clear.

4.

✓Humiliate Yourself
in Front of a VSB

Mom's new Fresh Savings was located right in the middle of Capitol Hill, which, just my luck, was the heart of the gay neighborhood in Seattle. According to the last census, up to 25 percent of all households in Capitol Hill could consist of same-sex couples. One. In. Four. That's a lot of gays!

Not even the drizzly gray gloom that seemed to constantly hover over the city could squelch how bright Capitol Hill was. There were rainbow flags and Human Rights Campaign decals hanging outside businesses on every block; guys were holding hands or just good old-fashioned making out when you walked along the deep green grass of Cal Anderson Park; and it was like my eyes were homing beacons for colorful, heart-shaped *Love Is Love* bumper stickers.

I couldn't believe it. We went from living hours outside any civilization to being smack-dab in the middle of it, and it was as gay as a Pride parade. Talk about winning the gay lottery.

Our duplex was right in the center of the party. Mom's boss knew a guy who knew a lady who owned a couple properties in the area, so we got a deal on a furnished place to rent. Thank gawd Mom got a raise, because even with the friend-of-a-friend discount, rent in the city was expensive. But how could you put a price tag on living in a gay mecca? My jeans and favorite denim jacket might have been damp from the rain, but nothing could dampen my mood as I walked the eight blocks to my new school.

Back in Eastern Washington, everyone looked and acted and dressed and dated exactly the same way. But as I stood in front of the main building of Capitol Hill High, a squat gray structure draped in the school's colors of blue and white, nothing could have been more different from Riverton. There were kids of every race, kids who sported religious emblems for things other than ProteBaptatholic, and—like shining beacons of love—kids with rainbow flags and HRC patches on their backpacks.

I was home.

It was such a surreal feeling. I immediately knew I belonged in this physical space even though I'd never been there before. There was this sort of tingling throughout my body, and my heart started to race like it had finally found the rhythm it'd been waiting almost eighteen years to beat. This was where I was meant to be. Where I'd finally find my queer community. Where I'd find the person to give me my first kiss, to become my first boyfriend, to cross off item eight with a condom and a flourish!

It was in that moment, nothing but a gleam of hope in my eye and a bit of horniness in my crotch, that I was shoved to the ground. Hard. The impact was enough to make the duct-taped JanSport backpack I'd had since eighth grade split down the middle. Granted, the bag was a real pile of crap, but that didn't make it any less jarring. Everything I owned exploded all over the sidewalk.

"What the frack!" I screamed. My left palm scraped the concrete, and my right landed directly in a pile of chewed gum. Whatever Stats Gods had started putting life in my favor by bringing me to this gay paradise were clearly no longer on my side.

"Shit, I am so sorry!"

I looked up to see what appeared to be a printer on wheels staring at me through googly eyes glued to its front. Two human hands kept shifting over its sides to get a good grip on the machine, the googly eyes shaking up and down with each new attempt at a hand position. The person holding it eventually gave up and set the printer down, revealing what Lu would call a VSB: Very Sexy Boy. He was Asian, had the best wave in his thick, black hair, and had the most gorgeous dark eyes accented by tortoiseshell square-framed glasses. You know those statues where you're like, *I've never seen a jawline that chiseled in real life?* His totally was. And—even though I was still on the ground—I could tell he was tall. Just the thought of having to look up at him to meet those mesmerizing eyes sent shivers down my spine.

VSB stuck his hand out. "Sorry about that. Let me help you up."

Under his sexy boy spell, I stuck my gum-gunked hand right into his. This was not the meet-cute Mom and Dad promised.

"Oh gawd, that's gross." I face-palmed with my non-gummed hand, my skin stinging from all the sidewalk scrapes.

VSB laughed, and oh. My. Gawd. My insides melted. You know how you always read books or see movies and the main character is like, "His laugh swept me off my feet" or "One deep chuckle emanated from the middle of his chest and it set my insides burning" and you roll your eyes like, *Yeah, right. Laughs don't have magic powers?* His totally did. He was a laughing, sexy sorcerer.

"Don't worry about it," VSB said. He wiped his hand on his jeans without any mind that half a wad of gum now stuck to his thigh. He knelt down and grabbed a handful of pens that my backpack had vomited. "Let me at least help you pick some of this up. I'm Albert, by the way. Albert Huang. I don't think I've seen you around before."

"New. I'm new," I said, nodding for some reason, and a stray lock of bangs stuck to my forehead. I instantly clocked that as strange because I never put enough product in my hair to make it stick to my skin. My signature face-palm hair billowing would be impossible.

I tried to pull the wayward hair from my face. *Oh frack*. I somehow got gum on my forehead and my hair was sticking to it!

"I'm Jay," I said, trying to very nonchalantly flick the gum off my forehead with my nonsticky hand. But whatever nonchalance I was trying to put out there was completely blown away by the fact that my cheeks were on fire. Choking-related accidents from things like chewing gum kill about 2,500 people a year. Right then I wished I could rip that gum from my forehead, cram it down my throat, and be one of them.

"Nice to meet you, Jay." Albert was about to hand me my notebook and more pens, but he stopped and motioned to my scraped hand. "That looks like it hurts. Maybe I should carry your stuff for you?"

Sexy and sweet! This was turning into the adorable meet-cute Mom said was written in the stars after all. But I needed to get my notebook back before Albert opened it and the moment was ruined by the Gay Agenda in all its purple, horny glory.

"It's fine," I said. "I'll just—" I snatched my notebook from Albert, ripped a page from the back, and dabbed the blood off my palm. I turned to the trash can behind me to throw out the paper and try to collect myself even the tiniest bit. This was my first shot to try to impress a boy. I could not let it end with bloodied hands and a gummed forehead.

I turned back around and met Albert's gaze. How come no one at Riverton had ever mentioned how good it feels for your insides to turn to jelly? Or how your insides could be melting while a very outer part of you does the exact opposite of liquefy? I suddenly realized that literally anybody I met that day could be the first person I saw without any clothes on, possibly even Albert. I would not mind at all seeing what his torso looked like under his Henley.

Albert's eyes went wide. Was he thinking about me shirtless too?

"You've got something on your face," Albert said. "Just a little blood. It must have been from your scraped hand. You know, when you wiped that gum off?"

This was definitely not the situation I'd imagined when I'd thought about a VSB inspecting my body for the first time.

I ripped another page from my notebook and blotted the blood from my forehead.

"Th-thanks." I reached forward and took the rest of my stuff from Albert.

"Don't mention it," he said. "My dad's a heart surgeon. He's shown me a lot worse than just a little blood." He bent over to get a solid grip on his printer-creature, his butt on full display. A VSB's derriere was just feet away from my face, but I was too embarrassed to really appreciate the view.

"Once I install the battery pack, I'll finally get to

use the wheels on this thing." Albert stood back up and smiled, big and openmouthed. He had one bottom tooth that overlapped another in his otherwise perfectly aligned teeth, like he'd worn braces but then stopped wearing his retainer. "See you around, Jay."

"Yeah." Could I have been any less smooth? I felt like that prepubescent dweeb who watched the suave and sexy kids from the sidelines all over again. Not only did I have zero idea how to flirt when confronted with a VSB, but I'd tried it with gum in my hair and blood on my face. At this rate, I'd be dead before I could even cross one item off the Gay Agenda.

Oh gawd, I would die a virgin.

I gave Albert a good head start before sulking into the office to grab my schedule. It took the whole way to the office to get rid of the rest of the gum on my fingers, and I figured it would take the whole rest of my life to get rid of the embarrassment from my Albert encounter. But as I looked down at my schedule to see that calculus would be my first class, numbers took over. The odds of the very first person I met at Capitol Hill High being gay were slim to none. There were almost *two thousand kids* in the school. If in some strange stroke of luck the 8-percent-of-the-population-is-queer stat finally came true, that would mean I had a one in twelve and a half chance of the first person I spoke to (read: Albert) being gay. Those were small odds that were totally in my favor. There was no way Albert could be interested in me because there was such a tiny chance he was gay. So it didn't really matter that I looked like such a fracking idiot in front of him. Maybe the Gay Gods were just giving me a chance to get the nerves out of my system. Then I could go full force into the Gay Agenda without any more buffoonery.

Phew. Close call.

5.

✓ Spill Your Secrets

I hadn't had first-day-of-school jitters in years. My new-school-year routine always went like this:

BACK-TO-SCHOOL SCHEDULE

1. Wake up from a heart-racing nightmare that I'd overslept and somehow missed all my finals even though it was the first day of school.

2. Make sure all my pens were in the right backpack pocket and organize my notebooks by color spectrum order.

3. Get to school and grab my schedule so I could label said notebooks appropriately.

4. Check what the fall play was going to be and volunteer to help the drama teacher with

costuming (my hoedown duct-tape and safety-pin talents are legendary).

5. Wait for one of Lu's journalism classmates to ask if I'd finally gotten action over the summer and begrudgingly mumble "no" while a headline blared over my head, screaming VIRGIN! VIRGIN! VIRGIN!

It was all so routine, so predictable, but at least I was a part of the Riverton community. And yes, while not everybody there fully understood who I was inside, or only saw me as the token magical unicorn gay friend, I'd been with them since kindergarten and they were familiar. How did I start from scratch?

I tried making eye contact with my locker neighbor, but they were instantly distracted by someone tackling them and making out like they were trying to swap bodies. It figured that everyone here was in SexTown too. Later on, somebody tapped my shoulder in calculus, but it was only to ask for an extra pencil. I couldn't muster up the courage to introduce myself to anyone, let alone ask them if they knew about the QSA and where I'd find all the gays.

There was also the horrible moment of being the new kid at lunch. I had no idea where to sit. I wasn't athletic enough to sit with the jocks, not musically talented enough to sit with the band kids, and my denim jacket was way too bright to sit with the goth group. Realizing that I might go my entire senior year of high school with zero friends made me really miss Lu. I ended up Skyping her from a wet bench in the quad outside the cafeteria.

"Everyone keeps asking where you are," Lu said. "It's really depressing having to repeat over and over that you've moved. Not that we're not all happy for you. Give me the scoop. Have you already met your future *boyfriend*?" She sang it like she was going to follow up with *sitting in a tree, K-I-S-S-I-N-G*.

"Well," I said, "that would require me actually talking to someone."

"What?!" Lu flung the phone screen around so her whole lunch table could see me. "Guys, tell Jay how much we love him and how cute and charming he is and how he'll have a boyfriend in no time."

"Lu!" I got what she was trying to do, but I did not need half the *Riverton Reporter* crew talking about what a virginal dweeb I was.

I was bombarded with a chorus of "You got this, Jay" and "Go get 'em, tiger."

"See?" Lu said, turning the camera back toward her. "We all believe in you. I know it's weird being the new kid, but just put yourself out there. There's got to be somewhere all the gays go, right?"

A huge gust of wind blew, immediately followed by something wet and slimy smacking me right in the face.

"Oh, frack!"

"Jay!" Lu yelled. "What was that?"

I cringed as I pulled away the mushy projectile.

"Ohmigawd," I said. "It's a sign."

Literally. A soggy one that had been beaten down by

the Seattle rain. Even though its words were faded, they shone like beacons from above.

QUEER-STRAIGHT ALLIANCE
First Meeting of the Year
Tuesday, September 7, Room 313 @ 2:45

"I found them," I whispered. "I found the gays."

—*mm*—

I stood at the door to room 313 after the last bell rang. My heart went a million beats per second. Stepping over the threshold meant I was about to step into the room that could hold the person who would become my first boyfriend. Or give me my first kiss. Or be the owner of my first number seven!

I did a quick bangs check in my phone's camera to make sure my hair was perfectly in place. When I looked back up, a familiar face glowed through the doorway. Sitting on the window ledge with the sun lighting him up like some arousing angel sent from heaven—or whatever awesome resort waits for us in the afterlife—was Albert.

My mind went into overdrive. *Albert Huang could be gay. Or bi. Or pansexual. Shit! I mean, yay, but, shit!* I'd looked like a complete fracking idiot that morning. If he was interested in dudes, the bloody gum fiasco had to have blown any possible chance he'd be interested in me. Then again, he could also be representing the *S* part of the

QSA, and then I'd have nothing to worry about. But honestly, I really hoped he wasn't straight and that number six could get an immediate revision.

JAY'S GAY AGENDA

1. Meet another ~~gay~~ kid. ~~Somewhere, anywhere . . . please!~~ in Seattle in, like, days!

2. Go on a date with a boy at the Space Needle and hold hands within the first ninety minutes.

3. ~~Go to a d~~Dance with a boy and have my first kiss slow dancing to Shawn Mendes while getting caught in a surprise Seattle downpour.

4. Have a boyfriend, one who likes to wrap me up in his arms and let me be little spoon, and maybe smells like coffee from all the cafés he goes to.

5. Fall in love with a boy, but wait for him to say it first so I don't seem too desperate, and maybe he says it for the first time at Pike Place Market or in the first Starbucks.

6. Make out **with Albert**, with tongue, and ~~hard enough that I'd get a little burn from his stubble~~ **run my fingers along that perfect jawline**.

7. See another penis besides my own, IRL, and do fun things with it!

8. Lose. My. Virginity!

9. Become part of a super-queer, super-tight framily.

There's this thing in statistics called the Gini index. It's all about measuring how wealth is shared throughout a whole country. It's on a scale from zero to one, and a country where everyone shares wealth equally is at a zero. If just one person controls all the wealth, the Gini index is at a one. For the Capitol Hill High QSA, hotness was not shared equally. The Sexy Gini index was all the way at a one, and Albert was the guy who controlled all that sexiness.

"I know," a voice whispered in my ear. "He's super hot, right?"

I was caught in the act drooling over a boy while blocking the doorway. Way to make a good first impression.

"Sorry." I moved to the side, my back still turned to whoever I was blocking.

"Don't worry about it," they said. "I haven't seen you around these meetings before. My name's Max Knudson. The *K*'s not silent, and neither am I!"

I turned to face whoever it was who introduced themselves with such magnetic sass. When I took in all his fabulousness, my mouth fell open. Max looked to be about my age, was my same height, and had long blond hair. Illuminating powder highlighted his white, freckled cheekbones, and he wore an outfit that looked almost identical to the one Mom had chosen for work that morning: dark blue, high-waisted paper-bag pants with a white blouse. He wore black booties and carried a blue-and-white tote bag with *What Would Dolly Do?* written on the side.

No guy in rural Eastern Washington would ever wear women's clothes. I loved color and wanted to be more adventurous with my style, but I always played it safe in a white Hanes T-shirt, jeans from Target, and my favorite Levi's jacket my parents bought me in ninth grade. It still fit because, sadly, that was the year I stopped growing at the national average of five foot nine inches.

Max followed my line of sight to his pants. "What? Did my belt come undone or something?"

"No, it's just . . ." Max lifted his eyebrows and peered at me down his nose. *Say something, Jay!* The longer it took me to get any words out, the more I looked like some closed-minded, denim getup, country hick. "You look great!"

"Thanks!" Max beamed. "Gendered fashion can be so limiting, don't you think?" He grabbed my hand and led me into the classroom, all skepticism vanished from his face. "Tell me your life story. Start from birth."

My mind ran through the list of Jay attributes as Max plopped into a desk in the front row.

JAY COLLIER QUALITIES

1. Hyper-organized list maker (as evidenced by making a list of my own personality traits).

2. Stats geek and mathematician (including a two-time Washington Association of Mathematics (WAM) regional champion at the annual WAMbledon math competition).

3. Reality TV aficionado (I could recite the MTV, VH1, and Bravo show schedules).

4. Three-time award-winning hoedown costumier (the only French word I know).

5. Inexperienced and getting-desperate gay virgin (Ugh).

I couldn't say any of these traits out loud. I'm super organized and outrageously type A? That will be read as totally neurotic. I'm into stats and math? Huge geek. Lover of reality show drama? I could practically see Chip pointing at me and saying I was a stereotype. Hoedown costumier? I couldn't sound any more country if I tried, even with a French word in there. And there was no way I was going into my sexual inactivity. I seemed so dull and boring. If I was going to make a new life for myself, I needed to be alluring and captivating so I could make friends and interest guys.

Max stared at me expectantly. "You look like the human personification of the computer-stalling color wheel." His eyes glazed over, and he said in a robotic voice, "Thinking, thinking, thinking."

"Ha, ha." I laughed robotically, only proving Max's point. I took the seat next to him and decided to just list the surface things that couldn't land me in loser new kid territory. "I'm Jay and I just moved here. I'm a senior. I'll be eighteen in a couple weeks. On the twentieth."

"Ooh, a Virgo. Let me guess. You're super organized, and you like to make lists."

Obviously, that was dead-on. I glanced down at my notebook, nervous that somehow it had splayed open and

Max could see the Gay Agenda. It was shut tight with my elbow resting on top of its cover. But if Max could guess my number-one personality trait just based on me being a Virgo, maybe there really was something to stars and astrology.

Max seemed to be okay with my neuroses, so I ventured a little further in the truth about Jay. "Sure, I guess I'm pretty organized. I also like drag and theater."

"Who doesn't?" Max said.

"Dressing up."

"Preaching to the choir."

"Sudoku, calculus, statistics." I face-palmed. Dropping math bombs was definitely taking it too far. I was coming across as the biggest nerd to the first person I'd spoken to without gum on my forehead.

But Max pulled my hand from my face, his eyes glowing with adoration. "Lord and Taylor, that was the cutest move I've ever seen! I'm obsessed with a good catchphrase, but a catch*move*! Love it!"

Finally, someone who appreciated the face-palm. Lu always said it was so dramatic, but Max knew what I was going for: sending a message with just the right amount of cute. There's this study that says it takes two hundred hours to become someone's best friend, but if things kept going this well between us, Max and I would be BFFs in no time.

It was such a relief that Max took the conversational lead after I hadn't been able to muster up the courage to talk to anybody. As he continued to ask me questions,

I fully intended to omit the most embarrassing detail of my life, namely, that I was a virgin while everyone our age seemed to constantly be naked with somebody else. But somehow Max was like a bloodhound sniffing out the scent of my boy-on-boy inexperience.

"So, you're gay, right?" Max asked, then immediately slapped his cheek. "Lord and Taylor, shut up, Max! I didn't mean to assume or anything, but I just kind of have a sixth sense about these things."

"It's okay," I said. "And your superpowers remain intact. I'm gay."

"And you mentioned you moved from outside of Spokane?"

I nodded.

"*Where* outside of Spokane?" he asked.

"Riverton. Most people haven't heard of—"

"Ohmigawd, you poor thing." Max covered his mouth in shock. "My mom's second cousin used to live out there and the one time we went to visit, I couldn't wait to leave. There's nothing to *do*. It's just farms and fields and"—he gasped—"no gays."

Max leaned in so close his hair landed on my shoulder. "But I mean, like, you *have* kissed a boy before, right?"

I hesitated, completely wanting to avoid the subject of my having never done anything with a guy, ever. But my silence only confirmed Max's suspicions.

"Don't you worry. Your life is about to change, Jay, because this place is swarming with gays." Max pointed at himself. "Gay." Then he pointed at a few of the guys chatting or taking seats. "Gay, gay, gay, gay, a couple fresh-men I don't know, aaaaaand gay. All openly, of course, because I'm not in the business of outing people."

Three thoughts went through my head: 1) That third gay on the list was Albert, so, hell fracking yes, it was con-firmed, 2) I could officially cross off item number one on the Gay Agenda (twice, really, since I'd met Albert that morning and now Max), and 3) Max knew which boys liked boys. He could save me from those awkward *Hey, are you gay?* conversations. With Max by my side, I could flirt with confidence and meet up with all those other high schoolers in SexTown ASAP.

"Okay, so true-confession time," I said.

"That's my favorite time." I swear Max was salivating.

I lowered my voice. "You were right about how barren Riverton is. I've never kissed a guy before." Max's eyes lit up and he opened his mouth to speak. *"Don't* tell anybody," I rushed to say before he could get the whole QSA's attention. "But I could use, like, a sort of guide." I thought back to my encounter with Albert and how stupid I looked. "Someone to help me figure out how to not come across like a total amateur while I cross items off my Gay Agenda."

Oh, frack. Oh, fracking shit balls shit! This is what happens when someone makes you feel comfortable after nearly a whole day of silence: you spill every single secret without meaning to.

Was there a stat on how many people die of embar-rassment?

Because I was about to become one of them.

6.

✓ Become Veep

"Oh. My. Gawd. Your Gay Agenda? Tell me everything!" Max was like a kid in a candy store, and I'd just produced the juiciest piece of candy he could imagine. I was the Willy Wonka of slipups.

"Really, it's nothing. I don't know what I was—"

"Please," Max interrupted. "You've let the cat out of the bag now, and I'm just going to keep asking until you say yes. Just like you can't stop yourself from making lists, Geminis are known for being nosy." Max motioned for me to hand over my notebook. "I know it's in there, Virgo."

I really wanted the QSA meeting to start already so I could avoid the question and pretend like nothing happened. I looked at the clock. It was only two forty. I had five minutes left of this torture.

Here were my options:

GAY AGENDA DIVULGENCE DILEMMA

1. Continue to deny Max and have him keep asking about it (which would inevitably cause a commotion that catches Albert's and the rest of the group's attention, then everyone would ask what all the hubbub was about, and the Gay Agenda would be revealed to the entire world).

2. Show Max the Gay Agenda (which would give him more insight into just what I want out of my first year with other gay guys, and potentially lead to crossing off more items with him as my guide).

3. Run.

There were too many people blocking the doorway to run, and if Albert learned about the Gay Agenda, I would move back to Riverton and live with Lu with only myself to blame for my virginity.

That meant there was only one thing left to do.

"Fine." I flipped to the Gay Agenda, then checked over both shoulders to be sure there was no one close enough to see all my gay hopes and dreams on the page. "The only other person I've shown this to is Lu, my best friend back home. So you can't tell *a single person* about this."

Max made an X over his chest. "It's an honor to be in such esteemed company as your best friend. I won't take this lightly." Then he snatched the Moleskine away from me.

When Max's hand closed over my notebook, I felt

a vise grip on my heart. It was like he was holding my soul. Like he could literally tear me to shreds. What if he laughed? What if he thought I was a skeezy perv?

But as Max's eyes roved farther down the list, his smile got wider and wider. When he reached the bottom of the agenda, he snapped the book shut and declared, "I accept the position as your Gay Guide, your Libido Liberator, and your Jizz Genie. I will make all your sex wishes come true!"

I was relieved and horrified at the same time. "Let's *never* use the title Jizz Genie ever again. Gay Guide will totally work if you have to have an official title." The vise grip left my heart. It actually felt kind of good to have somebody accept this mission head-on. "You don't think I'm some sex-crazed lunatic or something, do you?"

"Of course I do. But, like, we all are," Max said. "Except for our asexual friends, who can still get just as wrapped up in romance and relationships. The key is being a sex-and/or romance-crazed lunatic with confidence."

"You seem to have a lot of that."

"Confidence is key when you're genderqueer, or else the world will eat you alive," Max said, flipping his hair over his shoulder.

This was a time for my internet research to come in handy. I could finally use it now that I was out of the homogeneity of my hometown and able to meet a noncis-gender person.

"Cool," I said. "I go by he/him pronouns, and I'm a total safe space if you ever want to share yours."

Max gave me an *Oh, aren't you cute* look. "There's never a way to broach this topic without it sounding clinical, is there? I'm an open book, so none of the pronouns really feel one hundred percent right. But you can address your Gay Guide as he/him or she/her. My body is male, my energy is feminine, and I'm down for paying tribute to both."

"Got it," I said. "And thanks for accepting the position."

Max put his hand over his heart. "It's an honor you asked. And gave in to my pushiness. It's just that I could really use a project right now, and helping you get a hookup will be fun. For my first order of business as your newly appointed GG: What are you looking for in a man?"

I was prevented from pointing over Max's shoulder at Albert by Ms. Okeke—the World Lit teacher and faculty leader of the group—clapping her hands. "All right, everybody, settle down. We've got a lot of work to do and not a lot of time to do it. As most of you already know, the QSA is in charge of homecoming this year."

Everyone did the exact opposite of settle down. At Ms. Okeke's announcement, the whole room erupted in excited chatter. I let out a gasp thinking about crossing number three off the Gay Agenda (although unless it was outside, I might have to rethink the getting-caught-in-a-romantic-downpour bit). I'd probably even be able to give that item two check marks if I could get said boy—cough, Albert, cough—to come with me back to Riverton and go to the hoedown.

My eyes slipped toward Albert, and I SWEAR TO

GAWD he was already looking right at me. I was getting checked out by a guy! Me! Jay Collier! I mentally added a 1.5 to the Gay Agenda and crossed it off: *Get checked out by a VSB the stars may or may not have sent literally crashing into you this morning.* Check!

Here was my chance to make up for being a total klutz. I ran my tongue over my teeth to double-check I didn't have any leftover turkey sandwich in them from lunch. Then I let loose the "sexy smile" that I'd practiced so many times in the mirror: the corners of my lips turned up just enough so as not to seem too eager, and my mouth opened ever so slightly so that he could see just a bit of my tongue. I definitely wanted Albert to be thinking about what it would be like to make contact with my tongue.

All that mirror practice must have worked because . . . ALBERT SMILED BACK!

Max followed my line of sight. "Lord and Taylor, would you two stop being so cute already?"

I face-palmed, hoping to keep Max's attention on my face and nowhere near the bulge appearing thanks to tonguing-Albert thoughts.

"Do not let hormones take control of this club!" Ms. Okeke yelled over the chaos. We all eventually quieted down, with a scattered giggle here and there. "We've got to get planning right away because homecoming is October ninth. First thing to do is elect our president for the year. That person will oversee all the committees for getting homecoming up and running. Then they'll schedule various discussions once this dance debauchery dies down

– 68 –

and we can get back to our regularly scheduled queer-straight programming. Any contenders?"

Max immediately interlocked his fingers with mine and hoisted our hands in the air. Two gold bracelets jangled on his wrist as he waved our hands back and forth.

"What are you doing?" I was excited to become a part of an LGBTQ framily, especially after that lonely lunch earlier, but I didn't want to dive into the deep end like this quite so quickly.

"As your Gay Guide, I'm getting your name out there," Max whispered. "Now everyone will know about the cute, mysterious new boy at school." He turned to the class. "We're running on a Knudson and um, whatever Jay's last name is, ticket!"

My cheeks burned with a thousand tiny furnaces. "It's C-Collier."

Ms. Okeke wrote our names on the board. "Excellent. Nice to meet you, Jay. I'm glad to see a newcomer jump right in. Everyone say hi to Jay."

"Hi, Jay!" the group echoed.

Ms. Okeke motioned for me to stand up. "Tell us a bit about yourself."

At Riverton, just saying I was "the gay kid" made me automatically interesting since I was the one and only. I had spent so much time hearing that label that I'd taken it on as my number-one reason for being, hence, the creation of the Gay Agenda. But here, among all kinds of queer students who had real identities other than their sexual one, there was no way just saying I was gay would be enough. This was why crossing items off the Gay Agenda was so important: not only so I could get all the relationship firsts I'd been lagging behind on, but so I could stop obsessing so much over the lack of boy lips on mine, and get to focusing on what makes me me. I'd actually get to develop what makes me worthy of spending time with people other than being the token gay.

Ms. Okeke and the rest of the club kept staring at me, ready for my fascinating explanation of who I was that would completely blow them away.

"M-me?" I stuttered. "I'm new. Happy to be here."

Great. I was just replacing the label of "the gay kid" with "the new kid." I didn't give them any worthwhile information about myself other than demonstrating how I was not good at speaking under pressure. I sat back down as fast as I could.

Max looked at me like I'd said the most brilliant thing in the world. "See? He gets right to the point. We need somebody as organized as Jay is as we head into planning the biggest dance of the year. I've seen his list-making skills firsthand." Max winked at me and a whole new list started forming in my mind.

GAY GUIDE GUIDELINES

1. Absolutely <u>no</u> veiled references to the Gay Agenda in mixed company.

"Way to bring it back to the issue at hand, Max," Ms. Okeke said. "Would anyone like to challenge Max and

Jay?" She looked around the room, but nobody said anything.

"Oh, no," a girl finally cooed from the back of the class. "We all think that Max needs this. After what happened with—"

"I do *not* need the pity votes, Lisbeth," Max interrupted. "Not in these hallowed grounds of the QSA. I want to win this election fair and square."

Nobody moved. What could Max be getting pity over? Just eight minutes with him and he was already the most self-assured person I'd ever met.

"Ms. Okeke, make somebody else volunteer for president," Max commanded.

"I don't think you understand what *volunteer* means, Max," Ms. Okeke said. "I can't make anybody do anything." She faced the room once more. "Anybody want to reconsider running?"

After another silent pause filled with condoling looks at Max, Ms. Okeke called the easiest election I'd ever heard of in my life. "That settles it," she said. "Take it away, you two."

"Fine." Max's tone was sharp. Not at all the mood I was expecting after winning an election. He stood and pulled me up with him. I glanced at Albert, then immediately looked away when he flashed me that perfect smile.

"I am honored to serve as your party planner in chief," Max said, although the begrudging look that still lingered didn't make his statement seem so true. "In the spirit of our great country, I want you to know this is a dance-ocracy. I will take all suggestions to heart and put them to a group vote. And with Mr. Collier by my side"—he raised my hand high—"we won't let you down."

With that, Max got down to business. He actually reached into his tote bag and pulled out *a gavel*. Whether we got a fair election or not, he'd clearly planned on winning, but apparently not with pity votes, whatever that was about.

I didn't have time to think about it because Max started naming off committees and enlisted me to write down people's names as they volunteered for different duties. Max smashed his gavel on Ms. Okeke's desk along the way if people got too rowdy. There was decorating committee, drinks committee, ticket sales. Albert signed up for that last one, so I did, too. Maybe we'd fall in love while working the cash box together. Take that, Mom and Dad! Dance-ticket-selling romance definitely overrules made-up mechanical mishaps on the cuteness scale.

"I've saved the best for last," Max announced after everyone's name was listed under their respective duties. I had to admit, *Albert & Jay* looked really good together on the whiteboard. "It's time to come up with a theme for the dance and costume contest. As we all know, this is the most important decision, people. Whichever couple gets the most votes for best costume wins homecoming royalty."

I was starting to think Mom was right about stars aligning because in that moment, everything seemed to click. It was like the universe wanted me to cross off all kinds of items on the Gay Agenda. First, I was at a school with boys who liked boys who might want to make out with me on the dance floor. Second, I was a three-time costume-contest award winner. I could put those skills to use and make the most epic homecoming outfit so that everyone voted for me for best costume. Then I'd be homecoming royalty and could erase the "new kid" label for good. People would realize I'm fun and have interesting skills, and I'd never have to list WAMbledon champion under Jay Collier Qualities again. People would be clamoring to become a part of the Jay Gay Framily.

Now I had a game plan for item number nine.

JAY'S GAY AGENDA

1. ~~Meet another gay kid. Somewhere, anywhere . . . please! in Seattle in, like, days!~~ ✓

1.5. ~~Get checked out by a very VSB!~~ ✓

2. Go on a date with a boy at the Space Needle and hold hands within the first ninety minutes.

3. ~~Go to a d~~Dance with a boy and have my first kiss slow dancing to Shawn Mendes while getting caught in a surprise Seattle downpour.

4. Have a boyfriend, one who likes to wrap me up in his arms and let me be little spoon, and maybe smells like coffee from all the cafés he goes to.

5. Fall in love with a boy, but wait for him to say it first so I don't seem too desperate, and maybe he says it for the first time at Pike Place Market or in the first Starbucks.

6. Make out with Albert, with tongue, and ~~hard enough that I'd get a little burn from his stubble.~~ run my fingers along that perfect jawline.

7. See another penis besides my own, IRL, and do fun things with it!

8. Lose. My. Virginity!

9. Become part of a super-queer, super-tight framily **by impressing everybody with my epic costumier skills, erasing the "new kid" label, and becoming homecoming royalty.**

I knew just what theme was going to turn this goal into a reality.

"I've got an idea," I said. "For the dance."

All eyes in the room turned to me. My insides squirmed. This was my shot.

I'd had this idea saved up for the past three years since the chumps of the hoedown costume committee never used it, despite all the times I brought it up. Maybe it stemmed from just how suppressed I was as the only gay kid in Riverton, but I couldn't help but see so many bromances that really should have just been straight-up romances in hindsight.

GET TOGETHER ALREADY

1. SpongeBob and Patrick (I mean, come on, they can't go a single day without seeing each other?)

2. Hulk and Thor (I know I'm not the only one who's wondered what's under the Hulk's jean shorts, and

we all know what Thor's hammer really is)
3. R2-D2 and C-3PO (they literally finish each other's sentences, even when R2 speaks in beeps and boops)

All that time thinking about bro-couples that should be homo-couples led to my perfect theme. It was all about letting duos that should have been together finally have their chance.

"It's centered around that old cliché 'hindsight is 20/20,'" I said, grabbing my notebook to flip to the costume ideas I'd listed. "It could be all about the couples that we wish had stayed together or would finally see what everyone else does and become a thing already. You could make it gay, like shipping War Machine and Iron Man, or full of hope, like Romeo and Juliet without killing themselves. Or you could rewrite history and put our favorite couples back together, like Vanessa Hudgens and Zac Efron."

"They were so cute together," someone shouted.

"Wait." A girl angrily shot up from her desk. Her long hair was the same color as a fire hydrant. "I thought we agreed last year we would do an under-the-sea theme. I already dyed my hair for it!"

"I appreciate how strongly you commit to your name, Ariel, so we'll put it to a vote," Max said. "All in favor of Under the Sea?" Max looked around the room three times, doing his due diligence even though Ariel's hand was the only one raised. "All in favor of Homecoming in Hindsight?"

Hands rose throughout the classroom.

"It's decided!" Max slammed his gavel. "Start spreading the word now, folks, so people have time to really up their costume game. We'll meet every Monday and Tuesday, with a Wednesday gathering this week since Monday was a holiday. All committees should arrive tomorrow prepared to make a game plan for the dance. I declareth this session O-V-E-R!" He rapped his gavel with each letter for dramatic effect.

The space filled with talk about hindsight costume ideas as everyone filed out of the classroom. Even Ariel took part. She mentioned something about how she totally shipped Flotsam and Jetsam, and that the rest of us poor unfortunate souls wouldn't stand a chance against her outfit. At least I didn't make an enemy on day one at Capitol Hill High.

"Hey, great idea for the dance, by the way." I turned and Albert was looking right at my mouth with those perfect dark eyes. That sexy smile had totally worked.

"Thanks." He was standing so close. I had to say something, fast, or I was positive my lips would lunge forward with a mind of their own. "Where's your friend?"

Albert cocked his head to the side like a confused puppy. How can a person be outrageously adorable and smolderingly sexy at the same time? He was so fracking cute I thought my heart was going to explode. "Friend? What do you mean?"

"Your robot thingy from this morning."

"Oh, that!" Albert laughed loudly, making me melt all

over again. His laugh was the most carefree sound I'd ever heard, like he had every right to enjoy life as loudly and as much as he wanted. "Ms. Rochester, the robotics teacher, hates that her office is so far from the staff printer. She said anyone who could fix the situation with a robot over the summer would get extra credit this year. So I made a remote-controlled, battery-powered, wireless printer on wheels."

Albert could make robots, adding yet another item to the list of Albert Adjectives.

ALBERT ADJECTIVES

1. Sexy (I mean, he is a V, V, V VSB.)

2. Sweet (Who else would help pick up all my crap even though I had gum on my face and my hand was soaked in blood?)

3. Adorable (I'm talking puppy-dog-eyes adorable.)

4. Smart (Where do you even get started on building a robot?)

In short, he was totally swoon-worthy.

"Ever since I learned that you're four to six times more likely to get killed by a vending machine than a shark, I've steered clear of machinery of any kind," I said. Hopefully Albert would think I was funny and not too much of a stats geek. I wanted to hear that laugh again. "But the googly eyes you added were a nice touch."

It worked. Albert let out a guffaw, and my heart reached the ceiling.

"Thanks," he said, "but I'm not sure it was enough to make PrinterBot stand out. I was one of five remote-controlled printers. Ms. Rochester had no idea what she was bargaining for when she set that challenge."

I steepled my hands like a devious evil genius. "Or maybe she did. Her army of PrinterBots is finally complete! Mwahahaha!"

Albert's real laugh joined my evil one. It made his eyes shine beneath his glasses, and he had a dimple on his right cheek that accented his angular jaw. *Ohmigawd, get ahold of yourself, Jay. You can't fall for this guy after knowing him for only seven hours.*

But they were seven glorious hours.

"Anyway," Albert said, snapping me out of my internal love fest, "see you tomorrow."

"Sounds great." I waved. "See ya." The wave immediately turned into yet another face-palm. *See ya?* I sounded like a sixth grader who's never kissed anybody. Sure, the second half of that was true, but I didn't need to make it so obvious.

Max slammed his gavel, and I practically jumped out of my skin. "What the frack?!"

"I declareth that you and Albert should just go as yourselves to homecoming," Max said. "The two of you need to get it over with and get together already."

My breath caught in my throat. "Wait. Do you think Albert likes me?"

"Uh, yeah." Max put his gavel in his Dolly tote and hoisted the bag over his shoulder. "I'm not so sure you're going to need my advice, after all. I haven't seen Albert flirt with anybody since he and Kyler broke up last winter. He just walked right up to you like you had some sort of gravitational pull. What could that possibly mean?" Max winked. We both *totally* knew what that meant, and I could not wait to tell Lu. Maybe finding a date to the hoedown really wasn't going to be so hard.

Max handed me a piece of paper, then headed toward the door. "Okay, gotta run. That's my number. If ever you need me, your Gay Guide is only a text away. Later, Veep."

I stood there, utterly in shock about how well the whole day had gone. It seemed impossible that I could have met more than twenty queer kids in one day, having gone my whole life without meeting a single one. Then to click so well with Max and have the beginnings of my new framily underway? Not to mention that Albert could possibly *like* me? That he'd stare at my mouth like he wanted to devour it as much as I wanted to devour his?

Statistics would call this day an outlier. The majority of days would just be normal, emotionless days. Others—the outliers—go completely horribly (like, Jack-doesn't-get-to-climb-on-that-floating-door-with-Rose-after-the-*Titanic*-sank-despite-the-fact-that-he-totally-could-have-fit, kind of horrible), or they go perfectly, like my first day at Capitol Hill High. But I couldn't get used to the perfection. As outliers, those epic days are only supposed to happen very rarely.

Or maybe the Gay Gods wanted to throw a bone/boner my way, and my life was about to have a much more VSB-filled trend.

7.

✓ Have a Hoedown Heart Attack

I itched to Skype Lu the whole way home, but my walk back to our new place was only eight blocks from school. I had no idea yet who else lived nearby, or whether any of the teens I saw on the street went to Capitol Hill. I was *not* going to risk anybody overhearing all the giggling and squealing that was definitely about to go down.

The Seattle gloom had finally burned off, and I got to thinking how I'd love to explore the city with a boy in the very near future. I pictured going to the Space Needle, but the landmark's giant phallic shape shifted my thoughts to knocking items seven and eight off the Gay Agenda. Why did the city's most notable attraction have to be so boner-y?

I burst through our apartment door and collapsed on the full-sized living room couch. I unlocked my phone and

Skyped Lu, making sure my bangs were perfectly in place while I waited for her to pick up.

"Headline news: Chip and I had a fight." Lu always skipped hellos and got right to the point. She said it came from her journalism background, to always start with the most important information first.

But this information slapped everything I was going to say right out of my mouth with a perfectly manicured hand. How could I tell Lu about Max and the QSA and getting checked out by a *very* VSB when she was having her first fight with Chip?

"Jay?" She banged her phone against her coffee table. "Screw this old piece of shit!"

With each bang of the phone I pictured punching Chip in his stupid face. *Now* was when he decided to open the trunk to their metaphorical relationship car and let out the Spare Tire? I was hundreds of miles away and should be focused on making a whole romance vehicle of my own, not picking up the pieces of the wreck he left behind.

Lu's face reappeared, and the anger washed right out of me. She looked completely beaten down. Her hair was frizzy, she had on a perma-scowl, and I swear one of her neon-green nails was chipped. She never let that happen.

"I'm so sorry, Lu," I said. "What happened?"

"He says I'm becoming such a . . ." The sound of her nervous nail clicking filled the void. If I was with her it would be so much easier to take her hand and tell her everything would be okay, that Chip was the douchiest of douches. But digital comforting was going to have to be our new normal now, and it was seriously lacking.

"He says I'm becoming a burden, Jay," Lu continued. "I'm not kidding when I say we have no. Extra. Money. We see each other half as much as before because practically all my free time is spent working at the diner. When I do get to see Chip, he has to come out here because I can't drive to Spokane without a car. I can't pay for my own dinner when we go on dates. He has to pay for everything. To top it all off, I'm that girl who always smells like burger grease. He just called to say he feels like he never sees me anymore, and when we do see each other, he thinks I'm different than when we started dating. Yeah, I'm different, because my life is blowing up around me. So I blew up at him." She took a deep breath and tried to smooth away some of her frizz. "Gawd, I look awful. My life is such a miserable shit show, and now it's ruining my relationship too."

She said it in such a matter-of-fact way, which was never a good sign. The more emotionless Lu got, the worse she was feeling on the inside. Since she was describing the fight like she was reading a grocery list, I knew she was completely torn up about it.

"But it is what it is." We were at Red-Alert nonchalance. "I learned a long time ago that life isn't fair, and Chip doesn't need to deal with my bad luck."

Lu's never seemed to be able to catch a break. Her parents died in a car crash when their pickup slipped on black ice. We were just babies, and Aunt Carol was only nineteen when she took Lu in. Apparently one in seventy-seven people die in car wrecks every year, but Lu is the only person I know who's lost anybody in her family to one. Plus, it's a .02 percent chance that a child will lose both their parents before they turn eighteen, but Lu did. Regardless of the numbers, all the statistics are just a way to say she was dealt a really fracking shitty hand.

But Chip was not supposed to be a part of all that shittiness. What happened to him having perfect timing? To him being able to look out for her when I had to move away? Him having her back was what was supposed to make all those times I was made the Spare Tire worth it. Now it was like he'd let all the air out of me and Lu in one fell swoop.

I was still silently cursing Chip when Lu said, "The hoedown cannot get here soon enough. Maybe the distraction of the dance will remind Chip that I'm a fun person, if he even wants to come anymore. And you'll be here, which will make life seem normal again, even if it's just for a night. Speaking of which, I've been assigned the community beat for the school paper and got all the deets for the hoedown. It's October ninth."

October ninth. As in the very same October ninth as my homecoming. The homecoming at which I was going to dance with a boy, maybe kiss (hopefully make out), and be elected homecoming king because of my epic costuming skills.

I felt light-headed. My vision tunneled. I couldn't catch my breath. About one-third of the general population faints, and I was about to become a part of that group.

I had no idea what to do. I couldn't dump Lu and the hoedown after she just said she needed me there to lift her spirits. Especially not when a major reason Chip and Lu fought was because she couldn't afford anything. The prize money for the costume contest could at least get her a little extra cash. Sad stat: Two-thirds of American households would be sent into debt with a five-hundred-dollar emergency. I had a feeling Lu and Aunt Carol's emergency threshold was way less than five hundred bucks. Every dollar helped.

"Jay?"

"Oh, um . . . Is there a theme?" I asked. "I want to be sure we dress to the theme."

Fracking great. My first thought was to dig myself deeper into this mess.

"Roses Are Red, Violets Are Blue," Lu said.

"That's the lamest theme I've ever heard." Maybe she'd let me bow out of going if the theme was so stupid I couldn't come up with a legendary outfit.

"Yeah," Lu agreed. "The dance committee was really uninspired this year. It's supposed to be"—she put on a really affected, sarcastic voice—"emblematic of the Blue Bluff orchard surrounded by the red leaves of autumn. Ugh. I've got nail art covered if you can come up with the costume. And maybe, uh . . ." She drummed her nails against the coffee table again. "Maybe if you can cover the cost for it, that would really help me out. That way I wouldn't have to ask Chip."

I didn't hesitate at all. "Of course, Lu, don't even worry

about that." I'd have the worrier role covered while I figured out how to escape this dance dilemma.

"Great," Lu said, but I could tell she was bothered she even had to ask. "I'll pay you back with my portion of the winnings." She massaged her temples, the creases in her forehead the deepest I had ever seen them. "But tell me all about your first day. Did you meet any VSBs?"

My mind flashed back to Albert checking me out in Ms. Okeke's room, his eyes veering down to my mouth. I had met a VSB, one who's into other guys, and who Max said was totally into me, but I couldn't tell Lu all that now.

"You totally did, didn't you?" Lu said. "And now you feel bad telling me about him when I've just had a huge fight with my boyfriend."

She knew me so well.

Lu wagged a finger in front of the camera. "Nuh-uh. Don't do that. You get to be excited about the things that are happening to you even if my life is going to shit. Spill."

So I told her all about Albert. The smashing into each other, the gum stuck to my hair, the blood on my face. I told her about meeting Max, and how he suspected Albert thought *I* was a VSB, despite all my clumsiness.

"I'm totally going to Insta-stalk him," Lu said. "Do you think you're going to go to homecoming with him? When is it, by the way?"

My brain froze. Curse her journalistic instincts to always ask pertinent questions.

"Um, October nixteenth?"

"I don't think that's a date."

"Sorry." I cleared my throat. "October sixteenth."

I knew it was a lie, and that I shouldn't lie to my best friend. But six out of ten Americans think it's okay to call in sick to work even when you're not, so I decided to just call it a mental health day. A day in which I could take some time to *mentally* figure things out to keep Lu's and my friendship nice and *healthy.*

"That's perfect!" Lu said, finally perking up. "Hey, maybe Albert would want to come to the hoedown too. You should ask him."

"Will do." I laughed way too loudly. "Everything's perfect!" Another awkward laugh.

"Are you okay? You're doing that weird laugh like when Ms. Poffenroth taught us sex ed freshman year."

Fortunately, that's when Dad walked through the front door, giving me an excuse to get out of the convo before I made the situation worse.

"Yeah, everything's fine," I said. "Dad just walked in and"—awkward laugh—"you know how excruciating it is talking about relationship stuff when he's around. Gotta go! Bye!"

I hung up and face-palmed. "No, no, no, no, no! The odds are *never* in my favor."

"Rough first day?" Dad asked.

"Oh, no, actually the day was great. Just having a hard time with, uh . . . with my math homework." I didn't want to tell Dad about the dance dilemma because all my horny hopes in the Gay Agenda would have to be divulged, and that was *not* an option.

Dad whistled. "Homework on the first day. They're not kidding around at this new school, huh? I like it." He headed for the kitchen while I melted in despair on the couch.

The day had been great. I had crossed off the first item and a half on the Gay Agenda, and found potential friends and a group where I might belong. There was a guy who possibly liked me, if Max's suspicions and those tingles in my gut (and other places) were accurate. But in order to accept all of that and start the plans I'd been waiting my whole life to set in motion, I had to ditch my best friend *since kindergarten*. I wouldn't get to go to our last hoedown together, and I'd ruin Lu's shot at some extra cash she could really use.

Despite that, I couldn't stop myself from wanting to go to homecoming with a boy for the first time ever. This year was supposed to be all about knocking my firsts off the Gay Agenda. And if I won the homecoming costume contest, I'd have a chance to make my mark.

This was the Battle of the Ho's: homecoming vs. hoedown, and it was HOrrible.

I grabbed my notebook. It was time to add my first depressing item to the list.

JAY'S GAY AGENDA

1. ~~Meet another gay kid. Somewhere, anywhere . . . please! in Seattle in, like, days!~~ ✓

1.5. ~~Get checked out by a very VSB!~~ ✓

2. Go on a date with a boy at the Space Needle and hold hands within the first ninety minutes.

3. ~~Go to a d~~Dance with a boy and have my first kiss slow dancing to Shawn Mendes while getting caught in a surprise Seattle downpour.

4. Have a boyfriend, one who likes to wrap me up in his arms and let me be little spoon, and maybe smells like coffee from all the cafés he goes to.

5. Fall in love with a boy, but wait for him to say it first so I don't seem too desperate, and maybe he says it for the first time at Pike Place Market or in the first Starbucks.

6. Make out with Albert, with tongue, and ~~hard enough that I'd get a little burn from his stubble.~~ run my fingers along that perfect jawline.

7. See another penis besides my own, IRL, and do fun things with it!

8. Lose. My. Virginity!

9. Become part of a super-queer, super-tight framily by impressing everybody with my epic costumier skills, erasing the "new kid" label, and becoming homecoming royalty.

10. **Figure out a way to make my gay dreams come true and not destroy my bestie's life.**

8.

✓ Fashion Yourself into a Life Vest

The next day was my first block-B schedule. Unlike Riverton, which only had six classes a day every day of the week, Capitol Hill did eight longer classes, but you only had four each day to accommodate for the longer periods. This gave me block-A days, like the first day of school, and block-B days, which included Fashion Design. This school had a legit fashion course, the kind of artsy elective I only got to see on episodes of CW shows with kids who lived much more glamorous lives than me. Until now, that is. I figured it was time to move on to costuming with more sewing and less duct tape to guarantee an unbreakable best-costume winning streak. Now I just needed to decide which dance I was going to be making a costume for. I was at my locker mulling over the Battle of the Ho's when Max snatched my schedule from my hand.

"Yes! We have Fashion Design together *and* the same free period. We're going to devote it entirely to homecoming planning and Gay Agenda accomplishing."

My stomach flipped. I'd tossed and turned all night thinking of some way that I could be at two dances at once, but nothing came, including myself. "Helping myself out" was a usual nightly routine, since I was a nearly eighteen-year-old who had yet to meet another gay guy willing to help me out on the coming front. Basically, no coming meant I was seriously distracted. I was going to have to pick one dance over the other, and I just wasn't ready to make that choice yet.

I was *way more likely* to make out with somebody (and maybe knock off *more intimate* items on the Gay Agenda) if I went to homecoming. But I was also *way more likely* to break my best friend's heart if I didn't show up in Riverton. I couldn't lose Lu.

I took my schedule back so I could change the subject. "This says that Fashion Design is in S-I-F? What's S-I-F?"

"It's pronounced *sif*," Max said. "It's the Seattle Institute of Fashion, just a couple blocks down the street." He grabbed my hand, the same thin gold bracelets he'd worn yesterday bumping against my wrist. "Follow me."

We left the main building and walked into the morning gloom. Capitol Hill High was right in the middle of the city and made up of refurbished old buildings that weren't big enough to hold everything a school needed in one structure.

The campus consisted of the main building, the math and science building, the humanities building, the gymnasium, the auditorium, and apparently, the Seattle Institute of Fashion, all scattered among thriving businesses. We walked past a brewery, the Furry Friends of Dorothy pet groomer, and no fewer than four coffee shops until Max pointed to a structure that was as nondescript and gray as the Seattle sky. "Here we are," he said. It did not seem like a place where fabulous fashions were fashioned.

I held the door open for Max, but a group of at least a dozen football players knocked him aside as they barreled past to run into the building. Max threw up his hands so vigorously that his vintage Backstreet Boys T-shirt came untucked from his purple leggings. "Watch where you're going!"

"Max!" one of the players yelled. I instantly logged him in my list of Capitol Hill VSBs. He was Black, my height, and had short twists that were dark at the roots and bleached on top. He had round cheeks, like he still had a bit of baby weight, which was a cute clash to the adult biceps bulging out of his blue-and-white football jersey. A large number twenty-three was on the front over the Capitol Hill High lightning bolt mascot, and *Alexander* was written on the back.

Alexander let the rest of the football players cruise by. When the coast was clear, he approached Max tentatively. "I've been trying to get ahold of you the past couple weeks."

"Mmm." It was the shortest reply I'd ever heard from Max. Yes, I'd only known him one day, but he was so outgoing. Here he was all pursed lips and awkward looks at the sidewalk.

"How are you holding up?" Alexander asked.

"I'm great, Damon," Max said, reminding me that last names were on jerseys. I really should have paid more attention to *Monday Night Football.* "Honestly, great. People need to stop worrying about me." Max hooked his arm around my elbow. "Besides, I've got Jay now."

Damon looked as if he hadn't noticed me standing there. "That's right. I heard about you. New kid running the QSA with Max?"

Wow. Word got around Capitol Hill faster than Riverton, even with nearly eight times as many students.

"That's me," I said.

Damon turned his attention back to Max with such a tender look in his eyes. Did they used to go out? Maybe that was why Max was being so short with him: they'd had a jaw-dropping summer affair like the one I'd hoped for while it was actually Lu and Chip who were having one. But it must have ended badly if Max and Damon were so uncomfortable around each other.

"Well, I guess as long as you're okay," Damon said, opening the door to SIF. "You know you can always talk to me, right? Answer my calls sometime. Or Cami's. She's really been wanting to tell you about her first few days of college."

Damon gave Max those tender eyes again. If all that time watching *Ex on the Beach* taught me anything, it's that people didn't look at each other like that unless they used to bone. Max nodded in acknowledgment, and Damon walked into the building, but not before giving Max one last loving look.

I whipped to Max as soon as Damon was out of sight. "Okay, what was that all about?"

Max slumped, his shirt wrinkling at just the right place so the Backstreet Boys' brows were as furrowed as his. "It's nothing. We're going to be late."

Apparently he didn't want to talk about it. I decided to drop it, but I made a mental note to start a list of ways to pay Max back for being my Gay Guide. Maybe helping heal the rift between him and Damon would be the way to do that.

"We can't be at the right building," I said, taking Max's hint to drop the subject, then making sure the pale orange letters on the glass door actually read SIF and not GYM. "Shouldn't all those jocks be going to work out or something?"

Max walked inside and held the door for me. "Actually, athletes mean we're in exactly the right place."

"They do?" I wouldn't at all mind taking in the view of some football players over the top of my sewing machine.

"Fashion Design is the football team's art of choice." Max led me past a chipped front desk, through another set of glass doors with a peeling orange SIF logo, and down a creepy hallway with fluorescent lights and scuffed booger-colored tile. The interior design of this place seriously had me doubting the instructors could create runway-worthy fashion.

"It's a tradition that started a few years ago," Max continued. "All athletes at Capitol Hill must participate in at least one art program to remain on the team. The football seniors a while back thought it would be fun if they all joined Fashion Design and created outfits for each other that they had to wear at graduation no matter what."

Max paused before opening a beige door with chips falling off it and took a fortifying breath. He pushed the door open, revealing a room that looked more like a biology lab swarming with jerseys and sewing machines than a design studio. There was one empty lab table left with two gray and dingy Singers on top.

Max led the way, continuing on his football player explanation as if he hadn't stopped to compose himself before entering the room. "Despite the stereotypes you might see on TV, Fashion Design is chock-full of straight boys." He patted the stool next to him and I sat down, completely in awe at all the jocks in the room. The football players at RHS wouldn't have been caught dead in a Fashion Design class. Last year Justin Ridderbach practically quit school when he found out he had to join home ec.

"Well, there is *one* other gay guy who I know signed up for this class, but he's . . ." Max trailed off, chewing his cheek as he tried to find the right word. "He's difficult. So don't go thinking you'll find any gay romance here while you're hemming some skirts." He nudged my shoulder, a mischievous grin replacing his scowl. "You'll just have to stick with Albert."

I giggled when Max said his name. Like *actually.* *Fracking. Giggled.* "Ohmigawd, I can't believe this is how I behave when I have a crush on a real-life guy."

Max patted my back. "You're sweeter than a Snickers, Jay. It's what I like about you. We're all jaded city kids here, but everything is so new to you. You're like a gay baby. You're a gayby!"

"Thanks? I think?"

Ping! A pen smacked against my sewing machine. "Jeezus!" I whipped around to see who had thrown the Paper Mate projectile.

Sitting two tables back was a blond white boy with the most piercingly blue eyes I had ever seen. So piercing, he looked like he'd spear me straight through the head if he could. "*Shhh!* Mr. Bogosian is about to start." He pointed to the door, where a man—Mr. Bogosian, apparently—had just barely set foot in the room. *About to start* was a total overstatement.

"Fine, but you don't have to be such a jer—"

Blue Piercer raised a very aggressive finger to his lips. "SHHHHHH!"

It's always so ironic that people who insist others be quiet end up making way more noise than the people they were shushing in the first place. I swear that kid got spit all over his purple NYU Tisch School of the Arts sweatshirt. If Lu had been here, she would have done a great impression of him and shushed him right back with a fiercely nailed pointer finger. Unfortunately, I didn't have a sharpened manicure to do the job. So instead I turned around and rolled my eyes at Max, who fiddled with his gold bracelets while he mouthed, *Difficult*.

My mind reeled. If this shusher was the difficult guy, that meant he was the one other Fashion Design gay. Not Damon. So that summer affair I'd made up for him and Max was not a thing, since Damon was straight.

"Good morning, class," Mr. Bogosian said. He couldn't even be thirty yet. He just oozed cool as he walked to his worktable at the front of the room. He had olive skin and wore skinny black jeans, a gray T-shirt underneath a gray cardigan, and circular black glasses and had a perfectly flawless bald head. Even the way the light glinted off his smooth scalp was cool.

"For those of you who haven't met me, I'm Mr. Bogosian. I'm an instructor here at the Seattle Institute of Fashion, where we like to usher in the next generation of talent. That's why we provide this space to Capitol Hill High students each semester. I'll help you *SIF*"—he paused, waggling his eyebrows so much that I worried they might fall off—"through your designs and get you ready for the runway in no time."

I guess even cool guys tell terrible dad jokes. We were so under his spell, though, that we all laughed. One of the football players even shouted, "Aw, good one, Mr. B!"

"Thank you . . ."

"Julian Dasher, teach," the footballer finished.

"Thanks, Julian. Now I know you've all been waiting on *pins and needles*"—more eyebrow wiggling—"to find out what we'll design first. Drumroll, please." The jocks beat their hands against their worktables, the drumroll sounding way more like an earthquake. "Tote bags!"

Everyone went silent.

"What?" Mr. Bogosian asked. "I thought you'd all be *totes* excited."

Julian slapped his table. "You're on a roll, Mr. B."

Blond Butthead stretched his hand so high I thought the logo on his sweatshirt would crack. "Reese Buttersworth, sir. It's just that I was hoping for something more *dramatic*."

Mr. Bogosian polished his glasses on his cardigan. "Well, Reese, even the most well-known designers had humble beginnings. The wrap dress wasn't built in a day, you know. Just because we're starting with totes doesn't mean that one of you might not become the next Diane von Furstenburg or Cristóbal Balenciaga."

Julian threw his hand in the air. "Balenci-what-a?"

"Balenci*aga*," Reese said, and rolled his eyes before directing his icy glare back at Mr. Bogosian. "I'm hoping to be able to tailor my own outfit this year for the fall play. I was swimming in my tunic in last spring's *Oliver!* I guess the wardrobe kids just didn't understand how every moment onstage is a time to put your best foot forward."

I was so glad I hadn't signed up to help with outfits for the drama department. Reese would have eaten me and my duct tape alive.

"He's the Diane von *Worst*enburg," I whispered to Max.

"HA!" Max's laugh sounded exactly like the donkey back on the Steiners' farm in Riverton. I face-palmed as all heads in class whipped our way.

Not surprisingly, the most judgmental of all the looks came from Reese. "You two could use some help putting your best foot forward, if you ask me."

I wasn't sure exactly what I had done, but somehow, I had ended up on Reese's bad side in a span of two minutes. Where was all the gay camaraderie? If watching *High School Musical: The Musical: The Series* and daydreaming about cute boys serenading me had taught me anything, it was that we were all supposed to be in this together, right?

Mr. Bogosian walked toward a set of double doors in the back of the room. "Now, now, we all express ourselves differently." He opened the doors to reveal a massive storage closet packed to the ceiling with rolls of fabric in every color of the rainbow. "And the best way to do that is through fashion." Mr. Bogosian stepped to the side and made a sweeping gesture with his arm. "Pick whichever fabric speaks to you the most for this *tote*-ally awesome project."

The room was flooded with the sounds of scraping stools as the football team barreled toward the fabric closet.

"Come on," Max said. He grabbed my hand and led me to the back of the room. The football team had somehow dismantled the nice and orderly stacks of fabric in a matter of seconds. When we passed Reese's worktable, I noticed Max tense up and Reese's blue stare zeroed in on our clasped hands.

"Watch out!" I yanked Max down to avoid being hit by a five-foot-long roll of yellow velvet.

"Sorry," Julian said. A roll of white material and another of blue were tucked under his arms. "My bad."

"Take it easy, fellas," Mr. Bogosian called. "There's enough fabric to go around. We've got whole *football fields* of this stuff." He wiggled his eyebrows again, and a football player gave him a high five.

When most of the players had finally left the closet, it was safe enough to pick my material. I wanted to make something for Lu, a sort of pick-me-up tote considering all the crap she was going through. Or maybe it would end up being an *I'm Sorry for Being the Worst BFF* tote if I had to bail on the hoedown. Nothing says *Please forgive me for being a backstabbing best friend* like a tote bag, right?

I found a roll of neon green—Lu's favorite color—but of course it was on the bottom of the fabric mountain the football players had made. I grabbed one end of the roll and tugged. It didn't budge. I tried again, getting what I thought was a firm grip. "Come on, you fracking—whoa!" My fingers slipped, and I careened backward. Images of cracking my skull open on the nearest worktable flew through my head.

I braced myself for impact, but instead of oozing brains all over the fashion lab, I fell into a set of muscular, dark arms.

"Easy!" I was put on my feet like I weighed nothing at

all. It was the first time I had been physically picked up, and I realized that was definitely something I wanted to have happen again. And again. And again.

I turned around to find Damon. "Thanks."

"Don't mention it." Damon pointed at the neon-green material still stuck under the fabric mountain. "Need some help with that?"

I nodded, and Damon whipped the roll out of the jumbled mess like it was nothing.

"Here you go," he said. He propped it up on one end and handed me the other. It was just the two of us in the supply closet, and Damon's smile seemed so warm and welcoming. I thought now was as good a time as any to try to get to the bottom of the Damon-Max awkwardness.

"What was up back there with you and Max?" I asked.

Damon's smile vanished instantly. "I don't know. He hasn't been the same since the breakup. He's ignored my calls and my sister Cami's. That's how I know he's not okay. They've been best friends since they met in the QSA three years ago. He'd come over to our house every day, and was practically part of the family. Even when Cami left for college in Los Angeles a few weeks back, they still talked constantly. But then he got dumped and fell off the face of the earth. I'm worried. Everybody who knows him is worried."

That must have been what Max meant about pity votes. If everybody was worried about him, that's why they didn't run against him for QSA president, and why they'd be so quick to accept me as their VP when they'd never even met me before. But who could make super-confident Max so distraught that everyone was on high alert about it?

"Who broke up with him?" I asked.

With the worst timing ever, Mr. Bogosian called, "Back to your stations!"

"Listen." Damon sighed. "Look out for him, okay? I promised Cami I'd keep an eye on him, but he's not letting me do that right now. At least he's talking to you."

"Yeah, of course," I said.

Damon put his hand out, and I thought he wanted to shake on it. But Damon grabbed my fingers and moved his hand in some cool-kid fist bump that I knew absolutely nothing about. My hand just sat there like a limp noodle. I was completely mortified.

"Ohmigawd. I'm like, the least coolest person who ever existed."

Damon chuckled, but his smile didn't light up like it had before. "You've got to be all right if Max is hanging out with you," he said. "He could really use a friend."

My stomach sank while Damon walked away. I'd gone from Spare Tire to Life Vest, and it definitely didn't help me in choosing which side to pick in the Battle of the Ho's. If I abandoned Max for the hoedown, I'd be leaving him in a time of need just as badly as if I dumped Lu for homecoming.

"Excuse *you*," Reese sneered. "You're holding up the

whole class." His icy glare followed me the entire way back to my seat.

I couldn't concentrate as Mr. Bogosian walked us through the basics of sewing machines. Even his cringe-worthy puns ("Isn't this *sew* awesome!") couldn't snap me out of my funk.

After who knows how long, Max shimmied in front of me, the Backstreet Boys shaking along with him. "Earth to Jay! Are you in there?"

I rattled my head. "Sorry, what?"

"Time to go. Class is over. What are you thinking about?"

I watched Damon and the rest of the football guys leave. Would asking about Max's breakup make him shut me out like he had to Cami, Damon, and everyone else? I couldn't lose my Gay Guide before I crossed any more items off the Gay Agenda. I decided to let it go for now, just in case.

Max pointed to my forehead. "That scowl is way too deep for the gift I'm about to give you." His mischievous grin was back and he looked much happier now that everyone was gone.

"What is it?"

"I noticed that your Gay Agenda is all physical stuff and lacking any real gay culture." Max led the way out of the classroom, swinging his violet Michael Kors purse as he walked. "Being the magnificent Gay Guide and Libido Liberator that I am, I thought we could combine the two. I'm taking you to your first-ever drag show on Saturday. A drag queen DJ I love is hosting, and I want to hire her for homecoming."

I couldn't believe I'd never thought to add *See drag live* to the Gay Agenda. I'd only watched every single season of *Drag Race* twice.

"Aaaaand," Max added, "while we're there, I'm going to introduce you to a very sexy, very single boy."

His eyebrow wiggling rivaled Mr. Bogosian's.

9.
✓ Snag a Ticket to Your First Date

According to *Medical News Today*, one in four people suffer from halitosis. I prayed to Andy Cohen that I was not one of those people as Albert walked up to me that Friday before lunch. We'd be spending the next hour together, and I did not want to chase him away with some chronic bad breath.

Albert's head was down, looking at his phone, his glasses slipping dangerously close to the edge of his nose. I was caught between two warring urges—check my breath before Albert took the empty folding chair next to me, or gently nudge those glasses back up so I could touch his face. I decided the latter might be a little too serial killer-y for our first solo hangout. Breath check it was.

My breath was . . . fine. But I definitely wouldn't be

eating the tuna fish sandwich I'd packed for lunch. What the actual *frack* was I thinking, packing tuna when I'd be within breathing distance of a VSB?

It was Albert's and my first shift selling homecoming tickets. I'd already grabbed a cashbox from the office and set up a folding table outside the cafeteria. All that was left to do was write people's names down, take their money, and not embarrass myself in front of Albert. I'd even come up with a list of potential things to get some conversation started:

TOPICS TO CHARM ALBERT

1. R2-D2 and how everybody seems to understand what he's saying. (Is there some beep-boop robot linguistics course everyone in the Star Wars universe goes to? As the robotics expert, I thought he could enlighten me.)

2. How he chose tortoiseshell as the pattern for his glasses. (It was the perfect fit for him because they really made his eyes pop, and this topic would let me look into them even more.)

3. Costume ideas for Homecoming in Hindsight. (And maybe, just maybe, this would lead into him saying he didn't have a date and asking if I had a date, which I conveniently didn't, and yes, I would totally go with him.)

"Hey, Albert," I said.

He didn't look up. He kept walking forward, his head still in his phone.

"A-Albert?"

He was dead focused on whatever was on his screen. He took another step, and another, and if he didn't look up right that second he was going to . . .

BAM!

Albert slammed into the table, sending the cashbox flying. It clattered to the floor, but Albert didn't give any indication he cared about the commotion or the collision.

"Ow." Albert said it like *he* was a robot, an automatic response that he knew he should say for slamming into a table. But he still didn't take his eyes from his phone.

"Are you okay?" The impact was definitely going to leave a bruise.

"I will be in fourteen steps. I'm so close to hatching this thing." He waved his phone, and I thought he'd lost his mind.

"Um, your phone's not going to hatch."

Albert paced around in a circle and counted to himself. "One, two, three, four . . ."

He had for sure lost his mind.

I walked around the table and snagged the cashbox before Albert tripped over it. I mentally added and crossed *Save a VSB from smashing his perfect nose and crushing his adorable glasses* off the Gay Agenda.

". . . thirteen, fourteen." Albert threw his hands in the air like he'd just scored a touchdown and thrust his hips from side to side. "It's happening! Look!" He grabbed my shoulder and pulled me toward him. My whole body instantly lit on fire, every atom of my being aware that

I was held close to an extremely good-looking boy who might have a thing for me. If firemen came to douse me with water, I'd tell them no, I never wanted to be put out.

"The egg!" Albert said. "What's it going to be?"

I finally glanced at his phone. Albert hadn't lost his mind. He was playing Digimals, a huge video game franchise that now had a mobile phone version. A giant orange egg was cracking open on Albert's phone, ready to hatch into a digital animal.

"Please be Petaliabear." Albert moved his hips back and forth again. It was like he had no control over his body. He was so carefree and unself-conscious. It was really refreshing to see after obsessing so much over how I should look and act and if my breath smelled too much like canned fish. "Come on, Petaliabear!"

The egg exploded. Lying among the pixel shells was something that looked like a mix between a frog and a duck.

"Noooo!" Albert moaned. "Not Quackcroak. I've got like nine million of these things."

"If only your magic Digimals dance worked," I said while Albert continued shaking his hips.

"It usually does! Some say it's superstition, but I swear I've caught every Digimal I've ever hoped for when I do the Digihips."

Ohmigawd, he actually gave the dance move a name. Could he be any cuter?

All his hip thrusting made me think of the homecoming dance and what it would be like to thrust hips next to each other. "You may not have caught that Petal Bear or whatever, but you definitely caught my attention."

Albert's cheeks immediately bloomed with adorable pink spots, while mine burst into flames. If those firemen came by again to douse me, I'd tell them no, I needed to burn to ash because I couldn't believe my inner monologue had become an *outer* monologue.

"Ohmigawd, Albert. I—"

The bell rang, and the hallway was swarmed with students. They saw the "Homecoming Tickets" sign I'd taped behind our table, and before I knew it Albert and I were swept up taking cash and keeping track of who paid for who. I wished I knew more kids at school so I could get lost in the gossip of who was pairing up, namely the drama of some person named Graham breaking up with Forrest and asking Forrest's best friend, Tara, to the dance instead. But since I had no idea who these people were, I couldn't stop replaying in my mind that gawdawful moment when I'd told Albert that his *hips caught my attention.* Seriously? I didn't need to worry about being creepy by face-touching because all I had to do was open my mouth.

Despite the hour being so busy, it was excruciatingly slow. I kept glancing at Albert to see if he was skeezed out by me after my Digihips comment. Every time our eyes met, his darted away. I'd freaked him out and he couldn't even look at me. Not to mention whenever our hands went toward the cashbox or the roll of tickets at the same time, he'd snatch his fingers out of reach so that there was no way my creeper ass could touch him.

I'd totally blown it. Any fantasies of Albert being part

of the Gay Agenda needed to be crossed out of my mind in extra-bold mental marker.

The bell rang for the end of lunch period, and I smashed the cashbox shut. I had to get out of there fast. I didn't want to say or do anything else that would make Albert relinquish his ticket-selling duties so he'd never be anywhere near me again.

"Feel free to head out. I can clean up here," I said. This time it was me who couldn't lock eyes. I stared at the linoleum floor like my life depended on it.

"Do you play?"

I tentatively lifted my head. Our eyes finally met, and neither of us looked away. Albert was staring right at me, a smile on his lips.

"Play what?" I asked.

"Digimals. They're releasing a rare Digimal on Sunday for one day only. I was going to go out and see if I could find it. Would you want to join?" Albert swayed his hips again, that soft blush creeping up his cheeks. "There will be a lot more of this."

Holy shit. Albert was flirting with me.

I'd seen so many people flirt at Riverton. Lame compliments like in homeroom when Steven Rylie said what great handwriting Ashley Kearn had, or Steph Richardson telling Eric Andrews that his dribbling skills were, like, totally amazing. I'd rolled my eyes every time. But Albert playfully moving his hips at me made me feel more whole than I ever had before.

For years, I had thought of the Gay Agenda as a way

to fit in, to be part of the group that could talk about hand-holding and kissing and someday having sex. But seeing Albert look at me like that, flirting with me like that, I realized the Gay Agenda was so much more. It was about connecting with another person. I'd always felt like this overlooked, sexless, invisible *thing* that just had to stand by while everyone else was noticed. Sure, hand-holding and kissing and coming together all seemed like they would feel good when I eventually got to do those things. But I never knew that I'd feel more like a complete person when someone else recognized me as somebody they could want. Sexually, romantically, flirtingly, all of it. The Gay Agenda made me feel more complete. Like a human being worthy of love and connection instead of some lonely sideshow.

The next step toward that connection was accepting this Digimals date. Sure, it wasn't the Space Needle, but this was a real-life VSB asking me to go out with him! I'd hardly played a video game ever in my life, but I was not going to let that get in the way of crossing item number two off the Gay Agenda.

JAY'S GAY AGENDA

1. ~~Meet another gay kid. Somewhere, anywhere . . . please! in Seattle in, like, days!~~ ✓

1.5. ~~Get checked out by a very VSB!~~ ✓

2. Go on a **Digimals** date with **Albert** ~~a boy at the Space Needle~~ and hold hands within the first ninety minutes.

3. ~~Go to a d~~Dance with a boy and have my first kiss slow dancing to Shawn Mendes while getting caught in a surprise Seattle downpour.

4. Have a boyfriend, one who likes to wrap me up in his arms and let me be little spoon, and maybe smells like coffee from all the cafés he goes to.

5. Fall in love with a boy, but wait for him to say it first so I don't seem too desperate, and maybe he says it for the first time at Pike Place Market or in the first Starbucks.

6. Make out with Albert, with tongue, and ~~hard enough that I'd get a little burn from his stubble.~~ run my fingers along that perfect jawline.

7. See another penis besides my own, IRL, and do fun things with it!

8. Lose. My. Virginity!

9. Become part of a super-queer, super-tight framily by impressing everybody with my epic costumier skills, erasing the "new kid" label, and becoming homecoming royalty.

10. Figure out a way to make my gay dreams come true and not destroy my bestie's life.

It was time to attempt flirting back for the first time in my life.

"No fair," I tried. "You already know I can't resist the Digihips."

Albert's smile was so big it made his glasses slip down his nose again. Flirt accomplished.

"Great," he said. "Meet me by the Fish Market at Pike

- 111 -

Place at noon on Sunday."

"Fish Market. Pike Place. Got it." I nodded so much I probably looked like a bobblehead. But Albert didn't seem to care. He waved—actually, wholesomely waved—goodbye, and sauntered off, a little sway still in his hips. Images of my hands on them as we danced together at homecoming flashed through my mind. But I was getting ahead of myself. First thing first:

Our date.

My first date of all time.

It was finally happening.

10.

✓ Get Dragged into a VSB's Line of Sight

It's the weirdest thing how you can live in such a seemingly depressing place—gray skies all the time, rain from hour to hour—but have it still be so full of color. Seattle was like that. It was gloomy, and it rained an average of 155 days a year, but all that rain made it full of the greenest greens I'd ever seen. And maybe it was just a trick of the gray skies juxtaposed against bright, sequined outfits, but I think the gray made drag queens go out in the most radiant colors they could find. Or maybe they just looked so vibrant because I was seeing drag queens in real life for the very first time.

Or maybe I was seeing everything in Technicolor because I was going on my first date ever the next day.

"Have I mentioned I have a date with Albert

tomorrow?" I couldn't stop bouncing on my toes. I had this feeling like I constantly needed to move, like if I somehow ran fast enough, I could make time move forward and then, wham! It'd be Sunday, and Albert and I would be in First Date Delirium.

"Yes, you've mentioned it a time or two," Max said flatly. "And I'm happy for you. Thrilled. And while I fully support this date, all I'm saying is, you just finished your *first* week of school. Have all the fun with Albert you want, but keep your options open."

Max and I stood outside the Pride of Lions Lounge and Disco, waiting in line to get into their monthly drag brunch. Each time someone new popped in line, Max peeked over his shoulder to give them an up-down.

"Are you expecting someone?" I asked.

"Of course I am. I told you I'd be introducing you to a very single boy. But if you're too caught up with Albert and not interested . . ." Max shrugged his shoulders. "I guess my Gay Guide services aren't needed."

"No," I rushed. "You're doing great. I'm happy to meet anybody you want to introduce me to. And you're right. Maybe I shouldn't get too hung up on Albert so quickly."

Max beamed. "Trust me, you won't be sorry."

A big, burly bouncer was at the door looking at IDs. I kept obsessively checking my hair as we got closer to the front of the line. The rain was out in force, and the resulting mist continually crept under our umbrella and clung to my bangs.

"Lord and Taylor, if you keep doing that, your hair is going to fall out," Max said.

I unstuck a wet strand from my forehead. "I can't help it. This is my first real leap into queer culture, and I don't need the moment ruined by limp bangs. Besides, if it's always wet like this, I'm going to need practice on how to keep my 'do making me look . . . doable."

"Do you honestly think I would let you go in there with anything less than the perfect coif?" Max asked. "Besides, they don't call me Mary Poppins for nothing." I wondered who exactly called Max Mary Poppins while he patted his white feathered bucket bag. "The bag may change with the outfit, but the necessities don't. Serums, gels, sprays, you name it. Jizz Genie, remember?"

"I thought we agreed you'd never—"

"IDs."

We'd made it to the front of the line and the big, burly bouncer (who I could now see wore a name tag with the very unburly name *Lilli* on it) held out his hand. His stare was the most intimidating look I'd ever come across. If we'd been trying to sneak in at night, when Pride of Lions was twenty-one and over, his glare would have made me confess how sinful we were. Even with a sweet name like Lilli.

Max and I handed over our licenses. Lilli gave them a quick glance, then pulled the thickest black Sharpie out of his jacket pocket.

"Hands."

I held out my hand, palm up, fingers shaking. My

nerves were on overdrive. It wasn't just about being moments away from stepping through the threshold into my first drag show ever. It was about being in the presence of so many gay people for the first time in my life. I never knew until we got into that line, but there's an energy you can get from other queer people that lets you know you're part of the family. I felt it when a guy smirked at me in a way that said he thought I was cute, and when a lesbian couple beamed as they got in line behind us. Their smiles let me know I was welcome and part of the community. It simultaneously set me at ease and made me buzz, which resulted in shaking hands.

Lilli grabbed Max's composed and shake-free fingers, holding the Sharpie over Max's shimmer-enhanced skin.

"Do we have to do this every time, Lilli?" Max asked. "Garish permanent marker isn't really my look. I'd be happy to wear a tasteful brooch to declare I'm underage as opposed to something that looks like a kindergartener figuring out how to spell."

Lilli didn't say a word. He just marked Max's hand with a giant X.

"I guess that's a no," Max said, bitter. I wouldn't be surprised if his outfits involved gloves for the rest of the week.

Lilli pointed to my shaking hand with a meaty finger. "Flip it over," he commanded.

I turned my shivering palm upside down just before the longest, most bedazzled magenta fingernails came into view and grabbed my fingers.

"Oh, honey, you're shaking like a leaf. Thank gawd you didn't come for the Friday show. You think Lilli Putian's scary now, just wait until you see her in drag."

I looked up to find the most beautiful woman I had ever seen. She was wearing a bodysuit covered in sparkling scales in ombré shades of pink. They cascaded from her long elegant neck where gold dusted her ebony skin, all the way down to her pointy high-heeled boots. Even the headphones draped around her neck were covered in the sparkly scale pattern.

"The name's Tuna Turner," she said, caressing my cheek with a curved nail. "The fishiest drag queen DJ in the Pacific Northwest."

Max clapped his hands together. "This is my present for you, Tuna," he said, directing a flourish my way. He had that very mischievous glint in his eye, and any thoughts of Tuna were swept away by the nervous guppies that suddenly swam in my stomach. "He's a virgin."

"Max!" I entrust him with the Gay Agenda, then he goes and blabs to random drag queens about my lack of sexual activity? Guess I'd be going to prison a virgin because I was about to murder him.

"A virgin!" Tuna squealed. "Oh, Max, you're so good to me." She pinched Max's cheek, then cupped her hand around her mouth to yell, "We've got a first timer here, folks!"

Everyone in line looked up. Excited chatter—including way too many repetitions of the word *virgin*—rippled down the street. People in the lounge perked up too. Some even came back through the doorway to see firsthand the commotion caused by someone who'd had no boy-on-boy action. I needed to find out the stats about spontaneous combustion. I was fairly certain the odds of me bursting into flames were 100 percent.

Tuna pulled me behind her into the lounge and screamed, "HIT IT!"

Music blared from speakers over dozens of packed booths. Electric organs and saxophones blasted while Tuna struck a pose, hand on hip above a sparkly pink fin sewn to the side of her bodysuit. Words began in a slightly raspy, fiery voice, and Tuna lip-synced perfectly.

"Oh, I left a good job in the city . . ."

Tuna's magenta fingernails dug into my skin as she grabbed my hand with an iron grip.

"What's happening?" I asked. I looked with wide, terrified eyes into Tuna's. She batted her glittering lashes innocently.

"You're a drag virgin," she said. I felt a very brief sense of relief that all the first-timer talk was about attending a drag show. "We're rolling down the river, baby." She said it at just the right time so that she never lost her place in the lip sync. *"And I never lost one minute of sleepin' . . ."*

I knew I'd heard the song somewhere before, but I couldn't place it. Tuna's hair looked very familiar too: it was short in the back, but high and full on top, streaks of blond reaching for the sky. If the energy and exuberance of the song were turned into a haircut, this would totally be it. Her hair whipped to the side as she grabbed my free hand in hers and spun us around in circles.

"*Big wheel, keep on turning! Proud Mary, keep on burning.*"

Then Tuna was pulling me behind her, the faces of everybody in the lounge flying past.

"*Rollin', rollin', rollin' on a river.*"

We were rolling, rolling on a river of patrons. Their eyes were locked on us, their phones were out, and they all pointed at me way too much. I only ever got this amount of attention *in costume*, when it was like I had a shield of cardboard and duct tape and superglue. Just Jay on complete display like this was my worst nightmare.

We rolled back up the way we'd come. If people didn't get a good look the first time, they for sure would get a second shot at basking in my embarrassment.

A second verse came and went in the blink of an eye, but also slower than any song ever had a right to be. Tuna still had a grip on my hand, making sure I couldn't escape the stares of everyone inside Pride of Lions. I would have given anything for a pride of lions to come through right at that moment and eat me alive.

The "Rollin'" chorus came along again, followed by a bunch of "*Doot, doot, doot, doot*" that was punctuated by even more drums and saxophones. Tuna bent forward and thrust her arms out with the beat.

"Do it with me, baby, come on," Tuna yelled.

"Oh, I couldn't . . ."

"HOLD IT!"

The music scratched to a stop. Like, literally, a record scratch cut through the speakers.

"What's your name, honey?" Tuna asked.

"J-Jay," I whispered. "Jay."

Tuna faced the crowd. "JayJay here thinks he can't do Ms. Tina Turner's classic move." Even without a microphone Tuna's voice was as loud as if she was magnified by the speakers. "Who here thinks JayJay can do it?"

The crowd whistled and screamed. I looked at Max back in the doorway, hoping he could see the panic in my eyes and get me the frack out of there. Instead he was standing next to an inordinately cute guy, and both of them were pointing at me with the rest of the drag brunchers.

"There's only one way out of this, baby," Tuna said. "You ready?"

I couldn't speak past the frog in my throat, so I just nodded.

"HIT IT!" Tuna screamed again, and the music blared once more. All eyes were zeroed in on us—including Max's and Cutie McCuterson's—as the song picked back up.

This was it. If I wanted out of this, I was just going to have to play along.

That's when I had a vision of Albert thrusting from side to side without any care in the world. I needed to stop worrying so much and channel his Digihips.

The saxophones came to punctuate the *doots* again. In time with Tina, Tuna and I flung our hands forward, bent down, and thrashed our hair back and forth. My hair was fluffed just right to swoop and hit the beat.

"YEEEEES, HUNTY," Tuna cried, and the crowd roared like it was actually a pride of lions. My face was on fire, but this time from a good sort of embarrassment, something I had no idea existed. I was still absolutely mortified, but I felt in on the joke, like I was a part of something bigger. People were pointing and laughing, but in a *He's really going for it and look at his great hair-ography* type of way. Warm tingles cascaded through my entire body. For the first time ever, I put myself out there in front of a crowd, just Jay, and it went well.

Max was smiling bigger than I'd ever seen him smile, and that cute guy next to him had his eyes laser-focused on me. I didn't think it was possible, but my cheeks got even redder as he caught my eye and winked.

"Everybody give it up for JayJay!" Tuna lifted my hands in the air, the whooping and hollering picking up as she twirled me in front of the crowd. "You're officially initiated, honey. And I'm going to come to you if I ever need backup dancers."

Despite how exhilarated I felt, I didn't think backup dancer was going to be my career of choice.

Tuna gave me a kiss on the cheek before another song started and she got back to her hosting duties. I booked it over to Max before I could get pulled into another number.

"Lord and Taylor, that was fan-fucking-tastic!" Max said. He elbowed the cutie standing with him. "Don't you think, Tony?"

"Really, that was amazing."

Now that I was up close, I could see that Cutie McCuterson—er, Tony—wasn't just an inordinately cute guy, he was certifiably H. O. T. T.

HOTNESS OVERLOAD TONY TRAITS

1. Shockingly green eyes (that rivaled the emerald power of Seattle's nature)

2. Flawless skin (with the exact shade of tan I tried and failed to get over the summer)

3. Perfectly straight teeth (that looked very white against said tan skin and would make him the only reasonable choice for a model for both his orthodontist and the next Calvin Klein underwear ad)

"I had other newbies with me when I first came to this drag brunch," Tony continued. "I don't think I could have faced the crowd alone. You're very brave."

He smirked at me, but in that way that oozed *I'm into you*. It was how I'd felt earlier making eye contact with the occasional guy standing in line, only times a thousand. Tony was clearly sending signals, and if there was anything else that could have gotten me more worked up than thinking about Tony in an underwear ad, it was thinking about me and Tony standing in our underwear together.

Max poked me in the ribs. "Say something," he whispered.

"I'm Jay." It was the most creative thing that came to mind.

"Tony." He put his hand out, and we shook. Electric jolts bolted up my skin. I swear his touch made my arm hairs stand on end.

"Tony graduated from Capitol Hill two years ago," Max explained. He looked at our clasped hands and let loose a self-satisfied shrug. Tony kept clutching my fingers, a smirk perpetually playing at the corner of his lips. This was the most physical contact I'd ever had with a guy who was into me. And while it wasn't on a date at the Space Needle, and it happened before my Digimals date with Albert, maybe this meant I could technically scratch "hold hands" in item number two off the agenda.

I stared at our hands, positive we could power the entire city of Seattle with the energy buzzing between us. Tony's long fingers dwarfed mine. There was something about his hand being big enough to fold mine into his that sent a thrill through me. And his lingering contact had to mean that Tony was into it, too, right? Scientists say if someone gets into your personal bubble—as in, zero to eighteen inches away from you—they are more likely to be physically attracted to you. With Tony keeping my hand in his, I'd say we counted as zero inches apart.

Max was so right. I had rushed too quickly into thinking Albert would be the guy to cross all the items off the Gay Agenda with. Why focus on only one boy when there could be a whole smorgasbord of gays just waiting to give me my first kiss? Or first make-out? I'd

have to tweak the plan as soon as I had some alone time
with my notebook.

JAY'S GAY AGENDA

1. ~~Meet another gay kid. Somewhere, anywhere . . .
   please! in Seattle in, like, days!~~ ✓

1.5. ~~Get checked out by a very VSB!~~ ✓

2. Go on a Digimals date with Albert ~~a boy at the
   Space Needle.~~

2.5. **Hold hands ~~within the first ninety minutes~~
   a VSB after being pulled into my first-ever
   drag show by a queen named after a fish.** ✓

3. ~~Go to a d~~Dance with a boy and have my first
   kiss slow dancing to Shawn Mendes while getting
   caught in a surprise Seattle downpour.

4. Have a boyfriend, one who likes to wrap me up
   in his arms and let me be little spoon, and maybe
   smells like coffee from all the cafés he goes to.

5. Fall in love with a boy, but wait for him to say it
   first so I don't seem too desperate, and maybe he
   says it for the first time at Pike Place Market or
   in the first Starbucks.

6. Make out with Albert, **or Tony, or, you know,
   any guy who keeps himself in my personal
   bubble,** with tongue~~, and hard enough that I'd
   get a little burn from his stubble.~~ ~~run my fingers
   along that perfect jawline.~~

7. See another penis besides my own, IRL, and do fun
   things with it!

8. Lose. My. Virginity!

9. Become part of a super-queer, super-tight framily by impressing everybody with my epic costumier skills, erasing the "new kid" label, and becoming homecoming royalty.

10. Figure out a way to make my gay dreams come true and not destroy my bestie's life.

The Handshake from Heaven was interrupted by throngs of people pushing to get inside now that the drag brunch had started in earnest. Max and I wandered to an empty booth, Tony close behind. I hadn't been expecting the two of us to have company during the show, and now I was certain that I would definitely spontaneously combust if Tony sat with us and our knees happened to bump together. But just as I scooched across the tan velvet booth to make room for Tony, he waved to a group of guys sitting across the room.

"Those are my brothers," he said. "But you guys should come to our party next Friday. It's the annual Lambda Chi Fire and Ice Ball."

"Oh, you're frat brothers!" I blurted.

Those let's-get-in-our-undies vibes switched off from Tony almost instantly. "Don't ever say that. We aren't a *frat*. We're a *fraternity*. A brotherhood. You don't abbreviate it. You wouldn't call a country a cun—"

"Whoa, okay, I get it!" Lu would never forgive me if I let somebody say that word. "Lesson learned."

"It's all right." Tony's smirk crept back up his lips. "I'll give you this one. But just this once."

"We accept your invitation," Max said. "It'll be great research on how to really go all out with a theme for homecoming. And please excuse my friend here. He's new to flirting."

I glared at Max. There was another thing to add to the Gay Guide Guidelines: *no* mentioning to VSBs that I don't know what I'm doing around guys.

"If you come to the party, maybe we can practice together." Tony paused a beat. I swear he licked his lip, just the tiniest bit of tongue darting out to send my mind reeling. "Flirting, that is."

It wouldn't take Tony touching me to spontaneously combust. His words alone could do the trick.

"See you then," Tony said. Just before turning away, he smirked at me one last time. "Nice to meet you, Jay."

I tried saying *Nice to meet you too*, but thanks to becoming a boy-crazy drooling mess, my words came out in a mushy jumble. Fortunately, Tony was headed toward his *fraternity* brothers, so he didn't see me melt.

A server came by with waters, and I gulped mine like I'd been stuck in the desert for days. I needed to cool down.

"You're welcome," Max said. "For so getting you laid."

I choked, water flying out of my mouth. "Wh—*hack*— what?"

"I knew he was going to have a thing for you," Max said. "And clearly you've got one for him. Your mouth has been open so wide I could fit Mount Rainier in there. It's so on for the two of you at his party."

For the rest of the brunch, I couldn't stop thinking about all the Gay Agenda items I could do with Tony that involved no pants. When our server came to take my order, I nearly asked for pan*cocks* instead of pan*cakes*. As Tuna danced across the bar to her own remixes of Beyoncé and Britney and Whitney, I couldn't stop myself from occasionally looking away from her high kicks and catching eyes with Tony. And when Max pulled me over at the end of the show to ask Tuna if she'd be free to DJ the homecoming dance, I said "Bye, Tony" instead of "Bye, Tuna." Tuna followed the slip by snapping her magenta nails in front of my face. It took way too long for her movement to register.

"Max, honey, it's just as I expected," she said. "This one's dicknotized."

Yep. That's exactly what I was.

11.

✓ Have a Date Downgraded

The next day was surprisingly sunny for Seattle. Clear skies brought people down to Pike Place Market in full force. Vendors were lined up all along the street selling fresh flowers, local art, and handmade jewelry. Behind me was the Fish Market, where muscly guys tossed dead fish to each other and wrapped them up as people placed their orders for fresh salmon. If I had come down here for any other reason than to meet a VSB on my very first date, I would have found those guys and their fish-carcass choreography surprisingly hot. But seeing as how this *was* about to become my first date, I was too distracted by my heart racing a million miles a minute. The CDC says someone has a heart attack every forty seconds, and if my heart didn't slow down, I was about to become one of those people. The anticipation of Albert getting there was killing me. I peered through the throngs of shoppers and tourists, expecting him to appear at any moment with his perfect hair, perfect glasses, and perfect jawline, his sexy Digigeek-chic trifecta.

I don't know if it was from almost eighteen years of suppressed gay hormones or what, but I was like a dog with a bone(r). Even though Tony had had all my attention the day before, my body quickly switched back to the closest hot guy who might flirt with me. And when I finally saw Albert walk past the newsstand next to the Fish Market, his hair perfectly coiffed just like I expected, his glasses perched adorably close to the end of his nose once again, I nearly did have a heart attack.

Because he wasn't alone.

Three people walked in step with Albert. The first was a pale white girl with jet-black hair that fell nearly to her butt, the second an Indian girl with the fiercest hot pink eyeshadow that would make Max jealous, and the third was the Blue Piercer himself, Reese.

What. The. Frack. This wasn't a date. This was a group hangout. And with Reese Buttersworth, the ultimate boner shrinker, to boot.

Fortunately, none of them saw my distress because their heads were buried in their phones. Albert looked up when they neared the Fish Market and beamed when he saw me.

"Jay, hey!" He laughed, but in the presence of all this unexpected company, it didn't make me melt quite like it usually did. "That rhymes! And you made it."

"Ha, ha, yeah. Sure does. And sure did." Having a one-syllable name meant an inordinate amount of things rhymed with it. Gay Jay picked up steam for a hot minute when I first came out at Riverton, but Lu shut that down by writing a piece in the school newspaper about how a person's sexuality does not define who they are. I loved her for that. I didn't need people pouring salt in the wound every time they said my name by highlighting that I was the one and only gay kid in the student body. Today, however, I wanted the gay part of my identity in caps lock and bright lights since I'd thought I was going on my first GAY date.

"Guys, this is Jay," Albert said to the group.

"Hey, everybody." I tried to save face by smiling, showing teeth so that it looked like I really meant it. But I overdid it, my lips stretching too tight. I'm sure I looked like that psychotic clown in *It*, grinning maniacally before he tried to eat everybody.

"Good orthodontia." The pale girl with jet-black hair inspected my too-toothy smile. "Braces?"

Gawd, the only tooth interaction I wanted was Albert's teeth biting my lips in a hot make-out session. I'd seen it enough times in movies that it had to feel good, even if it did make your lip look like Silly Putty when it was stretched back from your face.

"Yep," I said. "From sixth grade to eighth."

Hot Pink Eyes bumped Braces Observer with her hip. "Regina, we've talked about this. Putting someone's teeth on blast is a really intimate thing. It makes people self-conscious." She looked at me pointedly. "Didn't it make you feel self-conscious?"

I caught myself running my tongue over my teeth. "Yeah, I guess it did."

"Sorry about her." She put her hand out and we shook. "I'm Shruti Dhawan. This overenthusiastic tooth inspector is Regina Walsh."

Regina threw her hands in the air. "I can't help it if I get distracted by great teeth. Albert, you didn't tell us he had such a cute smile."

"Seriously," Shruti deadpanned. "Did you even hear what I said?"

So Albert mentioned me to his friends. But Regina said he *didn't* say I was cute, so it had to be more of a *Hey, I'm bringing this new kid Jay around* kind of conversation instead of *I'm bringing this cute guy Jay who I might be interested in.*

"Well, I mean . . ." Albert's eyes met mine and he smiled even bigger than I had. "I guess I was distracted."

Or maybe this group hangout wasn't a lost cause. Albert was blatantly flirting with me again like he had when we were selling homecoming tickets.

"Okay, enough about distracting smiles and blah, blah, blah. We're on a mission." It seemed like Reese really loved to be a wet blanket. I wouldn't expect someone as soul-sucking as him to be friends with a guy as kind and smart and hot as Albert. "We've got today and today only to find a sparkly PomPom, and we've already wasted seven minutes!"

"Reese is right," Regina agreed. "We need to get serious."

I raised my hand and Reese nodded in my direction. "Good, yes," he said. "We need order, we need discipline, we need hand-raising."

It actually seemed like he might not hate my guts for a second.

"Um, what's a PomPom?" I asked.

Reese went right back to looking like he would kill me. "Only the most versatile Digimal known to Digikind. It can evolve into *eight* more powerful Digimals, all representing different elements. It's a cornerstone of the Digimal community."

"Plus, it's really cute," Shruti added. She showed me her phone. A fluffy purple Pomeranian wagged a tail that was very reminiscent of a cheerleading pom-pom.

"Aw, it's adorable!" I said.

"Adorable," Reese muttered. "I can't with you people." He pointed at Albert, back in Digigeneral mode. "Digihips. Now. We need the luck."

Albert thrust from side to side. "See," he said, grinning at me while he gyrated. "I told you these work. Sparkly PomPom, here we come."

We walked past the burly fish throwers and into the market. I don't know how they did it, but Albert, Reese, Shruti, and Regina were all able to keep eagle eyes on their phones without running into any shoppers, flower stalls, or the vendor selling hand-knitted cat figurines. I kept myself as close to Albert as I could so I wouldn't get lost in the crowd, which led to my elbows bumping into him pretty often. But he never pulled away. In fact, I think he bumped me on purpose a few times. He'd look up and smile slyly every time our elbows made contact even though we weren't jostled by someone nearby. I didn't know it was possible to flirt without any words, but I think we were officially flirting in some kind of elbow-tapping Morse code.

But when a particularly aggressive shopper with a basket full of healing crystals bulldozed through the crowd, I had to jump away from Albert and into Reese. He gave me that icy blue stare. "You don't have your phone out?" He looked to the sky as if he was asking the universe to smite me. "We need all hands on deck here. Sparkly Pom-Poms aren't going to find themselves." He put his hand out. "Give me your phone."

Reese didn't seem like the kind of guy you argued with, especially when on a Digimission. As Max put it, he was difficult, so I decided it was best to just do as he said.

While Reese was distracted with my phone, I whispered to Albert, "I didn't know you two were friends."

"Who? Me and Reese?"

I nodded.

"Yeah, he's been a part of the Digigang for a while. He stopped coming recently for acting gigs, but he's been a little down lately. I'm glad he's back. The Digihips always cheer him up."

I had a hard time picturing icy Reese feeling down about anything. He still had my phone, glaring at it while he tapped on my screen.

"What are you doing?" I asked Reese.

"Starting you a Digimals account," he said, then handed back my phone.

"This is my favorite part!" Regina said with a squeal. "You get to come up with a username."

"And it can't just be your name," Shruti added. "It's got to reflect who you are, what's in your soul. It stays with you forever."

"So," Regina asked, "who are you, Jay?"

The whole group stared at me. Shruti's head was cocked in thoughtfulness, Regina bounced on her tiptoes, Reese scowled with one eye still trained on his screen, and Albert's smile unleashed that irresistible dimple.

I peered down at my phone. Reese had created an avatar that actually looked just like me; there was even the swoop to my light brown bangs that took six weeks freshman year to figure out. But blinking right next to Digime was a cursor under the glaring question:

What's your name, Trainer?

The moment of truth when I had to declare who I was and what I stood for, not just to Reese and Shruti and Regina, but to *Albert*. A VSB I wanted to impress and keep flirting with. AlbertFlirt would be too obsessive of a name, though. And besides, that wasn't really what made me me. So I was back at that unanswerable question of what Jay stood for. Or, I guess I could have answered it, but with the world's most boring response:

Hi, I'm Jay, and I'm a hyper-organized, sexually very nonactive numbers geek.

"Um, well, I . . ." If I didn't say something quick, Reese would just grab my phone and make my username *Dumbass.*

"SPARKLY POMPOM, FOLKS, WE GOT EYES ON A SPARKLY POMPOM." Reese was off and striding through the crowd. "This is not a drill! I repeat, this is not a drill!"

Saved by General Reese!

Shruti lit up when she checked her own game. "He's right! Only point three miles away."

"At the Great Wheel!" Regina added. She grabbed my hand and pulled me into the crowd. "Come on, Cute Incisors. Let's go, Pearly Whites. Giddy up, Nice and Straight 32. Hmmm, no, that one might be read as homophobic."

"Regina, what are you doing?" Albert asked.

"Trying to come up with Jay's screen name, duh."

"You're doing it again," Shruti said. "And I doubt Jay has your same affinity for teeth, Gothodontist."

Ohmigawd that name perfectly described Regina: goth-tastic and obsessed with teeth.

Regina rolled her eyes. "What, I'm just trying to help, ShruteForTheStars."

Shruti turned to me and asked, "You don't happen to be into astronomy or anything, do you? Because I could help you come up with some space-themed usernames that are out of this world. Pun totally intended."

I shook my head. "Sadly, no."

Reese was now yards ahead of us and barreling down a staircase that led to the lower levels of Pike Place.

"PomPom's still at the Wheel," he yelled. "Let's move, move, move!"

Shruti took off after him, and Regina rushed to follow. "This isn't over," she said. "We'll come up with something, Mouth Guardian."

"Regina!" Shruti shouted from the bottom of the stairs.

"All right, all right, I'll stop."

I looked down at the cursor still blinking on my phone, ready for me to declare my soul to the world. Who knew that Digimals was going to send me into such an identity crisis?

I moved to follow Reese, Shruti, and Regina, but with my eyes still on my phone, I totally misjudged how deep the stairs were. I leaned forward way too far, my stomach lurching as my foot plummeted farther than expected. I might not have known what made me me inside, but Albert was about to see my literal insides if I fell down the stairs and broke my whole body.

A hand snatched my shirt and pulled me back just in the nick of time. My shoulder blades slammed into Albert's chest. My feet dangled dangerously over the step in front of me, but Albert had me tightly pressed against his pecs. His strong, firm pecs.

"I got you," Albert said.

I looked up, his face upside down from my vantage point. It was like that part in *Spider-Man* where Peter Parker slides down his web and kisses Mary Jane in a dramatic, upside-down, rain-soaked kiss. I would have given anything to re-create that scene.

Our eyes met. Electric tingles cascaded over my body just like they had with Tony, only this time the energy poured through my shoulder blades. They'd never felt so alive, and I was completely, totally, 100 percent here for it.

"What's your username?" I breathed. "Knight in Shining Glasses?"

I guess Albert wasn't bothered by my total cheesiness because he chuckled. The vibrations traveling from his chest to my back set my body on fire. "Maybe I should change it," he said.

Albert put me back on my feet, but even when my shoes were firmly on the steps, he didn't let go. His hands were now on my sides, keeping me steady, the perfect position to pull me closer and kiss.

"You good?" he asked.

"Mm-hmm."

"Should I let go?"

No. Never. I wanted him to pull me closer and get to number six right that very second.

"Sure," I said. "We should probably catch up with the group."

"Undecided," Albert replied.

Maybe he hadn't heard me. "Well, I don't want to keep

you from your friends, unless—"

"It's my username," Albert explained. "Undecided Huang. Don't worry about what the Digigang says. Coming up with your avatar name is really not as life-or-death as they make it sound. I mean, I'm as much of a gamer as the rest of them, but as for who I am inside, I'm still trying to figure that out. There's always so much pressure to know everything about ourselves right away, don't you think?"

He couldn't have said anything that rang more true in my soul if he tried. That must be how you know you've met your soul mate. When what they say or how they are just clicks somewhere inside you.

"Completely," I said. His words broke down a wall and made me want to open up. "I'm just the new kid. Who likes math and stats. Everything else—where I want to go to college, what I want to do for a living, who I want to be for the rest of my life—is still kind of up in the air."

"And can't I try a few things out before I make a final decision?" Albert said. "There are so many things I haven't been able to do yet that I don't think I can truly make an educated decision on who I am. There's a lot of firsts I still need to have. Do you know what I mean, or is that just me?"

Maybe the stars really *did* bring people together. All these years I'd been sitting on the sidelines worrying about being stuck in prepubescent purgatory, not having a kiss, a hand-hold, or a date, and still solidly having my V-card. But here was Albert, telling me that I didn't have to rush things. That I was okay to be me. He was quickly adding to his list of swoon-worthy qualities.

ALBERT ADJECTIVES

1. Sexy (I mean, he is a V, V, V VSB.)
2. Sweet (Who else would help pick up all my crap even though I had gum on my face and my hand was soaked in blood?)
3. Adorable (I'm talking puppy-dog-eyes adorable.)
4. Smart (Where do you even get started on building a robot?)
5. Unabashedly Albert (As evidenced by the prevalence of Digihips with no mind for who's watching.)
6. Accepting (Nobody else made me feel this safe to be me, exactly as I am.)

That last attribute was quickly becoming my favorite. He was so much more than just a hot guy. I didn't have to have the answers around Albert, and if his very public flirting meant what I thought it did, he still liked me even if I was my own attribute list in progress. Or working my way out of that prepubescent purgatory. He even mentioned he had some firsts of his own to accomplish. Maybe we'd be each other's firsts for a few things.

I considered telling Albert about the Gay Agenda right then and there. But sharing that I'd fantasized about us making out would be coming on too strong. I'd always imagined that the fun of my agenda would be crossing off items when they happened organically. I didn't want to force it, and telling Albert about the list felt like doing just that. I didn't want him to feel pressured to do these things just because I'd taken the time to write them down. It was different from telling Max, who just wanted to help set up situations that could lead to my great gay liberation.

"I totally get it," I finally said. "Let's just be ourselves and go where life takes us."

Albert's eyes met mine. He was still a step higher than me. His glasses slipped down to the tip of his nose, but he was too distracted to care. I swear he was thinking all the same things I was. That there was something between us that just clicked. That when the time felt right, a few firsts could be shared together. And maybe that time was now.

Albert leaned forward.

This was it. He was going to kiss me! My first kiss was finally going to happen after all this time.

Albert's lips parted just slightly as he gently pulled me forward. He was going to put his mouth against mine and item number three—minus the dancing—would be—

PIIIIIIIIING!

Albert's text notification was outrageously loud. He snapped back, startled, when his lips were only centimeters away from mine.

Item three was still firmly a part of the Gay Agenda.

"It's Reese." Of course it was. "They're wondering where we are."

"PomPom waits for no one," I panted. I was out of breath. My heart was pounding. *PomPom, PomPom,*

PomPom, PomPom. It was like my aorta was rubbing it in that I'd just missed out on my first kiss thanks to a digital dog.

We left the market and walked the few blocks down to the pier. The Great Wheel, a massive Ferris wheel, loomed over the water and looked back on the city. In a perfect world, I'd be pulling Albert onto the ride and we'd make out as we were lifted into the air. But now I questioned everything after our kissing close call. Had he actually been going to kiss me? If he had, why would he pull away so quickly? Maybe I made up the tension between us. Albert could have just ignored the text. I must have been totally misreading his signals.

I could just see Reese, Regina, and Shruti fist-pumping in the distance. They'd probably caught a sparkly Pom-Pom. At least the day was a success for someone.

Before I could go any farther and join the group, Albert caught my hand and pulled me to a stop. "Hey," he breathed.

He looked so serious. No. That's not right. He looked . . . smoldering.

"Hey," I said.

"Can I tell you something?"

Oh gawd. He was close again. Really close. Close enough I bet he could feel my heart beating against his shirt. *PomPom, PomPom, PomPom, PomPom.*

"So, about back there," Albert started.

The only way I could cool off now was to jump off the pier and into the Puget Sound.

"The Digigang can get pretty intense," he continued. "Maybe we could do something just the two of us some-time?"

Yes, yes, yes! That was exactly what I wanted. Alone time, just him and me, and with as little clothes as he wanted.

"Like . . . a date?" It was the most forward I had ever been in my life. But I didn't want any confusion this time. No more group hangouts where I went through an iden-tity crisis again.

"Yeah, like a date," Albert said.

Holy. Fracking. Shit.

Albert's smile took over, and I wanted to kiss down his jaw all the way to that dimple. How would he react if I just seized the day and went for it?

I gasped. "That's it!"

I looked down at my phone. The cursor was still blink-ing under *What's your name, Trainer?*

I typed in my idea and showed the screen to Albert.

"SeizeTheJay," he read.

That's what our whole talk had been about. Waiting for our firsts to happen and figuring ourselves out in the process. The only way to get started on that was to seize the day, to actually do those firsts and discover the people we were meant to be.

"What do you think?" I asked.

"Well . . . you're actually really leaving me hanging on that date."

It was a massive face-palm moment. "Yes!" I shouted,

too loudly since Albert was so close. He winced, but his smile never wavered, and I lowered my voice to not-eardrum-destroying volume. "I'd like that. A date. I'd like that a lot."

"In that case, here's what I think about your username."

Albert thrust his hips from side to side. The Digihips. I think that meant he liked it.

12.

✓ Find Yourself in a BFF (Best Friend Fiasco)

There was one downside to having such an epic weekend full of hot guys and electric tingles: I was going to have to tell Lu. Normally, I would have been ecstatic to tell her about Albert asking me on a date and Tony inviting me to his Lambda Chi party. But this time, I had a feeling Lu wasn't going to like the end of that story. Because the next day, when Albert and I continued to communicate through elbow Morse code while selling dance tickets again, I realized that I didn't want to give up on feeling this electricity at homecoming. Especially not after the way Albert looked at me when he solidified the time for our first date that upcoming Saturday, the day after the party where Tony might or might not want to hook up. I felt like I was just about to step into gay paradise, and heading back to

Riverton during the middle of this would be taking a solid leap out of it. I knew Lu was depending on me since she and Chip were having a rough time, but what about me finding *my* Chip? Finding the guy who I wanted to spend as much time with as I could, like Lu did with Chip over the summer? After all, she was the one who said she didn't want to continue our award-winning hoedown duo in the first place. Maybe if I helped them get over their rockiness, Lu wouldn't need me as a Spare Tire.

While I walked home after the QSA meeting that afternoon, I went through all the things I would tell Lu to explain why the hoedown just wouldn't work this year.

HOMECOMING IS THE LEAD HO BECAUSE. . . .

1. I'd found a couple guys who made my whole body turn into an electric power plant. (Maybe this could take a global warming angle since this was sustainable energy. Too much?)

2. Lu was going to ditch me for Chip, and I went along with it. (By the laws of quid pro quo, she had to do the same for me.)

3. I had yet to dance with a boy, and this was my chance. (And if Albert happened to ask me, he'd want to go to homecoming, not to the hoedown with strangers hundreds of miles away.)

I knew she'd get it. She had to. Lu and I understood each other on everything, even if we didn't always like what we had to be so understanding about.

My thumb was hovering over the Call button when a notification popped up on my phone. I'd set up a Google Alert freshman year when Lu started working for the school newspaper. I still got pinged whenever anything with her name on it was posted so I could read her articles right when they went up. Normally, her words filled me with a sense of pride that my bestie was pursuing her journalistic journey one piece at a time. But with this alert, there was no bursting pride. Just horrible pins of dread.

TOUGH AS NAILS NAILING SHUT DOORS
By Lu Fuhrman

Local nail salon Tough as Nails is closing its doors permanently after twenty-three years in business. Owner Leslie Lovett cited a lack of customers as the reason.

"With the opening of Nailed It in Deer Park, we've lost a lot of clients," Lovett said. "It's just too much for this old gal to keep up with."

Nailed It opened last year. Its updated equipment and offerings of custom-made espresso drinks were noted as big draws to former Tough as Nails patrons.

"They've got, like, a thousand options for polish color, too," Riverton High School senior Monica Delancey said. "It's really the only place to go."

Carol Fuhrman, the sole nail technician at Tough as Nails, is available for in-home nail service and can be contacted at CarolDoesUrNails@gmail.com.

Lu never tried to be funny in her articles. She always said journalistic integrity was everything. Avoiding "being cute" was rule number one, so with an article title like "Tough as Nails Nailing Shut Doors," Lu was not feeling this assignment at all. Was not feeling her life at all.

I couldn't blame her. I called her instantly.

"You read the article, didn't you?" Straight to the point, as always.

"What are you going to do, Lu?"

"More shifts at the diner, what else? Eau de burger grease is my life now."

There she was, trying to be funny again. Not good.

"And Aunt Carol? Maybe she could get a job at Nailed It?" I was grasping at straws, but it didn't feel right not to offer some kind of solution.

"We don't have a car, remember?"

Frack. This was bad. This was so, so bad.

"But who knows. Maybe I'll be able to buy some beat-up junker with our hoedown prize winnings," Lu continued.

Those pins of dread increased to knives. Lu was *literally* depending on us taking the costume contest prize money to get out of this mess. Hopefully Chip was doing his job as her boyfriend and making her feel better in all of this.

"How's Chip been handling it?" I asked.

"He broke up with me. Over the weekend."

"Oh gawd, Lu. Why didn't you tell me?"

Lu was silent, the only sounds coming through her

phone the background noise of the diner: the milkshake mixer running on high, the cash register bumping open, Derrick yelling, "Order number eight, your Belly Buster is ready." Life was so normal back in Riverton for everyone but Lu. She seemed to have the odds stacked against her even worse than I had as the only gay guy at our school. At least I'd had Lu all those years. Now Lu had to weather this shit storm alone. She didn't have me; she didn't have Chip. Maybe homecoming wasn't the lead Ho after all.

Lu finally sighed and said, "I've just decided to stop focusing on the negative. So the first positive is that we get to go to the hoedown together again. Have you come up with any great ideas?"

I'd been thinking so much about boys that coming up with costumes for Lu and Chip slipped my mind. I knew I could come up with something good, though, while deciding what exactly I'd do about the dance dilemma.

"Absolutely," I said vaguely. "We got this." I'd think of something. I would.

"Okay, I'm heading into work. Talk to you later. Love you."

"Love you too, Lu."

It was the truth. Lu was the person I loved the most in the whole world. But when I hung up, I wasn't sure that love was enough. Even though I wanted to figure out this whole mess, find the perfect hoedown costume to make Lu win the prize money, and have our relationship back to normal like it was before Chip, I wasn't entirely certain that I could. Because while my heart was full of

Lu in that moment, butting right up next to her were all my hopes and dreams in the Gay Agenda. I wasn't sure I could give those up yet, even if Lu needed me right now. But if I chose the Gay Agenda over Lu, there was one thing I knew for sure:

It would break her heart.

———

I had to run to SIF to make it just in time for class the next day. I'd overslept after a night worrying about all the different ways the dance dilemma could play out, and I didn't come up with any solid answers. I thought for a minute that I could just invite Lu to homecoming, but 1) where were we going to find the money to get her over to Seattle, and 2) an entire weekend away from the diner would mean at least two missed shifts. I eventually drifted off into a fitful sleep, but I woke up in a sweat after a nightmare where I told Lu I was ditching her. She scratched my eyes out with her perfectly manicured nails, screaming, "Headline news! You're dead!" The only thing I could think to do was fill Max in on this conundrum and see if he had any good ideas about how to fix it.

I huffed and puffed down the horrifying SIF hall, through the chipped fashion lab door, and plopped myself on the stool next to Max. "I need to tell you som—"

"I'm so glad you're here," Max interrupted, and he grabbed my hand like he needed me to keep him steady. His eyes were swimming with tears. Apparently I wasn't the only one who'd had a rough night.

"What happened?" I asked. "Are you okay?"

"Lord and Taylor, I am *not* going to cry." Max quickly wiped his eyes and cleared his throat. "I was not going to do this, but there's something I need to tell you. Can I vent?"

"I'm your man." After how quickly he jumped on helping with the Gay Agenda, I owed him one.

Max opened his mouth to spill, but Mr. Bogosian walked into the room. "Okay, everyone," he called. "Now that we've covered the basics of sewing machines that *most* of you seemed to grasp . . ." His eyes flashed to the back of the room, where Julian held a bandaged thumbs-up.

"It's all good, teach," Julian said. "I barely felt that needle."

Mr. Bogosian cringed. "Good. Let's *tote*-ally get started. This time accident-free, please. We do not need a lawsuit on our hands. Everyone grab your fabric while I pass out patterns."

I focused all my attention on Max as the football players rushed to the back of the room. "What's up?"

Max's frown perfectly matched the basset hound's on his forest-green sweater. "Dance drama. I'll tell you after class." He sulked behind the jocks and grabbed his pink tiger-stripe fabric.

Dance drama? It had only been a week, and I thought things were going smoothly when it came to homecoming. Tuna had signed on as DJ, and we'd already made enough money in ticket presales to cover her fee and pay for refreshments. What could be going wrong?

"Jay?" Mr. Bogosian said. "You okay? Where's your material?"

I jolted out of my seat way too fast, making my stool topple over with a *clang.* "Sorry, Professor. I mean"— awkward laugh—"Mr. Bogosian. I'll just . . ." I bent down and picked my stool up, then ran to the back of the room.

"Come on, everybody, let's pick it up!" Mr. Bogosian clapped his hands. "These totes won't make themselves."

I moved so fast to get back to my seat that I didn't pay attention to where I was going and stubbed my toe on the leg of my worktable. "Shit!"

"Real smooth," Reese fake-coughed into the sleeve of his baggy NYU sweatshirt. His insults were as unoriginal as his wardrobe. I'd hoped that we might slowly move toward becoming friends since we'd shared in the victory of catching a sparkly PomPom, but Reese was back to his spiteful self.

Mr. Bogosian glared at Reese instead of me for swearing, solidifying him as my favorite teacher. "Reese," Mr. Bogosian said, "it sounds like you're eager to share with the class. Why don't you help me demonstrate how to cut the patterns we'll need for this project?"

Max slumped in his seat. I couldn't figure out what was up with him.

Mr. Bogosian walked to Reese's worktable and demonstrated how to fold our fabrics in half, then lay the patterns for the tote bag and pin them into place before cutting.

"Does everyone see the placement of the main tote pattern on Reese's fabric?" Mr. Bogosian asked.

Max sank even deeper on his stool. Maybe it was the way the light hit his sweater, but he looked like he was turning a little green.

"Placement is key so that we use our fabric as efficiently as possible. Okay, Reese, place the handle pattern as close to the main pattern as you can, again so we really utilize the fabric and don't waste anything." The class watched the pattern placement while I watched Max get greener and greener. This was definitely not a trick of the light.

Mr. Bogosian eyed Reese's movements. "Excellent work, Reese."

A deep gurgle emanated from Max's stomach.

"Max," I asked, placing a tender hand on his shoulder. "Are you feeling oka—"

BLEEEEEEEEEEEEEECK!

Max threw up everywhere. I clattered back from the table just in time to avoid getting hit by the thick, chunky wave of orange vomit.

"Ohmigawd," I whispered. The average person throws up about .2 gallons of puke whenever they upchuck. I'd looked it up after I went a bit overboard on rum and Diet Dr Pepper at Lu's place once. But Max heaved *gallons*. Plural.

"Holy shit," Julian said. He sounded completely in awe. "That has to set a world record."

"M-Max?" I tried putting my hand on his shoulder

again, but he leaped up before I could comfort him. He grabbed his now-puke-splattered *What Would Dolly Do?* tote and ran from the workroom.

"Max? Max, wait," Mr. Bogosian called. But the door slammed shut, the sound echoing down the hall as we all sat in stunned silence.

Mr. Bogosian looked *tote*-ally bewildered. Everyone did. "Somebody should make sure he makes it to the nurse's office."

I whipped my hand in the air. "I'll do it." But I wasn't the only one to volunteer. Damon had his hand up too.

"Thanks, gentlemen." He stared wide-eyed as Max's puke started dripping on the floor. "I'm not even sure if janitorial has mops big enough for this."

As I followed Damon toward the door, Reese said, "As we say in the theater, the show must go on. We shouldn't derail the whole class just because Max loves attention."

"Jerk," I called back just as the door slammed shut behind me. It might not have been the most mature thing, but it still felt really fracking good to say. *Max loves attention?* Who in their right mind would want a spew spotlight?

"You're not wrong," Damon said. "Reese can cut kind of deep when he's upset. He and Max both have a hard time holding it in when they're heartbroken. Max more literally, I guess."

"Heartbroken? Reese?" I doubted that any kind of emotion could creep through Reese's icy demeanor. It still baffled me that Albert and Reese could be friends, even with the Digimals connection.

Damon motioned back toward the workroom. "I didn't think they'd be able to last in the same class very long. Did you notice how sad Max looked every time Mr. Bogosian said Reese's name?"

"Wait a minute." My mind ran through a whole list of Max interactions: those fortifying breaths before entering the workroom, calling Reese *difficult*, everyone in the QSA and Damon checking to make sure that Max was okay. Everything clicked in one massive lightbulb moment. "Did Max and Reese date?" I couldn't believe it. I mean, Reese was just so . . . rude and snobby and bitchy. He didn't seem like sweet, social Max's kind of guy at all.

Damon looked completely bewildered. "He hasn't told you?"

I shook my head. "He just made a veiled reference to Reese being difficult. That was it."

"Typical Max. He likes to avoid his problems at all costs. He shut his mom out our entire freshman year after she divorced his dad." Damon sighed, but not in that way like he was frustrated or stressed. He sighed like he was hurt.

"Still no word to you or Cami?"

"Nope," Damon said. "And he missed our first game of the year. He always shows up with blue-and-white pom-poms and a number-twenty-three jersey. The guys love it. He and Cami made them a couple years ago to cheer me on when I got put on the freshman team sophomore year. I love football, but I totally sucked, and the stupid-ass comments I was getting about being the Black guy bad at sports were getting to me."

"Those people are assholes," I said. I thought the city with its greater diversity would be a more aware place, but classmates making gross jokes about stereotypes wasn't just limited to the country.

"Yeah," Damon continued, "but I kept at it because Cami told me to stay true to myself and do what I want. She and Max put their fashion skills to use, made some outfits, and became my cheerleaders. But I guess Max is too upset to feel like cheering for anything. Especially with all the Twitter GIF shit that went down."

"GIF shit?" Dread settled in my gut. Social media could be the best, but it could also eat you alive.

Damon nodded. "A breakup was bad enough, but then . . ." He pulled out his phone and showed me a tweet from some account called Splitsville. Its bio read: *Home of your messiest breakups and craziest exes.* The pinned tweet featured Max sobbing uncontrollably over a basket of fries. His jaw dropped open, chewed-up potato and ketchup falling out of his mouth over and over and over. Text spelled out what Max was saying: "You're leaving me? WHYYYYY?" And sitting right across from him was Reese, looking totally oblivious to the devastation he'd caused in Max's heart.

"This is bad," I said. "Really bad."

"I mean, everyone loves Max, so as soon as this made rounds, people were instantly on his side," Damon explained. "But that just made it worse for him. He hates looking weak in front of people. So when his friends reached out to make sure he was okay, he shut us out, like he thought if he never addressed the GIF or the breakup then it didn't happen. Except, he's really embraced you, I guess. You know what, I shouldn't go check on him. I'll probably just make it worse, somehow, but . . ." Damon stared down the hallway like he thought if he looked hard enough he could see Max through the walls. "Just let him know I'm thinking about him, all right?"

"Yeah, you got it," I said, my mind spinning while Damon moped back to the workroom.

This was a real Best Friend Fiasco (a horrible new meaning of BFF). Lu and Max were the closest people to me, and both of them were imploding while I was on the cusp of making my gay dreams a reality. Maybe there's some kind of cosmic love equation to keep everything balanced. In order for me to add any romance to my life, others had to subtract it from theirs. First Lu and Chip, now Max and Reese with Damon and Cami as collateral damage.

I never thought I'd say this, but sometimes math really sucked.

13.

✓ Have Someone's Back While Someone Else Has Your Backside

Max was nowhere to be found at Capitol Hill High. He wasn't in the nurse's office, he didn't show up at lunch, and I had to head the QSA meeting alone while the group finalized ideas for dance decorations. I decided to check his house when I walked home. We realized after the drag brunch that we lived just a couple blocks from each other, which would always make the *I was just in the neighborhood* excuse for stopping by actually true. Sure enough, Max was lying on his four-poster bed, hidden behind drapes of purple taffeta.

"Who let you in?" His voice sounded weak from crying.

"Jules. She told me you threatened to dye her hair back to brown if she let me up." Max's stepmom made neon hair look natural. It was hard to imagine her without a bright blue pixie cut, but it was also hard to imagine Reese and Max dating.

"Are you all right?" I motioned toward Max sprawled out on his violet sheets. "Is this about the dance drama you mentioned? Is it something to do with Reese?"

Max's breath hitched. "I was trying to get through senior year without ever having to talk about him again."

"Damon told me about your breakup. He showed me the GIF."

"Who does Damon think he is?" Max said with a scoff. "If he thought I was ignoring him before, I'm going to go Elsa-level frozen on him now. Why does he *insist* on making my senior year about my heartbreak?"

Max grabbed a picture frame on his bedside table. It held a photo of him and a girl with dark brown skin in identical cheerleading outfits sandwiching Damon between them in a massive hug. That must be Cami. They were all laughing their heads off as Damon was clearly trying to squirm away from the love fest. Max's eyes softened for a second when he took in the photo, but then his expression hardened and he put the frame back, facedown.

"I really think they're just trying to help," I said. Damon had looked just as pained about the shakeup of their friendship as Lu and Max looked about the breakup of their relationships.

"Well, I've asked them to help by letting me pretend my relationship never happened. But Damon keeps saying I'll get over it faster if I talk about it, and it's like Cami thinks that since their mom is a therapist she's now licensed in marriage and family counseling too. I'll get over this if I forget I ever had a boyfriend! I made my entire junior year about being in love, and what did that get me? A broken heart and the world's most humiliating GIF. I am not going to let my last year of high school get hijacked by Ree—" He stopped, his eyes welling again. "I can't even say his name." Max threw a pillow over his face to muffle his sobs. "Gawd, I'm so pathetic."

I pulled back the curtains and sat next to Max. "No, you're not."

"But I am, Jay, I am! I'm going to say this once, and then you're never going to hear it from me again: I'm miserable without him. I can't stop looking at his Insta." He flung his pillow aside and pulled out his phone. Pictures filled the screen of Reese with a guy at the Space Needle, at Pike Place Market, at the Great Wheel on the pier. "Look at Reese's new boyfriend, *Spencer*. He posted these last night. I mean, it hasn't even been a month since we broke up! Then I saw him this morning, and with all that pent-up energy thinking about him and Spencer together, I just fucking lost it. Spew tsunami, everywhere. If he had any doubts about dumping me before, I think going full-blown *Exorcist* wiped them out."

"Why did you guys break up in the first place?" I asked.

Max sniffed and rolled his eyes. "He got an *agent* over the summer and said he had to get really serious about his craft. Aka, he had to dump me because a relationship was getting in the way of his career." He wiped his nose on his sleeve. "Do you know what the worst part is?"

I shook my head as Max and his sweater basset hound turned to me with tear- and puke-stained eyes.

"He's actually good. He's a fantastic actor."

I hoped Reese could put those acting skills to good use someday and pretend to be a nice person.

"I was surprised you guys used to date," I said. "Reese is just so . . . He's such a . . ."

"A royal asshat?" Max finished. "Yeah, I know. But he wasn't always this way." Max got a distant look in his eyes, like he was remembering a time before hysterical-crying, openmouthed fry-chewing GIFs existed. "He was so charming and nice and, *ugh*, talented. We started dating sophomore year when we worked on the spring musical together. He complimented the way I tailored his jacket, and I told him he was a great Kenickie in *Grease*. I totally fell for those ridiculously mesmerizing blue eyes." He jangled the gold bracelets he always wore. "He even gave me these. One for him and one for me, to symbolize us always being next to each other."

The guy Max described sounded totally different from the Reese I knew. He actually seemed sweet. Loving. But then Max's faraway look turned from nostalgic to *I want to punch something.*

"What a crock of shit," he said. "I thought I'd be able to get over him. Ever since he got that agent, he's become a complete self-centered ass. Plus, he didn't join the QSA this year, which I thought was because he was having a hard time seeing me. I know it sounds awful, but it made me feel kind of good that he might actually regret breaking up with me. I've kept wearing these bracelets so he knows I would take him back. But then he goes and gets a boyfriend just *weeks* after we break up, and Stella, who's in drama, said Reese auditioned for all the lead roles in the fall play. Apparently he was fantastic at every single one of them. That only proves one thing."

"What?"

"He's with Spencer, but he still nailed all his auditions. Reese didn't need to be single to focus on his career. He just needed to be away from *me*."

Max buried his face in his pillow again. He sobbed so hard that the mattress shook. I had no idea what to do when people cried. Lu avoided tears at all costs so I didn't have much practice in the right way to console someone.

"Is . . . is there anything I can do?" I asked. "I mean, just because you're my Gay Guide doesn't mean I can't help you out too."

"Let's just keep moving forward with the Gay Agenda. Living vicariously through you is nice, actually. It makes me stop thinking about him." Max's phone beeped, and he peeked at it from under his pillow. "Gawd, look. Reese just posted a picture about going shopping for a homecoming costume with *Spencer*. We did that together last year. He loves homecoming. Wait. That's it!"

Max snapped up so quickly I had to bounce back so his head wouldn't smash into mine. "*That's* what you could do!" he said. "You're the costume master! Go with me to the dance and let's beat Reese at the contest. He would hate losing the homecoming royalty title to us! Plus"—he looked at me with his sad, puffy red eyes—"I couldn't face going to the dance alone while Reese is all over his new boy. I could really use the moral support."

Something tugged at the corner of my mind. If I decided I didn't want to go to the hoedown, this might be the way to make Lu understand. She once told me she'd never sign up for any music classes like band or choir because they held concerts outside of school. It meant that kids would invite their moms and dads and she'd be alone since Aunt Carol couldn't take time away from Tough as Nails. Closing it down for the night meant potentially losing a customer and money they couldn't afford to lose (an entirely moot point now). To Lu, standing around after a concert while everyone was surrounded by people who loved them gave her the worst feeling in the world: being alone. She wouldn't want me to put Max through that.

Not to mention Lu was a total hot commodity; if she put her mind to it, she could find a new date to the hoedown in no time. I could come up with an outfit she could still use with her new date, while Max and I went and won homecoming royalty. That way, Max could rub it in Reese's face when we were crowned, I'd gain some popularity at my new school (plus the opportunity to dance with Albert, or maybe Tony if things went well at the Lambda Chi party), and Lu could still get the hoedown prize money.

It was a win-win-win.

The more I thought about going to homecoming with Max, the more I realized it was what I wanted to do most. But I still didn't want to hurt Lu's feelings and kick her while she was down. I spent the next couple days trying to come up with the right wording to lessen the blow.

LET LU DOWN EASY LIST

- Lu, I know I said I'd go to the hoedown, but I've got a new friend who really needs my help . . .
- Look, Lu, you won't make out with me on the dance floor, but maybe Albert will . . .
- I'm trying to make a name for myself here at my new school, and you don't spell Jay with L-U . . .

How exactly do you let your best friend know that you don't have their back? Even if I was helping out Max, I was still choosing my new life over my old one, and that couldn't be easy to hear. It seemed totally understandable to me, but when I put my reasons for choosing homecoming and my life in Seattle down on paper, I sounded more heartless than I meant to.

Luckily, Lu wasn't free to talk until our virtual Saturday sleepover that weekend. I'd still have some time to find the perfect wording. But the *Let Lu Down Easy List* took up so much of my brain that I couldn't concentrate at all in Fashion Design. Max was back to his chipper self, leaving me feeling like I might unleash a spew tsunami of my own thinking about Lu's disappointment. I was so out of it that Mr. Bogosian had to physically shake my shoulder to get my attention so I'd grab my tote in progress.

Damon and his two BFFFs (Best Football Friends Forever), Julian and Navin Mehta, were talking at the back counter with their backs to me, blocking my tote.

"We have got to kill it against Bellingham tomorrow," Navin said. "They wiped the floor with us last year."

Julian held up his bandaged hand. The top of his thumb peeked out of the wrappings, pink and swollen. It was still healing from his sewing machine accident the week before. "I don't think Coach is going to let me play with this thumb."

"Guys?" They were too deep in conversation to hear me, but I could just make out a corner of neon green in between Damon and Julian. I bent down and tried to non-chalantly grab my bag through them, but it was farther away than I expected.

"Everything's going to be fine," Damon said. "You got this. We got this."

I stretched forward, just centimeters away from snagging my material. How these guys didn't notice I was between them was beyond me. Their football focus was unshakable.

Damon wrapped up his pep talk. "We're going to win!" he yelled.

Then he slapped me on the ass.

"Hello!" I shouted.

I couldn't stop myself. It was a totally involuntary surprise-butt-slap exclamation.

I froze. Julian and Navin froze. Damon froze. And

Damon's hand was still on my butt. His grip was solid and firm, and, I know he said he wasn't the greatest at the game, but if his grasp on a football was anything like the grasp he had on my left butt cheek, he couldn't be all that bad. My ass stung from the slap, but I actually kind of liked it. It was more tingly than painful. The sensation sent my crotch into overdrive, and I realized I might be a guy who's into spanking.

Then Julian cracked up, snapping me back to reality.

I jolted upright. "S-sorry about the interruption."

"Jay!" Damon looked mortified. A couple beads of sweat formed on his forehead, glistening against his brown skin. "I'm the one who's sorry. I totally didn't mean to—" He pointed at my butt. "I thought you were Julian. We slap each other's—" He pointed at Julian's butt. "It's a thing football players do. Sometimes." Damon flashed me an embarrassed grin.

"Don't, um, w-worry about my butt. I mean, it. Don't worry about it." I couldn't talk right. I was too aware of the tingle that still lingered on my ass. When I was confronted with a nonstraight person who wanted to touch my butt, I definitely wanted a repeat of this tingle. "I ju-just needed my tote."

"Here." Damon grabbed the pile of neon green. "Sorry."

"No problem." I snatched the fabric from Damon so I could get out of there fast.

"Seriously," Damon said, "I'm not one to randomly slap guys' asses, except for the team. We have standing ass-slap permission. That will never happen again. Your butt is totally for you and whoever you give permission to slap it. Like a boyfriend."

That's when it clicked.

A boyfriend.

Number four on the Gay Agenda.

That would be the explanation Lu understood. How many times had she told me she wasn't available over the summer because she had to spend time with Chip, *her boyfriend*? To her, boyfriend time trumped friend time.

"Damon, you're a genius!"

"I am?"

"Yes! You actually slapped some sense into me."

There's this thing in statistics called regression analysis. Essentially it tries to come up with the likelihood of something happening to two different groups of people with all things the same except for one big difference. Like, are people who are guys and six feet tall and two hundred pounds more likely to get married if they're left-handed or right-handed? So here was my regression analysis: I had two equally hot guys—Albert and Tony—and I was spending time with both of them this weekend. Whoever I had a better time with could be the guy I pursued as my first-ever boyfriend, giving me an understandable out for the hoedown.

Let the Boyfriend Bonanza begin.

14.

✔ Make Out with a Scorching-Hot Snowman

TGIF: *Thank Gawd It's Frenching!* was on repeat in my head all day that Friday. I kept checking Instagram to look at Tony's profile and imagine what making out with him would be like. I felt a smidge guilty when Albert and I sold homecoming tickets again and he said how excited he was for our date the following day. I told him I was, too, which was 100 percent the truth. I just left out the part about going to a party where I'd be seeing an equally hot guy who might want to suck my face off.

I had come up with a list of what I thought were some real doozies to fit the Fire & Ice theme.

FIRE & ICE COSTUME IDEAS

1. A chimney with Santa coming down it.

2. Daenerys Targaryen, mother of dragons, and a
    White Walker from Game of Thrones.
3. A Sno-Cone and the devil.

While I was pretty pleased with myself, Max put the
kibosh on all of them. A chimney would be too cumbersome in a crowded fraternity house, he'd never watched
a second of GoT, and there wasn't a Sno-Cone's chance
in hell he'd let either of us wear those "tacky devil head-
bands." So instead we picked clothes out of Max's closet
that could work for fire and ice sprite outfits. There was
nothing clever about it, but Max wanted to be fashionable
and show off his makeup skills. I didn't want to disappoint
the person who had introduced me to the guy who might
or might not be making out with me later that night, so I
went along with it.

"Hold still!" Max yelled. The eye pencil in his hand
was once again about to skewer my cornea. "I hope you
have an eye patch. If you keep fidgeting, you're going to
have to go to this party as a pirate."

"It tickles!" I squealed.

"But I'm an expert, so *quit. Moving.*"

"You being an expert doesn't stop me from hating it
when people touch my face."

Max had picked me up from my place a couple hours
earlier. I told Dad I was going to stay the night, so he
didn't have to wait up for me. I felt a little bad leaving
Dad all alone on a Friday while Mom was away district-
managing some Fresh Savings stores in Eugene, Oregon,

but he was keeping himself busy. He'd decided to take up being an Uber driver to explore our new city while getting paid to haul people around. So I decided not to worry about it, and honestly, the possibility of getting to make out with somebody overruled feeling bad for Dad. A guy's gotta get kissed at some point, right?

Max and I were crammed in his extremely tight bathroom, with me perched on the rim of the bathtub while Max sat on the toilet. He'd already decked his face out in red, orange, and yellow flames, and he was doing mine in white, blue, and silver.

"Okay, all done." Max pulled me up so I could look at myself in the mirror.

"Wow," I breathed. Max had somehow put the silver in all the right places so that it reflected in my hazel eyes. The white highlighted my cheekbones, and the blue expertly covered every little blemish on my face. I was ice, but I felt on fire. "You made me look so good."

"Thanks," Max said. "But I just accented the features that were already there. This"—he waved his hand over my face—"is all you. Tony's gonna go crazy."

Gawd, I sure hoped so. I was coming up on two weeks in Seattle with all kinds of gays around me, but no gay action. I had waited practically eighteen years for this, but in the presence of so many guys who like guys, patience was no longer a virtue of mine. It was like when you go through half a romantic comedy and nobody has kissed yet. The audience in my mind was screaming, *GET TO THE KISSING ALREADY!* If things went as planned, I might be kissing *two* eligible bachelors in a twenty-four-hour time span. First Tony, then Albert.

Thinking of Albert got me picturing his excited look at the ticket table that afternoon. Twinges of guilt flashed in my stomach. "Should I feel bad that I hope Tony makes out with me even though I'm going on a date with Albert tomorrow?"

"Absolutely not," Max said. He even stamped his foot for emphasis. "In the immortal words of Queen Bey, if he liked it, then he shoulda put a ring on it. You're fair game until someone gives you the DTR."

"Please tell me that's not some STD I don't know about," I said.

"DTR," Max repeated. "Define. The. Relationship. Until someone specifically asks you to be exclusive, you're not. For all you know, Albert's running around right now with somebody else too. And if he is, you can't be mad. You're *both* fair game."

Maybe that's where the saying *All's fair in love and war* came from: people over the centuries doing their own boyfriend regression analyses until they got to the final DTR.

"Okay, let's move," Max said, doing one last mirror inspection. "Hmmm. It's missing something."

Max pressed on the mirror so that it popped forward. He snagged a small package out of the medicine cabinet, touched his face a couple times, then leaned back. "Lord and Taylor, that's perfect!"

Max turned toward me. He'd put on a pair of huge false eyelashes with red tips.

"Love it!"

"I am *fire*, after all." Max's floor-length red skirt flicked from side to side as he sashayed out of the bathroom. "I've got to look hot."

—*mm*—

I'd only ever been to one "party" before. And I didn't even go to it, technically. I'd picked Lu up in Mom's car because everyone was too tipsy off Pabst Blue Ribbon to drive, and Aunt Carol was having a girls' weekend in Idaho. Lu had texted me to come get her ASAO, which I assumed meant ASAP. When I'd pulled up, there were nine people huddled around a barrel fire in the middle of the Steiner farm, and country music blared through the speakers of Aaron Shepherd's pickup. I wouldn't exactly call it the most exciting party of the year.

The party at Lambda Chi Alpha, however, was *nothing* like that. The house was on Fraternity Row, a street packed with cars and lined with gigantic brick mansions with imposing pillars stuffing their porches. Purple and yellow UW flags hung in practically every window, and people swarmed the Lambda Chi yard. They had gone all out. There were people dressed as firemen and fire extinguishers, as dragons and snowmen, as Tabasco sauce and ice cream.

"I love everyone here," I said to Max as we pushed our way through the crowd of college kids. "Nobody held back!"

The fraternity was crammed wall-to-wall with people.

They were packed on the stairs, dancing in the living room just off the foyer, and streaming into the dining room toward a loaded table of drinks. A massive bowl steamed with dry ice right next to a mountain of red Solo cups and an ice luge in the shape of a polar bear. Somebody dressed as Olaf from *Frozen* was pouring vodka into the polar bear's mouth, while a girl in a volcano costume took the shot out of the ice bear's butt hole. Ten other people were lined up to take their turn at the icy bear butt.

More than 50 percent of Americans get cold sores. I'd bet anything that ice luges were the leading source of infection.

"TONY!" Max screamed.

The guy dressed as Olaf looked up. It was Tony. Sexy, scruffy, green-eyed Tony. He might have been a snowman, but he was the hottest thing in the room.

"Max! Jay!" Tony handed the bottle of vodka to a girl next to him and yelled, "Man the asshole."

Tony ran over, and when our eyes met, a jolt barreled through my body. It was like those scenes on the CW where the whole world goes into slow motion as two lovers' eyes meet, the electric energy passing between them bringing everything else to a halt. I could see with laser focus every millimeter of Tony's mouth as it moved into that sexy smirk. Any worries about what may or may not be transferred through lips went out the window. I just wanted his lips on mine.

That initial jolt was nothing compared to what I felt when Tony pulled me in for a hug. It was like a bolt of lightning slammed into my crotch and instantly made me hard. I had a feeling number six would be off the Gay Agenda in no time. Maybe even number seven.

Tony motioned to the steaming bowl of punch behind him. "Can I get you guys some Polar Potion?" he asked, never breaking eye contact. That smirk was still on his lips and it was mind-numbingly distracting.

"Sure," Max said, while I could only nod. All my blood was in the lower hemisphere of my body, leaving not a single drop in my brain to help me find words.

Tony grabbed three Solo cups and ladled them full of the neon-blue juice. "We didn't get to talk much the other day. Tell me about yourself, Jay."

He held a cup out for me, and I moved to take it. Just before my hand made contact, Tony adjusted *his* hand so that when I grabbed the cup, my fingers completely wrapped around his. He smirked again and caught my eye. He'd totally done that on purpose.

"Oh, um." I had to shake my head to clear my thoughts. "I just moved here from Riverton."

Tony scrunched his forehead, his thick, dark eyebrows coming together like super-hot commas. I didn't know that punctuation marks could be so sexy. "Where's that?"

"B. F. N!" Max shouted, pausing between each letter for dramatic effect.

Tony laughed, but I had no idea what Max meant. "What's that stand for?"

"Butt-Fucking Nowhere!" Max screamed, then took a big gulp of Polar Potion.

Just like that, I was thinking about butt-fucking in front of a VSB who I would not at *all* mind being naked with.

"It's not quite as far as that makes it sound, but yeah," I said, trying to get my thoughts away from Tony's dick. "Riverton is in the middle of nowhere."

I took a drink and OM-fracking-G it was the worst thing I had ever tasted. It was like battery acid in blue raspberry Kool-Aid. But I had to keep it together and not spit the juice out.

"Welcome to Seattle." Tony clicked his cup against mine. Even though I wasn't an experienced partier, the rules of cheersing meant I had to take *another* drink of the horrible potion. I took a gulp and swallowed it down fast, but it wasn't fast enough to stop myself from cringing.

Tony pointed to my cup and pat my back, creating more VSB contact tingles. "You get used to it after enough parties."

I giggled.

Two boys made it official: I was a giggler when I had a crush on someone. Thank gawd the music was loud so Tony couldn't hear me sound like a sixth grader playing spin the bottle.

"Speaking of parties," Max yelled, "we need to do research on sticking to a theme with gusto." He threw his arm over my shoulders. "Jay and I are leading the homecoming committee this year and need some inspiration."

Tony set his cup on the luge table, where an ice-cream cone was taking an inadvisable amount of shots. "Yeah, I can help with that. Let me, uh . . ." Tony bit his bottom lip. "Show you around." Even though there were loads of volcanos in my vicinity, that lip bite made me the one on the verge of an eruption.

Tony reached down and locked his fingers in mine, a jolt going through me once more. The hairs on my arms literally stood on end. "In this crowd," he said with a wink, "we'll get separated if we don't hold on to each other."

I looked back at Max with wide eyes. He batted his false eyelashes and gave me two big thumbs-up. *Best Gay Guide ever,* he mouthed. He then fluttered his fingers goodbye, backed away, and got lost in the crowd.

I was alone and holding hands with a VSB. Well, as alone as you can be when you're smooshed between hundreds of people dressed like dragons and iced lattes. I was no longer impressed by all their costume creativity. They were preventing me and Tony from finding a nice secluded place to make out.

"So, inside is where we've got the Ice portion covered," Tony said, making a sweeping motion with his hand. There were papier-mâché ice caves complete with stalactites, the ground was covered in fake confetti snow, and then there was the polar bear ice luge and bright blue Polar Potion.

"Pretty impressive," I said. I had to remember that functioning human beings actually had conversations. They didn't only think about what it was like to lock lips with seductive snowmen.

"Yeah, the pledges did a good job setting it up. But I'd rather go somewhere"—Tony raised one of those sexy commas on his forehead—"with more heat." He licked his upper lip in the most tempting way possible. The tip of his tongue caressed his full, pink lip, his mouth opening in the most graceful yet animalistic way.

"I'd like that," I squeaked, unable to take my eyes off Tony's mouth. It took everything in me not to go all Animal Planet myself and pounce on him right then and there.

Tony pulled me through the house until we made it to a set of sliding glass doors. They led out into the backyard, but people clogged the opening. Firemen and ice princesses tried to push outside while others tried to get back in the house.

"Outside is Fire," Tony explained. Through the glass doors I could see tiki torches, a makeshift volcano slide, and tables packed with red and orange Jell-O shots. "But I know a place that's even hotter."

How could one person say so few words but pack them with so much sexiness? Was there some sort of hot magic class where all the spells instantly turn people on? *Abracaboner!* It had to be a thing, and Tony had to have aced it. He was a wizard when it came to giving me a hard-on with the shortest of sentences.

I tried licking my lips like Tony, but it didn't pan out. I had to dodge the corner of a human-sized box of Hot Tamales, so I ended up just running my tongue over my teeth. I would definitely fail the sexy magic class.

I cleared my throat. Maybe I could at least come across as mysterious and suave with my words if not my tongue. "Maybe there's somewhere we could . . ." *Jeezus, Jay, think!* "Make. The heat. Ourselves?"

I would have face-palmed if my hand wasn't in Tony's. What the hell was that?

"Great minds." Tony ran a finger up my arm, electric shocks cascading over my skin. He was so smooth and effortless despite the fact we were constantly being jostled by costumed college kids. "I know just the place. Ready?"

Frack yes, I was ready.

"We'll have to push through the crowd. Hold tight."

Tony squeezed my fingers and surged forward. We burst onto the deck outside. His grip was so tight that I followed along right behind, but I couldn't stop myself from tripping over someone's shoe and falling forward. "Frack!" I was going to fall flat on my face. Visions of my nose slamming into the ground and bursting with blood were flashing through my head when, suddenly, Tony's free hand found my flailing arm. He yanked me out of the crowd, but pulled with such force that my chest rammed into his. We were face-to-face, the cool, misty outside air doing nothing to lower my temperature. Our mouths were so close that I was breathing in his Polar Potion–scented breaths.

Tony's lips parted, and something came over me. Whether it was a magic spell from Tony's sexy sorcerer skills, or some romantically aware part of my brain that knew this was the perfect moment, it didn't matter. I closed the distance and pressed my mouth hard against Tony's.

Everything around us faded away. No music. No chatter. No fire hydrant careening down the volcano slide. I could only focus on the feel of Tony's lips against mine.

I was kissing a boy. I WAS KISSING A BOY. Sure, it wasn't while slow dancing to Shawn Mendes, but oh fracking well.

Tony opened his mouth. He did it in such an assertive, deliberate way that mine followed suit. In the blink of an eye, his tongue was against mine.

My mind blared again with *Thank Gawd It's Frenching!* His tongue was wet, confident, bonkers-making perfection. He even had the lightest layer of stubble. The scratch of his whiskers against my face made my nerves go wild.

There went item number six:

JAY'S GAY AGENDA

1. ~~Meet another gay kid. Somewhere, anywhere . . . please! in Seattle in, like, days!~~ ✓

1.5. ~~Get checked out by a very VSB!~~ ✓

2. Go on **any** ~~Digimals~~ date with Albert ~~a boy at the Space Needle.~~

2.5. ~~Hold hands within the first ninety minutes.~~ a VSB ~~after being pulled into my first-ever drag show by a queen named after a fish.~~ ✓

3. ~~Go to a d~~Dance with a boy and ~~have my first~~ kiss slow dancing to Shawn Mendes while getting caught in a surprise Seattle downpour.

4. Have a boyfriend, one who likes to wrap me up in his arms and let me be little spoon, and maybe smells like coffee from all the cafés he goes to.

5. Fall in love with a boy, but wait for him to say it first so I don't seem too desperate, and maybe he

says it for the first time at Pike Place Market or in the first Starbucks.

6. **Make out with** ~~Albert, or Tony, or you know, any guy who keeps himself in my personal bubble, with tongue, and hard enough that I'd get a little burn from his stubble. run my fingers along that perfect jawline.~~ **the hottest snowman this side of the North Pole.** ✓

7. See another penis besides my own, IRL, and do fun things with it!

8. Lose. My. Virginity!

9. Become part of a super-queer, super-tight framily by impressing everybody with my epic costumier skills, erasing the "new kid" label, and becoming homecoming royalty.

10. Figure out a way to make my gay dreams come true and not destroy my bestie's life.

It was better than anything I'd ever imagined. Tony pushed me into the deck railing, his hands against my cheeks. White and blue and silver paint smeared against his palms. I suddenly didn't mind someone touching my face anymore as he pressed harder and deeper with each kiss.

The velvet carrot nose on Tony's costume rubbed against the top of my head, over and over and over. But I didn't care. He had a whole other protruding carrot thing going on that drew all my attention with each press of his body against mine.

For years, I'd wondered what this moment would be like. What it would feel like. Who it would be with. My mind was on such an overdrive of sensation that I couldn't really make sense of my thoughts, or even know where Tony's lips ended and mine began. But there was one thing I knew for sure:

This was totally worth the wait.

15.

✓ Get Ghosted by Your Bestie

I don't know how long we stood there making out. All I know is that when one of Tony's fraternity brothers pulled him back, creating enough space for cold air to whoosh between us, it wasn't long enough.

"Yo, dude, your Little is puking all over the den! Chunks everywhere!"

Tony looked to the sky in exasperation. "Fuuuuuuck." He nodded back toward the house with a silver-smeared chin. "I have to handle this."

"Okay," I panted. My chest heaved as I tried to catch my breath.

Tony put his hand in my pocket, and if anything was going to make me explode, it was his fingers being just centimeters away from my dick. Thankfully before any spontaneous ejaculation could occur, Tony pulled out my phone and handed it to me. "Take my number. Let's continue this next weekend. Saturday?"

I licked my lips. They felt wrong without Tony's stubble rubbing against them. Why did people ever waste time talking? All my mouth wanted to do was mash itself against Tony's sexy smirk.

"Yes, please," I said.

I unlocked my phone and Tony entered his number. He put it back in my pocket—there was that combustion feeling again—and leaned in for one last, hard kiss. "See you then."

I wondered if there was an actual vat of ice somewhere at this Fire & Ice party. If not, I was definitely going to melt.

~~~

"I don't know why everyone isn't kissing all the time." Max and I were in the Uber back to his house. "Tony was just so . . ." There was nothing in the English language to describe him. What word captured the ability to set each and every one of my nerves on fire?

"Based on Tony turning your face into a Picasso, I'd say he liked it too," Max said.

"Thank you for introducing me to him." I ran my fingers over my still throbbing lips. "How'd you know he'd want to make out?"

"Tony has always had a thing for guys with killer hair. I had a hunch he'd think you were cute."

Max winked as he reached over and ruffled my bangs. It made me think of Tony running his hands through my hair. And there I was with a boner again.

"But how did you know he would bypass just thinking I was cute and head straight to making out?" I asked. "It's like you have some sort of superpower."

"Let's just say that Tony is a very physical kind of guy." Max grabbed my hand, his red nail polish stark against the white makeup covering my skin. "Look, Jay, just so you know, Tony isn't really a relationship type of person. He was kind of known at school for being . . . easy, which is such a judgmental word, and that's not the vibe I'm going for here. I'm all about sex positivity, and while Tony does get around, I have it on good authority that he is always safe, consensual, and sexy. Maybe I should have told you before. But as your Libido Liberator, I just wanted your first make-out session to be no strings attached with a guy I was pretty sure would be down for it. I thought you'd like that too." Max cringed. "Did I read the room wrong and totally screw up?"

So Tony wasn't into relationships. I guess that instantly took him out of the boyfriend regression analysis. But if he was still interested in having some fun, that didn't mean we had to stop. I could just focus on giving Albert my heart and giving Tony any body part he wanted.

I brushed my fingers against my lips again. I never wanted the phantom Tony tingles to go away. "It *was* a good make-out session," I said. And it didn't make it any less good that Tony had kissed a lot of people before me.

In fact, his experience might have been what made it so good. He knew exactly what to do and just how to make my whole body go wild. Plus, I was the one to make the first mouth-to-mouth move. Tony being into it made me feel that much more like an actually attractive senior instead of some middle schooler who would forever be on the sidelines while everyone else was locking lips. "You did good, Max. Gay Guide of the Month Award."

"Only the month?" Max smacked my knee. "Lord and Taylor, I am underappreciated."

My phone vibrated with a text from Tony.

We never made it up to my room. Guess I'll have to show you next week 😊

My stomach turned, a mix of excitement and nerves and horniness bubbling in my gut. I showed the text to Max.

"Looks like I might have gotten you more than your first kiss," he said.

I wondered if that could really be possible. Was I just a week away from crossing off at least one of the penis items on the Gay Agenda?

"Okay, yeah. Gay Guide of the Year Award," I said.

"Damn straight. Or . . . damn gay."

"I have to text Lu about this. If anyone would appreciate that I'm going to go out with a college boy, it would be her."

I pulled up Lu's and my texts, ready to let fly the scruff-filled kiss news. I stopped short when I saw our last text exchange about Chip, full of all the *Eat Shit* GIFs we could find. Would it be heartless to send her a text about Gay Agenda accomplishments when her love life had crumbled? But then again, she'd been the one to say that just because things weren't going so hot for her didn't mean that I couldn't share when things were going well for me. So I decided to embrace the moment and just go for it.

I'VE BEEN KISSED!

I set my phone down and turned to Max. "I don't know what it is you want to do when we graduate high school, but if it doesn't include matchmaking, you're wrong."

"So far the plan is fashion stylist, but I'll be sure to include matchmaking services on my website," Max said.

We pulled up to his house and I looked down at my phone. No response. The subject of MY FIRST KISS was definitely *drop everything and get back to me ASAP*-worthy. Maybe if I added more of the juicy details, Lu would text back.

He was dressed as a snowman!

I never knew snow could be so hot!

Plus, he had stubble!

You were so right that it feels amazing!

And we're seeing each other again next weekend!

I think I won't be a virgin much longer.

I was probably being a little overenthusiastic, but I was on a high from the combo of making out and a cup full of Polar Potion.

When we got to Max's place, we tiptoed up to his room so we wouldn't wake his parents. They were so much more easygoing than Dad would be. Max straight-up told them we were going to a party, and they said as long as we Ubered and texted if anything "completely unruly" went down, we were fine to go.

Up in Max's room, I checked my phone again as I grabbed makeup-remover wipes. Still nothing from Lu. What was going on? Sure, it was one in the morning on a Friday night, but Lu wasn't the type who went to bed early on the weekend.

I *said* I might lose my virginity! I typed. **Text me!**

Max pointed accusingly at me through his taffeta curtains. "Jizz Genie tip: don't text Tony again tonight. You don't want to look desperate."

"We said you wouldn't call yourself that, and for the record, I wasn't texting Tony. I was texting Lu about kissing a guy for the first time."

"Oh, that reminds me. *Don't* mention to Tony that he's the first guy you ever kissed. That's a lot of pressure. So many gays don't want to have the responsibility of teaching someone everything about what it's like to be with another guy."

I didn't think I'd have to worry about blurting any of that to Tony. The next time I saw him I intended on making sure my tongue was too tied up with his to say anything Max put on the Do Not Let Slip list.

I dove through the draped taffeta and plopped next

to Max. "I'm totally on board with pretending I have this secret sexually experienced identity if it means Tony will want to make out more."

Max laughed. "I'm not saying to lie or anything. It's not secretive so much as . . ." He looked toward a wall that he'd completely covered in pictures of his favorite runway looks. "Think of it as having confidence. No matter how well-made the clothes are, no outfit is sexy unless you're completely sure of yourself in it. When I came out as genderqueer, runway models were the secret to my success. Even if it was a struggle at first, I learned to exude their power and self-assuredness. Do that and you're golden."

I caught my reflection in the mirror of Max's vanity. I'd removed most of my makeup, but missed a section around my lips that was smeared by Tony's mouth. "I mean, Tony didn't seem to have any issues with the way I kissed."

"Exactly," Max said. "Don't overthink it. You've got this really cute country-boy thing about you. It's very endearing."

I glanced at my phone again, hoping I might have missed hearing the ding of a text from Lu.

Nope. Still nothing.

Studies show that the average person doesn't start losing friends until around age twenty-five. I was still seven years away from that, and honestly didn't think there'd ever be a time when Lu and I weren't BFFs who spent hours on the phone talking about me, Tony, and Tony's tongue.

But ever since I moved away, Lu and I were talking less and less. Maybe I wouldn't have to worry about telling Lu I was bailing on the hoedown. Maybe she was going to bail on *me*. I'd thought the chances of that ever happening were a big, extra-bold **zero**.

It looked like all my friendship stats were completely wrong.

16.

✓ Find a Guy Who's Got (Video) Game

I still hadn't heard from Lu by Saturday afternoon. I stared at my phone the entire time I got ready for my date with Albert, my lips still buzzing from making out with Tony. This was exactly the kind of moment when I needed my best friend: to talk about how bananas it was to go from the world's most massive gay dry spell to making out with a college boy and going on my first date within twenty-four hours. It made me pretty mad, actually, that I'd spent so much time over the summer listening to her go on and on about Chip, but she couldn't be here for me the week-end I was crossing off some serious items from the Gay Agenda. I knew she was having a rough time, and it was a very real possibility that it stung that my life had this

- 189 -

whole upward trajectory when hers was going downhill. But she shouldn't say she wanted to hear my good news and then not follow through when I had news to share.

I put the finishing touches on my bangs, then grabbed my phone from the bathroom sink. Maybe if I texted Lu the seriousness of the situation, she'd finally stop giving me the silent treatment.

About to go on MY FIRST DATE EVER, I texted. **Could really use some support.**

If we both had iPhones, I'd get that nifty "delivered" message as soon as my texts made it to Lu. But she and Aunt Carol had gotten some good deal on Androids a few years ago. Up until now, text delivery had never been a problem. Lu would type back right away, making a received note irrelevant. My stomach burned with bitterness at her radio silence when it should have been fluttering with butterflies.

The doorbell rang.

Footsteps stomped down the hall.

Oh no. Dad was answering the door. He was always such a stoic and serious guy. I could just imagine the kicks he'd get from freaking Albert out by interrogating him with horrifying questions.

HIDEOUSLY EMBARRASSING QUESTIONS DAD COULD ASK ALBERT

1. What are your intentions with my son?
2. When was the last time you were tested for STDs?

3. Are you aware of the firestorm that will rain
    down on you if you break my son's heart?

I raced down the hall and grabbed the doorknob just
before Dad could reach it.

"Why all the excitement?" Dad asked.

"No reason," I said. "Just, you know, eager to hang out
with new friends."

Dad peered through the peephole and let loose his
knowing grunt. "This wouldn't happen to be a *special*
friend that you're hanging out with, would it?"

I had to avoid this conversation at all costs. "Sorry,
Dad, I'm going to be late."

I flung the door open.

"Ready?" I asked. Without thinking, I grabbed Albert's
hand to pull him away from the house before Dad could
get to those embarrassing questions. But as I moved to
shut the door, it jammed against something very solid.
Dad's steel-toe boot was in the doorframe, and just as I
expected, he was staring Albert down. It hit me that I
was *holding Albert's hand* so Dad was for sure going to hop
right into STD questions.

"You must be Jay's friend," Dad said, putting his hand
out to shake. "I'm Rick Collier, Jay's father. Nice to meet
you."

"Nice to meet you too, sir. I'm Albert." Albert let go of
my hand and shook Dad's. He was tall enough that they
were at the same eye level. They smiled pleasantly at each
other. Albert didn't seem nervous, and Dad wasn't being

weirdly intimidating. Everything was going surprisingly well.

But then Albert moved to let go. Instead of doing the same, Dad squeezed his hand tighter and dropped the smile from his face.

Oh, frack.

"Albert," Dad said. "Albert what?"

I. Was. Mortified. "Dad. Don't," I pleaded.

Albert stared at his hand, lost to Dad's vise grip. "Albert Huang, sir."

"And what do you do, Albert Huang?"

Albert looked to me, his eyebrows raised. All I could do was cringe. "I'm so sorry," I mumbled.

But Albert was much more composed than I was. "I'm a student, Mr. Collier."

"At my son's school?"

"Yes, sir."

"Any criminal history?"

"It's all been expunged from my record. So technically, no."

Dad cracked the tiniest smile. Albert was winning over my extremely annoying, extremely nosy dad.

"Great. Let's go." I grabbed Albert's hand and yanked him from the front porch. I didn't stop our mad dash until we were around the block and outside the radius of Dad yelling anything embarrassing after us.

"Ohmigawd, I'm so sorry about him," I said. "He just wants to give me a hard time because this is my first date, and I guess you could call me a virgin at this whole gay thi—" I stopped and planted a huge face-palm. I couldn't believe I'd just said that. Not only had I called myself a virgin—which of course instantly made me think of what sex with Albert might be like—but I'd also let slip that I had zero experience with guys. Max said that was a huge no-no. I had seriously messed this up.

Albert nudged my shoulder. "Can I tell you something?"

It took everything in me to pull my hand away from my face. "I'm sure it can't be any worse than what I just said."

Albert laughed, making my heart feel like it was going to fly out of my chest. It blew my mind that Albert could give me such a physical reaction without even trying. Last night, Tony lit my whole body on fire, but he had to exude *we're going to make out* energy to do it (not that I'm complaining). Albert, however, just had to smile and laugh. He left me so twitterpated that any lingering worries about totally humiliating myself left my mind.

"This is my first date in a long while," Albert said. "So it's practically like I'm a virgin too." He smiled again, letting loose that dimple. Gawd, I wanted to kiss it. And his mouth. Especially his mouth.

Then what he said actually sank in. I was shocked. He was the prime VSB of the whole school. People should have been lining up to date him! "How is that possible?" I asked.

Albert shrugged. "My last relationship kind of put me off dating. I haven't felt a connection with someone in a while. It's just that I'm . . ." He paused for a long time, then sighed. "Never mind. It's too heavy for a first date."

"No, what is it?" I wanted Albert to feel as at ease with me as I felt with him.

"Okay. Remember PrinterBot?" Albert asked.

"It's kind of hard to forget your first head-on collision with a robot."

Albert laughed again while my heart sprouted wings and took off into the drizzly sky.

"I'm the Chinese kid who likes robots," Albert continued. "And video games, for that matter. And people seem to think that gives them the right to peg me for a stereotype. I've heard some ignorant comments from guys I was interested in after my ex about how I must get straight As and like Panda Express. Or that because I'm a gamer, I'm somehow feeding the stereotype. But I like figuring out how machines work and kicking ass at a game. I don't want to be judged for what I enjoy. Sometimes people's judgment can just really kill the mood, you know?"

"I get what you mean," I said. "I'm a gay guy who likes theater and *RuPaul's Drag Race* and watching old episodes of *Will and Grace*. But just because I like certain 'stereotypically' gay things doesn't mean that every gay guy who walks the earth is exactly the same. I tried to explain this at my old school all the time. I was the only out guy, so me liking all these things that my straight friends assumed were *gay* things only reinforced the stereotype for them. It got really annoying hearing this stuff from people outside our community, but for you to be getting these racist judgments from guys you thought about dating? That's horrible. I'm sorry you went through that."

Most of my gay stats research talked about our issues living in a heteronormative society, but it looked like straight people weren't the only ones who needed to examine their problematic behavior.

"Thanks," Albert said. "Honestly, that comment you made on the first day of school? The stat about vending machines killing more people than sharks? It was such a dorky thing to say, and—"

"Ugh, I am such an idiot," I interrupted.

"No, no," Albert said. "I don't mean dorky in a bad way. It was perfect." His eyes practically pulsed with sincerity. It took everything in me not to tilt my head up and kiss him. "It felt like such an authentic statement. Like you were being unapologetically Jay. It made me think that I could just be myself around you."

It was a relief that Albert liked it when I embraced the stats-loving geek that I am inside. I didn't have to do all the romance equations of *these words + this flirtatious action = sexually attractive Jay* when I was around him.

"The feeling is so mutual," I said. We stood there, staring at each other with stupid grins on our faces. I think we both could have stood there all day, but Albert eventually pulled his eyes away, and led us down the street. "So, for our date, I thought you might want to see the city from the Space Needle."

It was like Albert could read my mind and knew the

landmark was on the Gay Agenda. Visions of making out at the top while a rainbow appeared over Mount Rainier flew through my mind.

But then a whole new vision joined it: It was Jimmy Arlington in fourth grade coming back to Riverton Elementary after spending spring break in Seattle. It was a big deal when anyone went somewhere we deemed far away (any place other than Spokane). Jimmy had bragged about going to the coolest video game arcade he'd ever seen. A plan began to form in my mind that I thought Albert might like.

"There's someplace else I've been interested in seeing too," I said. "I think it's called GameWorks?"

Albert's mouth fell open. "Seriously?"

"I've never been, and I'm not sure if it's still around, but I've heard it's a great place to play video games."

Albert looked like he was finally getting a puppy after begging for one for months.

"It's this really cool arcade that is three floors of games," he explained. "It's one of my favorite places. You really want to go?"

"Absolutely. If it's your favorite place, let's do it. I want to see Albert's Seattle."

This was not the first date I'd expected when thinking about crossing it off the Gay Agenda. But this feeling of wanting to make a boy I liked happy was new and exciting, and I wanted to see where it went.

"I do have to warn you, though, I am not a gamer at all," I added.

That smoldering look came over Albert. "That totally won't be a problem. I can teach you."

—*m*m—

We sprinted the last couple of blocks to GameWorks when it started to pour, providing the optimal rom-com environment for a rain-drenched kiss. In my hunt for real-world stats, I'd found that a very large number of people's highest-rated kissing scenes include rain because 1) it adds drama to an already heightened emotional moment, and 2) it makes people's clothes cling to them so that dramatic moment suddenly turns sexy. I totally got it as Albert's shirt wrapped closer and closer to his torso with each passing second.

The exterior of GameWorks was pretty nondescript: it was all beige stone occasionally streaked with gray from city soot clinging to the constantly wet walls (I guess rain doesn't make everything sexy, after all). But when Albert held the door open for me, the inside was a totally different story. It was tech overload. There were beeps and boops and blasts coming from every direction, with flashes of light going off as people blew up androids and aliens and Death Stars or whatever. In the center of all the arcade games was a three-story video wall. People in roller-coaster chairs were hoisted up and down the three levels as they shot at zombies coming to maul them.

"Whoa," I breathed.

Albert put his hand on my shoulder and my whole body buzzed. "It's beautiful, isn't it?" he said, gazing longingly at a *Grand Theft Auto* game.

My attention was entirely drawn to his face. "Yeah, it is."

We stepped up to buy tickets. The bored attendant grunted out that it would be $150 for two two-hour unlimited play passes. *Holy hell!* I had no idea video games could be so expensive.

I rushed to pull out my wallet. A couple people had asked me at Riverton, "But, like, who pays on a gay date? You're both guys so there's no chivalry. Can you be a gentleman to another gentleman?" Even with no experience, I had always insisted that each person could just pay for themselves. I was about to put that into practice now that I was actually faced with who would be paying for who. It seemed like a lot to expect Albert to pay seventy-five dollars for me to play games I knew absolutely nothing about. But Albert waved my wallet away.

"This is on me," he said.

"I couldn't ask you to pay that much!" I was extremely aware of other people's money now that Lu didn't have any. "Besides, it was my idea to come here."

"I'd like to do this for you," Albert said.

Turns out, you can be a gentleman to another gentleman, gay chivalry does exist, and there was no limit to the amount of times Albert could make me swoon.

"Thanks." Our eyes met and we were grinning at each other like dumb kids all over again. How long would it be until our grins were on top of each other while we kissed?

"Do you guys want the tickets or what?" the attendant

asked, totally killing the moment.

Albert's cheeks flushed. "Sure, yeah." He handed over two hundred dollars and walked away.

The attendant waved a few bills at Albert's retreating back. "Don't you want your change?"

"Oh. Whoopsie." He actually said *whoopsie!*

Albert snatched the cash and shoved it into his pocket. "You're making me nervous," he said. "I'm never nervous. What are you doing to me, Collier?"

This was actually happening. After almost eighteen years of waiting for another boy to make it super clear that he liked me, here I was standing next to a guy who said that *I* made *him* nervous. I knew that with Tony I had already done so much more than what I was about to do, but that didn't stop my heart from racing with excited jitters.

My hand shook a little as I took a deep breath and grabbed Albert's hand.

Technically, hand-holding was already crossed off the Gay Agenda, but this moment felt even more monumental because I had taken the lead, and it was extremely intentional. Was my hand way sweatier than I wanted it to be? Yes. But even still, there was something so magical about standing there with a hot guy's hand in mine, all of our attention on each other instead of having to dodge six-foot-tall fire hydrants like I had at the Lambda Chi party.

Albert looked down at our hands, then back at me, then back at our hands. Maybe I should have waited longer; I had always planned for ninety minutes to be the appropriate hand-holding wait time. But I'd rushed it within the first ninety *seconds* we were in GameWorks, and now I'd totally freaked Albert out. He probably thought I was some obsessed kid who was going to start calling him my boyfriend from this moment on.

"Sorry," I mumbled, loosening my grip.

"No," Albert said. He squeezed my fingers so I couldn't let go. "I like it."

"Whoa. Whoa! Oh frack! WATCH OUT!"

Albert and I zipped up and down the three-story video wall, my stomach lurching every time my seat whipped up another level. It turns out I'm a very vocal video game player. I screamed whenever a zombie popped out or my seat moved, and each time I shot a monster's head off, I whooped in victory. The latter happened very rarely. I was lucky Albert got us unlimited play cards because I was getting eaten by zombies more often than I was shooting them to pieces.

"Albert! On your left!" I had already been knocked out by an undead little girl, but Albert had made it to the boss level. If he made this shot, he would win the game.

Albert held his plastic blue gun like he was an actual marine sent to destroy the zombie hordes invading America. He whipped to the side and decimated that rotting bastard.

"Gotcha!" He holstered his gun as a military head

honcho congratulated us (read: Albert) on our heroism.

Our seats lowered to the first level and we walked back to the game floor. "I don't know how you play that without screaming," I said. "You're so calm and collected when zombies try to tear out your throat."

"It just takes practice," Albert said. "You'll be a pro in no time. We'll just have to keep coming back."

My mind burst into squeals louder than a Shawn Mendes concert. *EEEEEEEEE! Keep your cool, Jay. Keep your cool.*

"I'd like that."

Albert looked at his phone. "We only have ten minutes left before our play runs out."

"What should we do?" I asked.

"I know just the thing," Albert said, and grabbed my hand. We had reached the point in the date where lacing our fingers together had become our default position. How had my hands ever functioned outside of his?

We passed racing games with people riding life-sized motorcycles, then veered left at a row of Skee-Ball machines. We finally stopped at a little fort-looking game that you had to climb inside to play. "Jurassic World" was plastered on the side with bloodthirsty dinosaurs chasing A-list actors.

Albert pulled me inside without a word. Suddenly it was just the two of us, the flashes and lasers and other gamers disappearing as we sat together in our own private cave. All the sounds of GameWorks were replaced by Bryce Dallas Howard explaining that we were dino hunters looking to stop the Indominus rex. I never knew that talk of a carnivore hell-bent on eating every human in sight could be so romantic.

With a gentle tug, Albert pulled me closer. His pressure was tender but firm, lifting me just enough so that I slid over effortlessly. Our thighs pressed together, my body aware of every single atom that touched Albert. Our faces were close enough that I could see my reflection in his glasses, but I wanted to be even closer. Albert must have felt that, too, because he leaned in, stopping when his lips were just millimeters away from mine.

"Is this okay?" he whispered. There was something about him asking permission that made my already flying heart rocket to the moon.

I nodded at supersonic speed. This was more okay than anything had ever been in my entire life.

Even though it could have only taken .002 seconds, it was like everything went in slow motion. Albert's eyes zeroed in on my mouth. His fingers curled around a belt loop on either side of my hips. His lips parted just slightly, then he closed the distance, his mouth finally landing on mine.

Talk about tender but firm. Albert's lips were soft as he took my top lip between his, pulling slightly with just enough pressure to make every single nerve ending pulse. He wasn't frenzied, like Tony. He was measured and slow, taking his time to pull back before dipping his mouth again to wrap my lips up in his once more. It was like he was savoring me, wanting to taste not only my lips, but my soul. He wasn't just putting his body into this kiss. He was putting his heart into it too.

I kissed him back, letting my tongue dip just slightly into his mouth. My taste buds flooded with the flavor of his spearmint gum. Albert gasped when my tongue hit his, then pressed his own against mine. I wanted to taste him forever.

Albert moved a hand from my belt loop onto my leg. The blood pounding in my heart moved between my thighs. My whole body wanted him, my entire soul too, and it hit me that an item on the Gay Agenda always should have been to find Albert. To find the guy who could set my spirit and my sexuality on fire all at the same time.

Nothing could make me pull away from this kiss, this moment. Nothing could make me—

"THIS HAS GOT TO STOP!"

I snapped back. "What was that?"

Albert chuckled and nodded toward the screen. Bryce Dallas Howard was screaming about dinosaur carnage.

"Sorry," I said, the blood rushing from my crotch to fire up my cheeks. "I don't know anything about games, remember?"

"That's okay." Albert squeezed my thigh and pulled me into him. "I'm happy to be your teacher."

He took my mouth in his again, his tongue lightly

brushing over my lips.

I'd take all the lessons he wanted to give.

JAY'S GAY AGENDA

1. ~~Meet another gay kid. Somewhere, anywhere . . .~~
   ~~please! in Seattle in, like, days!~~ ✓

1.5. ~~Get checked out by a very VSB!~~ ✓

2. **Go on** ~~any Digimals~~ **a video game** date with
   Albert ~~a boy at the Space Needle~~ **and learn just
   how much game Albert's really got.** ✓

2.5 ~~Hold hands within the first ninety minutes a VSB~~
   ~~after being pulled into my first ever drag show~~
   ~~by a queen named after a fish.~~ ✓

3. ~~Go to a d~~Dance with a boy and ~~have my first~~
   kiss slow dancing to Shawn Mendes while getting
   caught in a surprise Seattle downpour.

4. Have a boyfriend, one who likes to wrap me up
   in his arms and let me be little spoon, and maybe
   ~~smells~~ **tastes** like ~~coffee from all the cafés he~~
   ~~goes to~~ **spearmint, and who ignites my soul and
   my sexuality.**

5. Fall in love with a boy, but wait for him to say it
   first so I don't seem too desperate, and maybe he
   says it for the first time at Pike Place Market or
   in the first Starbucks.

6. ~~Make out with Albert, or Tony, or you know, any~~
   ~~guy who keeps himself in my personal bubble, with~~
   ~~tongue, and hard enough that I'd get a little~~
   ~~burn from his stubble. run my fingers along that~~
   ~~perfect jawline. the hottest snowman this side of~~

~~the North Pole.~~ ✓

7. See another penis besides my own, IRL, and do fun things with it!

8. Lose. My. Virginity!

9. Become part of a super-queer, super-tight framily by impressing everybody with my epic costumier skills, erasing the "new kid" label, and becoming homecoming royalty.

10. Figure out a way to make my gay dreams come true and not destroy my bestie's life.

17.

✓ Finally Get Through Call Waiting

"HAPPY BIRTHDAY!" Dad pounded on my mattress with both fists, his classic go-to method for waking me up. He'd use it when I wanted to sleep in on the weekends, but he wanted me to help with chores around the property. I so did not miss country living.

"Whassat?" I rubbed the crust from my eyes and tried to muster enough energy to sit up. I was exhausted. I'd been thinking about Albert for the past thirty-six hours. I hadn't slept Saturday or Sunday night reliving that perfect kiss with him—and maybe imagining what doing more with him would be like too.

Dad held out an everything bagel with strawberry cream cheese, my favorite combo. A candle perched in the hole of each half. "I wanted to catch you before you head out to school," Dad said. He sat down on my bed, looking at me with big, very un-Dad-like doe eyes. "Eighteen years old. You're officially an adult."

"Yeah." I yawned. "I can buy cigarettes and gamble." And buy porn, but I didn't need to bring that up to Dad.

"Both of which you *won't* do," Dad said, flicking my knee. "But you can and will vote." He handed me the plate. The smell of freshly toasted bagel was enough to give me the boost I needed to sit up.

"Thanks, Dad." I blew out the candles, wishing for a fully crossed-off Gay Agenda with no casualties. Number ten was especially on my mind. I still hadn't heard from Lu, and it was really freaking me out.

I took a bite of the perfect mix of savory and sweet to lift my spirits. "Where's Mom?"

"She had to go into work early again," Dad said. "Apparently there's been a mix-up on milk orders at the Fresh Savings in Bellingham."

I gasped. "Not a Dairy Disaster!"

"And there's only one woman for the job," Dad mumbled. The slump in his shoulders could only mean the Dairy Disaster led to a Depressed Dad.

"You miss Mom, don't you?" I knew he was super proud of her for getting this new job, but the romantic in him hated that she'd been traveling so much.

Dad waved his hand dismissively. "No, no. She's doing what she needs to provide for this family." He paused, his forehead furrowing deeper by the second. "Okay, maybe I miss her. A lot. We're in a whole new town and I'd love to explore it with her."

"It's just barely been two weeks," I said with my mouth full. "There's still plenty of time to explore." I swallowed, finishing the first half of the bagel while Dad grabbed the second and took a bite.

"Hey!" I tried to swipe it back.

"You'll understand when you find the man of your dreams," Dad said, dodging me even though his look was faraway, probably imagining some romantic getaway with Mom. "When you find your perfect match, even one day without them is too much."

I had an inkling of what he meant. I couldn't stop thinking about when I'd get to kiss Albert again.

"Anyway." Dad reached into his back pocket and pulled out a white envelope. "From your mother and me."

I opened it and saw an Alaska Airlines gift card. "What's this for?" Mom usually had a no-gift-cards-as-presents rule. She said they were too impersonal and didn't require thought.

"This new life happened so fast," Dad said. He gazed out the window like if he squinted hard enough, he'd be able to see our log home back in Riverton. "We wanted you to know that you can fly back to visit Lu whenever you want while you adjust."

I wasn't so sure that Lu would even want me to visit. She never took more than fifteen minutes to respond to a text, let alone three days. But she'd been MIA from texts, phone calls, a "Call meeeeeeeeee" email, and when

I Skyped for our digital Saturday sleepover after my date with Albert. WT actual frack was going on?

"I should clarify and say you can fly back as long as you don't miss school," Dad continued. "Speaking of which, get dressed. Just because it's your birthday doesn't mean you get to miss out on your education."

—*ww*—

I kept checking my phone on the way to school because Lu normally made a big deal about birthdays. This had to be the day she stopped shutting me out. But I didn't get the annual wake-up call of her singing "Happy Birthday," so maybe not.

"Happy birthday, Virgo!" Max pranced up next to my locker, then slapped a hand to his mouth in shock. "Lord and Taylor, you look terrible!"

"Good morning to you, too."

"No, sorry, it's just . . ." Max circled my face with his hands. "What's going on here? I thought you had an epic weekend of locking lips with hot guys."

"It's Lu. I haven't heard a peep from her since last week," I said.

"You don't think she's mad about how well things are going for you when she's just broken up with Chip, do you?" Max asked.

Leave it to him to call things out exactly as they were. "Yes. That's precisely what I think."

"Well, you've done all you can to get ahold of her, right?"

I nodded.

"Then that's all you can do," Max said. "She'll come around eventually."

I wasn't so sure. Lu was known for her stubborn streak. She used it to her advantage a lot. Like how she got all her newspaper pieces in on time despite not having a laptop of her own to work from home, or how she always got people to give her quotes for her stories. For her gender-pay-gap article, she'd shown up on Donald Raben's bus route for three whole months before he'd finally caved and told her what he made as a bus driver. How long would she hold out when it came to me?

Max fished through his typewriter-shaped Kate Spade bag. "I have just the thing to get your mind off this." He pulled out his phone and opened Instagram with a picture of Reese and Spencer. Reese was wearing some sort of cream-colored tunic thing and held a lightsaber, while Spencer had on tight black pants and a black vest over a white long-sleeved shirt that also fit nice and snug over his body. "We'll come up with ideas for how we're going to beat these little asshats in the costume contest."

The reminder of the dance only sent my thoughts reeling further. If Lu did ever decide to end her silence, I was going to have to break it to her that I wasn't going to the hoedown.

"Reese and his"—Max rolled his eyes—"*boyfriend* are going as Luke Skywalker and Han Solo. According to Reese's Insta, they're the 'quintessential couple that should have gotten together in hindsight.' Really the only thing quintessential about that costume is that Reese is for sure the spawn of the most evil force in the universe."

Max seemed more and more comfortable saying Reese's name, so I thought he might be more willing to discuss his breakup issues. I opened my mouth to ask if he wanted to talk out his feelings, but Max held his hand up to stop me. He wasn't wearing his twin gold bracelets anymore. "No," he said. "We're not talking about it, remember? I'm fine."

I figured I should drop it or risk Max pushing me away like he had Damon and Cami.

"Okay, gotta go," Max said as the warning bell rang for class. "Let's brainstorm something great that will kill their costume idea like Emperor Palpatine killing Darth Vader. Later, may the Force be with you!"

Max left and I turned to head to calculus but came face-to-face with the school secretary, Mr. Hammond.

"Jay?" He was standing so close I could smell the coffee on his breath.

I coughed. "Y-yes?"

"Follow me, please. There's been an emergency. You're needed in the office right away."

"What's going on?" I asked.

Mr. Hammond didn't answer. He just kept speed-walking toward the office.

I was in too much of a Best Friend Fiasco mindset to have any idea what this could be about. My mind raced through the possibilities: Grammy or Gramps was in the hospital; Dad got into a car accident while Ubering someone through town; there really was some Dairy Disaster at Fresh Savings and Mom got taken out in a massive milk mishap.

Mr. Hammond ushered me through the glass doors of the office and into an empty cubicle. "I've put them on hold." He pointed to a phone where a blinking red button flashed in time with the pounding of my heart. "Just hit that button there, and she should be waiting for you."

I swallowed. My spit took so long to make it down my throat it felt like it was filled with rocks. "Okay," I breathed. Mr. Hammond gave me a sympathetic pat on the back and left. I picked up the receiver and with a shaking finger pressed Line 2. "Hello?"

"OM fucking G, it's taken me ages to get ahold of you!" Lu shouted. "Do you have any idea how hard it is to find phone numbers these days without a cell phone?"

"Lu!" I yelled, then quickly slapped my hand over my mouth. I didn't want Mr. Hammond to come racing back to discover this wasn't an emergency at all, but a chat with my bestie. "Where have you been?"

"Our, uh . . . our cell phones got shut off on Friday. We're behind on payments. Without my phone, I had to wait until I got to class this morning to google the number for your school. Ms. Bellinger's letting me use her phone. She says hi, by the way." Ms. Bellinger was the pre-calc teacher. Ever since I'd won my second WAMbledon title, I could do no wrong in her eyes. "Things are tighter than ever."

"Oh, Lu—"

"Don't. I know how bad it is." She sighed so heavily I could practically feel it through the phone. "Carol's hardly getting any private clients. But I'm taking as many shifts as I can at the diner, and we should have the cell bill paid by my next payday. And that's enough about that, okay? It's your birthday! Tell me everything that's going on with you."

"I can't go to the hoedown." The words just fell out of me, like my brain decided before my heart that this was the time to rip the Band-Aid off. I wanted to wait until things were going smoothly in Lu's life to tell her about the dance, but at this rate, Lu's life would never be back to normal.

A truck roared in the background, followed by a ton of laughter. "Sorry, Jay, Ms. Bellinger's windows are open, and you know how Travis Massey loves to rev his truck. He's so *macho*. What did you say?"

So much for ripping the Band-Aid off quickly.

"I said . . ." *Deep breaths, Jay, deep breaths.* "I can't go to the hoedown. With you. Or anyone. Because I'm not going."

More truck rumbling. More laughter. But nothing from Lu.

"Lu?" I tried. "Can you hear me?"

"I heard you," she said flatly. "I just can't believe what you're saying."

"Look, I know it sounds bad. It's just that homecoming is the same night as the hoedown, and—"

"I thought you said it was the week after. On the sixteenth."

Of course she hadn't forgotten that detail. This was Lu Fuhrman, star journalist of the *Riverton Reporter*, known for her ability to get facts straight.

"I got the date wrong," I lied. But it was just a tiny white lie. It didn't change the fact that the dances were on the same night, and how long I had known the dates conflicted was irrelevant. Wasn't it?

"That's unfortunate," Lu said. "Aren't you the guy who has a way with numbers? The Jay I know makes lists and writes everything down. It seems really unlike you to mess that up."

She was 100 percent right.

"I could still make a costume for you and somebody else," I offered. "It'd be like I was there all along." I thought if I just skipped over the date snafu, we could come up with something productive.

"I don't want to go with anyone else, Jay. I want to go with you. This was about us being together."

My anxiety was suddenly wiped away with a fiery burn. Was that really what this was about? *Us* going together? She was the one who had been planning to go with Chip instead of me.

"I don't know, I just kind of feel like this is a case of sloppy seconds," I said, not caring about the bite in my tone. "What if Chip was still with you? Would we even be having this conversation?"

"Are you kidding me, Jay? Chip was my *boyfriend*. That's who you're supposed to go to dances with. Your boyfriend."

Boyfriend. There it was again. If you had a significant other, you could get away with almost anything. You could ditch your best friend again and again, just like Lu had over the summer. It didn't matter whether or not it was right. Having a boyfriend was like some X-Men ability that absolved you of everything.

So I decided to use the power for myself.

"Well, I'm going to homecoming with my boyfriend," I said. It technically wasn't a lie if my plan was to get a boyfriend before the dance. It hadn't happened yet, but that didn't mean it wouldn't.

"Jay, that's . . ." Lu hesitated. Would she be happy for me? Or would she focus on the fact that I was bailing on her? We'd spent so many hours talking about what it would be like when I finally got to experience a relationship for the first time. For all she knew, it was actually happening. This was a big moment. She should be there for me.

"That's huge," Lu finished. "I'm really happy for you."

I instantly felt guilty for ever doubting her, and for thinking she'd shut me out after a huge weekend of Gay Agenda milestones. There was no way she would have ignored that on purpose. "Thanks, Lu."

"Is it Albert?" she asked.

This time my heart spoke before my brain. "Yeah." He kissed me like he wanted to give me a piece of his soul. That had to mean he eventually would ask me to be in a relationship. Then this whole conversation with Lu wouldn't really be a lie.

"That's great," Lu said. "You should go with him to

homecoming. You're right. I would have done the same thing."

She sounded resigned. Lifeless. Not at all like herself.

"Listen, my phone will probably come back on sometime next week," she said. "Then I'm going to be pretty busy for a while." I could hear Lu clack her nails. She was nervous or sad or . . . lying. "Shifts at the diner, interviews I've got to do for the paper. I'll call you whenever I'm free. Okay?"

"'Kay."

"Happy birthday, Jay. Sounds like it's been a pretty good one."

She hung up. I stared at the phone long past when the dial tone kicked in. I'd gotten what I wanted: a way out of the hoedown. I was all clear to cross numbers three and four off the Gay Agenda, like some cosmic birthday gift from the Gay Gods.

But why did I feel so awful?

~~~

That awful feeling lingered all day. Albert wasn't around at lunch to help lift my mood either. He had something to do with the Robotics Club, so he had to skip selling homecoming tickets, and Max was out getting decorating supplies for the dance. This was not the way I pictured ringing in my eighteenth birthday: alone and feeling like I'd just made a big mistake.

I felt terrible all the way into my last period of the day, Civics and Current Events. I was trying to distract myself by coming up with costume ideas for Homecoming in Hindsight when my thoughts were interrupted by a knock on the door. Mrs. Gakstetter stopped her talk about electoral college votes and how that messed-up system works to shout, "Come in!"

Nobody opened the door. Instead, another knock.

"I said come in!" Mrs. Gakstetter yelled.

Again, nobody entered. Just another knock.

Mrs. Gakstetter stomped to the door and flung it open. "What do you wan—Oh!"

She leaped out of the way as something zoomed past her. I couldn't make it out from my seat in the back corner of the room, but people started laughing instantly. Julian from the football team shouted, "Hey, it's R2-D2." Then he turned around and pointed his still-bandaged hand right at me. "And he's coming for Jay."

"What?" I stood up so I could get a better view of whatever was cruising past the first row of desks.

It was Albert's remote-controlled printer on wheels. Sitting right on top was a GoPro, and duct-taped to the side was a brand-new purple JanSport backpack. There was an envelope pinned to it that said, *HAPPY BIRTH-DAY, JAY.* I still hadn't found the time to get myself a new bag with the distraction of boys and making out with hot snowmen and video game romances. Albert had clearly noticed. Yet another reason why he was such a good choice for first-boyfriend status.

PrinterBot rolled to a stop by my desk, its googly eyes shaking. It looked so ridiculous that I couldn't help but laugh, even though I was *totally mortified* that the whole class was staring at me.

I grabbed the backpack and opened the attached envelope. The card inside had a birthday cake on it in the shape of a rocket ship blasting over the planet. Penned-in dinosaurs were drawn over the continents. I flipped the card open to find this note:

Hope your birthday
is out of this
JURASSIC
world.

It was the cutest thing anyone had ever done for me. Beneath Albert's name was a P.S.:

Max may have let slip it was your birthday. My (selfish) wish for you is that we get a lot more time together.

Then PrinterBot did a twirl to reveal another sign taped to its back.

Homecoming?

This was the kind of birthday present I had fantasized about. I was getting asked to my first dance by a VSB who made my insides quiver. And sure, Max and I were technically entering the costume contest together, but that didn't mean Albert and I couldn't re-create our soul-shattering smooch while slow dancing to Shawn Mendes. I'd explain the whole situation to Albert. I had a feeling he'd understand why I wanted to have Max's back.

I looked into the GoPro, where Albert had to be watching from the other end.

"I'd love to." I nodded for good measure, just in case the camera didn't carry sound.

Mrs. Gakstetter's clogs clacked angrily as she made her way to my desk. "Jay? What is going on here?"

I glanced at the googly-eyed PrinterBot and smiled.

"Just a little bot of romance."

18.
✓ French Kiss After French Films

always wondered how two people could go from spending zero time together to becoming virtually glued at the hip, conjoined-twins-but-actually-lovers. Like at Riverton, one second Monica Delancey and Liam Petrus were both single, then they'd made out at the Steiner bonfire, and *wham!* Nobody saw them apart ever again.

After our date and homecoming arrangement (Albert was totally fine if I entered the costume contest with Max as long as I saved my dances for Albert), Albert and I became those annoyingly into-each-other lovebirds, constantly strutting our feathers and catching eyes and laughing at the dumbest things while we sold homecoming tickets each lunch period. Ms. Okeke told us we didn't have to take every single ticket-selling session, but with one cheesy, grin-inducing look, Albert and I both said it was fine, we'd handle all the shifts.

So, I'd gone from being the only gay boy on a lonely island, to being on a folding-table island with a VSB while the rest of the world floated by. Regina and Shruti would stop and hang with us most days, and they'd always leave with eye rolls that said *You're gross, but it's actually pretty cute.*

I liked it. I liked being cute and gross.

And I liked being conjoined, the feel of Albert next to me, the sound of his laugh when I said something that really wasn't funny. Sometimes we just had to guffaw or giggle or grin like that terrifying clown from *It* to just get the energy out that came from having somebody you clicked with on every level—personality-wise, romance-wise, kiss-me-again-wise, maybe-can-we-please-take-off-our-clothes-wise.

Albert's and my heavy flirtation made the week go by in a blur, and many of my concerns didn't seem all that bad anymore. Lu would come around eventually, and then we'd laugh about how dumb it was that we could get upset over something with a name as ridiculous as *hoedown*.

My time with Albert also made one very important milestone slip my mind: my date with Tony. Which is why I gasped when I got a text from him while Max and I brainstormed costume ideas during our free period that Friday.

"What is it?" Max asked. "Did inspiration strike?"

"No," I said, handing over my phone. "Look."

We still on for tomorrow 😉

That damn winky face sent phantom scruff tingles to my cheeks. And other tingles down south.

"What do I say?" I asked. "I mean, I should turn him down, shouldn't I? Albert and I have been hanging around so much, it doesn't feel right."

"You've got to be kidding." Max looked as bewildered as the parrots dotting his shirt dress with wide-eyed stares. "What did I tell you last weekend?"

"If he liked it then he should've put a ring on it."

"Exactly. You and Albert are going to a dance together and you've been on one date. It's not like you're engaged or anything. You're single and you get to *be* gay for the first time in your life. And I mean *be* like capital B, Biblically."

Maybe Max was right. I could play the field a bit before I got tied down. And going on a date with Tony didn't mean I had to stop seeing Albert. I could have the best of both worlds until Albert came up with another cute way to suggest boyfriendship like he had with the PrinterBot dance proposal.

I opened my texts and replied to Tony.

Absolutely.

His response came back almost instantly.

Pick you up at 7.

⟿

"Are you sure this doesn't scream virginal country boy?" It was the next night, and I stood in front of my bathroom mirror picking at my denim jacket.

"I mean, sure, there is a country vibe, but now that you've upgraded to a V-neck shirt underneath, it shows just the right amount of chest," Max said. "Country is your look."

"I'm second-guessing everything." I gave myself another up-down in the mirror while Max inspected me from the back.

"Your butt looks so good in those jeans," he said clinically, like an art expert analyzing a gallery selection. "You're welcome to borrow them again at any time."

Despite Max's assurances, I still had doubts about my overall look. "But he's so tan and I'm so fracking pale. I'll look like a ghost next to him."

Max put his hands on my shoulders. I was surprised he could lift his arms with the huge shoulder pads on his blazer. "You're going to be fine," he said. "You know what always helps me when I'm nervous?"

"What?"

"Picturing Mr. Bogosian's butt."

"I do not want to be thinking about Mr. Bogosian's ass right now!"

"Suit yourself," Max said. "I happen to find Mr. B's derriere quite uplifting. If ever I'm in a bad mood, Bogosian butt flashes through my head and voilà! My day is instantly better."

All the butt talk made me think even more about what could go down that night. I was nervous. But I was also unbelievably excited. I felt like it was the night before

Christmas and I'd be gifted Tony's eggplant emoji in the flesh. Number seven was so going to get crossed off the Gay Agenda. Maybe even number eight.

I had to stop thinking about it or I'd explode in the pants Max had let me borrow, which didn't seem appropriate in loaner jeans.

My phone buzzed.

Here.

"It's Tony!" I screamed.

"Whoa, whoa! Calm down, or you're going to mess up all our hard work." Max swooped my bangs back into position, then gave me a final inspection. "Lord and Taylor, you look great. Now, remember, just be yourself, but no mentioning that this is only your second date, or that you've never seen a wiener before. And if Tony starts talking about things you know nothing about, just nod along and say, 'Yeah, I totally agree,' and everything will be fine."

"Got it," I said, fidgeting with the hem of my shirt. "You're the best Gay Guide a guy could ask for!"

Max swatted at my hands. "It's Jizz Genie, and don't wrinkle that!" He opened the bathroom door and pushed me into the hall. "You'll be great!"

I practically sprinted past the living room with a speedy wave to Mom and Dad cuddled on the couch.

"Hey, wait a minute," Mom said, picking her head up from Dad's chest. "Look at you!"

"So this is City Jay?" Dad took in my outfit, and that doe-eyed expression came over him again. It was like he was seeing me in a whole new light, which was weird because I really wasn't dressed *that* differently: the V-neck was new, and Max's jeans were tighter and more artfully bleach-splattered than my usual Levi's.

"I guess you could say that," I said.

"You look so . . . so . . . hip."

"Dad, it's not hip to say 'hip.'"

"You look hip and *handsome*," Mom added. "Your date is going to think you're so cute."

I face-palmed, worried that if my parents thought I was *cute* then I wasn't at all exuding the *let's take off these pants* vibe I wanted Tony to pick up on. "Ugh, gawd, okay, gotta go!"

"Be home by midnight, Jaybird!" Dad called.

I raced out of the house. Just as I was about to shut the front door, it was pulled back open.

"Mom?" She stood in the doorway, a shimmer of tears in her eyes. I instantly felt guilty for leaving the house when she finally got to stay home and not travel for her new job. But when I'd told her I had a date with a cute college guy (and that Max vouched for him, so that Dad would get off my case), the lovey-dovey romantic in her had insisted that I not stay around for my "silly old mom," as she called herself. "Are you okay?" I asked.

Mom waved her hand and wiped her eyes. "I'm such a sap. I'm fine, I'm just . . ." She sighed. "I'm so excited for you. I know it wasn't always easy in Riverton. I just wanted to say, you deserve this. Go out there and have the best time." She pulled me in for a hug, tugging my head down to rest against her shoulder even though I was a good seven inches taller than she was. "Thanks, Mom." My words were muffled in her shoulder. If she didn't let go soon, Max would come out and kill her for messing up my hair. "I've got to go now."

"Oh, all right." She pulled away, mussing my bangs with that mom sixth sense that let her know it would annoy me. "Just a heads-up, next time you go out, I need to meet this boy. I know he's in college, and you're technically an adult now, but that doesn't mean I don't need to give the go-ahead on who's allowed to see my only son."

I looked over my shoulder at Tony waiting in his shiny black BMW. "Okay, Mom. You got it. I should go."

I turned to head to Tony's car, but Mom reached out and stopped me. "One more thing," she said, then paused, pursing her lips. "Well, two. Since he's in college, I expect alcohol is more involved in his life than yours. If he drinks, *do not let him drive you home*. If you drink, be safe, Uber back here, and don't tell your father." Then she reached in her pocket and pulled out a condom.

I wanted to throw up.

I looked over my shoulder again, horrified that Tony might be able to see that *MY MOM WAS GIVING ME A FRACKING CONDOM!* My parents really were perfect for each other: they'd both made it their mission to humiliate me right before a date.

I snatched the square purple Durex wrapper and shoved it in my pocket. "Mom!" I whisper-shouted. "What if Tony saw that?!"

"What? Is it a crime that I want my only child to be responsible? You boys are young and hormonal. Just because I'm your silly old mom don't you think for one second that I don't know what hormones can lead to."

"Ohmigawd, ohmigawd, ohmigawd. I have to go right now."

Mom wriggled her fingers in the air. "Ta-ta. If you need any more, I put a whole box under your bathroom sink."

And with that, I ran to Tony's car. Of course, I couldn't stop thinking about the condom in my pocket. Which made me think of that condom going on a penis. Tony's penis. Cracking open my notebook and crossing off numbers seven and eight from the Gay Agenda thanks to Tony's hard penis.

Hello, boner.

I vowed never to let Max dress me again. His pants were too fracking tight, and with a condom in my pocket, I had a feeling I was going to be worked up all night.

I opened the passenger-side door and plopped down, hoping there'd be some significant AC to cool me off. "Hey," I panted. Why was I already out of breath?

As soon as I shut the door, Tony leaned over and gave me a kiss. There was no hesitation. He was just so confident and smooth. The kiss was hard and scruffy and longing, like he wanted to devour my entire body. Just like I remembered.

Tony's lips totally didn't help my boner situation. I wondered if I'd be able to make it through the date without spontaneously ejaculating.

"Been looking forward to this," Tony said, leaning back and pulling out into the street.

"Me too."

He smiled and bit his lip. I wanted *so badly* to be the one biting it. I figured lunging on top of him would have increased the odds of us crashing by about a million, so I decided to glance out the window and find something to take my mind off ravishing Tony. Of course the first thing that caught my eye was the Space Needle towering over the city. Giant phallus, giant phallus, giant phallus.

We pulled up to a stoplight, and Tony put his hand on my leg. The throbbing in my pants increased tenfold. "Hey," he said. He was a man of way fewer words than Albert, but somehow, he made one syllable sound so sexy.

I swallowed. "Hey."

Tony leaned forward and planted his mouth on mine again. Nothing about him was tender. He was forceful, like if he pressed hard enough our mouths could fuse together. I turned my whole body toward him so that he could get as much of my lips as he wanted. I lifted my hands to run through his hair and—

HOOOOOOONK! HONK, HONK, HONK!

"Oh shit! Green light!" I said, lurching back in my seat. "No distracting the driver, right?"

Tony gripped the steering wheel with one hand, using his other to roll down the window and flip off the honker. "Whatever. Fuck that guy." He floored it and we sped forward.

"Yeah. F-f-fuck him." I took a deep breath, trying to

get some composure back so I could function as a talking person and not a walking erection. "So, off to your place?"

Tony smirked. "Excited, huh?" He put his hand on my thigh, dangerously close to my crotch, and squeezed. "We'll get there. I have to make a stop first. But I promise I'll make it fun."

My mind went wild when he winked, imagining all the ways Tony could define *fun*. I tried to come up with something to say so I didn't come across like a drooling moron, but there was no easy rapport like I had with Albert. I was too worked up to speak, afraid that the first word out of my mouth would be *sex* or *dick* or something along those lines. And Tony didn't say anything either. He'd just occasionally look over and stroke my thigh, or bite his lip, and oh gawd, the sexual tension was so thick in that BMW you could have choked on it.

We finally pulled up to a bright blue building with a large sign that read "The Grand Illusion" and a tiny sign attached to that that said "Cinema." My heart and one other attentive body part sank.

"A theater?" I blurted. A public place meant there was no possibility of any nakey-time fun.

"I know, a bit of a drag, but I'm dangerously close to failing my film criticism class. My professor said I could get some extra credit if I did a write-up of some movie they're showing. But the plus side is this place is dark. Quiet." He looked right into my eyes as he grasped the outrageously phallic gearshift to put the car in park. "Intimate."

It was the sexiest extra credit assignment I'd ever heard of.

We climbed out of the car, the typical Seattle mist clinging to my arms. It did nothing to dampen the electric heat that went through me when Tony grabbed my hand and pulled me toward the theater.

"This place used to be a dentist's office," Tony explained. "But now they play movies instead of filling cavity holes and . . . drilling."

"I could tell you're a film buff by your deep love of *Frozen*," I said, trying to replace the naked dentist movie flying through my head with wholesome images of Tony fully clothed in a Disney outfit.

We entered the lobby. The place looked nothing like a cinema or a dentist's office, but more like a cute little house. The room's hardwood floors and older charm looked a lot like our duplex's living room, actually.

Tony laughed. It was scratchy and raspy, the audible manifestation of his scruff rubbing against my face while we made out.

"I bought that costume on Amazon and threw it on," Tony said. "I'm not much for dressing up, but the Lambda Chi rule is anyone who doesn't has to help the pledges clean." He pulled out a twenty as we approached a woman sitting at a folding table with a tin cashbox and a roll of tickets. "One, please."

My vision tunneled. *He wasn't into dressing up?* He had to be joking. Costumes were like the *one thing* besides statistics that I was good at. It's a good thing Tony just wanted to hook up because I could not be boyfriends with a guy who didn't want to go all out for a theme.

The woman handed Tony a small stub. "Here you go, darlin'. One for you too?" She shook her roll of tickets at me. "Ten dollars."

When it came to chivalry points, Albert got that one over Tony. Not that I expected anyone to pay for me, but still.

We ordered a tub of popcorn (I paid) and took it into the screening room. It was the only room in the place that resembled anything close to a theater, and an old-timey one at that. The room was pretty small with about thirty antique seats all covered in red velvet, and deep red curtains on either side of the screen. It looked like we were alone, the perfect setup to suck face with no one bothering us.

We sat in the back corner, and as if on cue, the lights dimmed. Make-out time!

I was instantly hard again. I turned to Tony, and he was already looking at me. He had a sexy eyebrow comma raised, his head cocked to the side. "So," he said.

"So," I breathed.

Tony leaned forward, the springs in his chair creaking loud enough that I hoped they covered the hammering of my heart.

His lips were just barely on mine when a beam of light blared through the room. A man in a beret had the flashlight on his phone glaring in front of him as he barreled into a seat just two down from ours.

"Seriously?" Tony moaned, his seat creaking again as he leaned back. "He's gonna sit right ther—"

"Shhhhhh!" The bereted bastard insisted on ruining the moment.

Tony scowled in the guy's direction, then bent forward and whispered in my ear, "Don't worry. This can be fun."

He moved his hand up the inside of my thigh, slowly, confidently, his pressure just perfect. It was a good thing I had a tub of popcorn in my lap to hide the Space Needle in my pants.

Tony leaned over, clearly going in for another kiss.

CREEEEEEAK. Those chairs needed some serious WD-40.

"Shhhhh!" Popcorn projectiles landed at my feet.

Okay, so kissing was going to be out of the question.

Thankfully, Tony kept running his index finger up and down the inseam of my jeans. Nothing had felt this good in my entire life, which was the saving grace for the ridiculous movie that played. It was just a kid running around the streets of Paris following a red balloon, occasionally saying, *"Ballon!"* and pointing up at the thing while it floated out of his reach. I did not get it at all.

But it was still the best movie I had ever seen because Tony's hand kept getting closer and closer to *there*. Just like the balloon in the movie, I could've popped at any second.

Tony's hand lingered just centimeters away from my crotch when the credits finally started to roll. "Wasn't that great?" he said with a smirk.

I couldn't get a word out. I could only nod.

"It's the only short film to ever win an Academy Award for Best Original Screenplay." Bereted Bastard was back, clearly a French-and-horrible-film enthusiast.

"That so?" Tony asked.

"Mmm. And next they're showing—"

Tony held up his hand. "Unfortunately, we have somewhere to be." He locked his fingers in mine and pulled me up. "Don't we?"

His eyes gleamed when he grinned, telling me that somewhere he mentioned was in each other's pants.

Tony led the way out of the theater, back into the drizzly streets. My skin was so hot that I'm sure I was surrounded by a cloud of steam. "Sorry about that," Tony said. "Usually the old French films aren't so crowded."

"Usually? You come here a lot?"

Tony shrugged. "I've needed extra credit on more than one occasion. It's typically just me and whoever I bring along. Like I said, intimate."

So Tony brought guys there often. At first, it made me feel kind of cheap. Like I wasn't worth the energy for Tony to come up with something original to do. But then I remembered that Max did say Tony was sexually open. I guess theater stroking was his preferred method of foreplay. And to be honest, he was really good at it. The way he'd gotten me so worked up just by running a finger down my leg made me want to know what other moves he had. Immediately.

I stepped forward and kissed him, hard.

Tony's stubble rubbing against my lips drove me wild

every single time. The prickles against my face sent shivers along my spine, and all I wanted to do was kiss Tony until I collapsed from being completely out of breath.

We stood there in the Seattle mist, getting drenched in dew and spit. When he pulled away, my whole body cried out for him to get back within mouth's reach.

"Campus isn't far," Tony said, that signature smirk spreading up his lips. "Ready to see my room?"

Oh yeah. I was ready.

19.

✓ Go All the Way

The Lambda Chi Alpha fraternity looked way different when there wasn't a party going on. There was no ice luge, no cascade of people streaming up and down the front staircase, and the floors didn't shake one bit with bass. There was still the lingering smell of beer and boy, though.

"Yo, Tony, what up!" someone called when we stepped inside.

Tony gave one of those effortless, sort of bro-ish nods of acknowledgment that would have looked like I was spasming if I tried it. "Hey, Keegan."

I looked over to see about a dozen guys sitting in front of a massive TV with controllers in their hands. Toad and Princess Daisy and Wario zoomed along the screen in a game of *Mario Kart*. My thoughts drifted to Albert. What would he think of me coming to a fraternity with a college boy and a condom in my pocket?

"Come play with us!" Keegan said.

"Can't." Tony grabbed my hand and pulled me up the staircase.

Keegan peered over his shoulder and caught us dashing up the stairs. "Gonna go play with your own joysticks, huh?"

All the guys in the room went "Oooooooooooh!" while I face-palmed. Yeah, I wanted us to play with our joysticks, but I didn't want the whole fraternity talking about it.

Tony rolled his eyes when we reached the second floor. "They're idiots."

With Tony's fraternity brothers out of sight, it really didn't bother me so much, especially because now I could practically feel the condom pulsing in my pocket. Or was that something else?

I squeezed Tony's hand. "It's all right."

Tony led us down the hall, which felt like it went on forever. We passed door after door, but none of them led to his room. If we didn't get to his dorm stat, I was prepared to throw him against the wall and pounce.

"How many people live here?" I asked.

"About fifty guys," Tony said, *finally* stopping in front of a door with the names Tony and Victor plastered on it. A bunch of tally marks were Sharpied under Tony's name, twelve in all.

"What are those for?" As a guy who likes to keep track

of things, I thought this might be something I had in common with Tony other than wanting to get it on.

"Oh, it's stupid. Vic likes to keep track of . . ." Tony's eyes wandered while he thought. "My visitors."

Visitors. Meaning hookups. "So, I'm number thirteen."

"Does that make you uncomfortable?" Tony asked. "I thought we were both here for a good time." His eyes roved down my body. When they got closer to my waist, I could practically see his visions of pulling my pants off. Everything about his demeanor—from that damn smirk to the way he'd applied just the right amount of inner thigh pressure to drive me bananas—told me he knew exactly what to do when he finally ripped them from my legs. Maybe me being his thirteenth visitor just meant he was practiced and would make the night epic.

"Lucky number thirteen," I said.

Tony laughed with a rasp and swung the door open, revealing a space that was not nearly as sexy as I thought it'd be. Two twin beds were shoved against opposite walls, a small chest of drawers at the foot of each. Crammed between the beds were two desks covered with textbooks, laptops, the paraphernalia of college students. The left side of the room was covered with posters of European soccer teams. The right side had a bunch of black-and-white photographs, a man's washed-out silhouette in all of them. When I looked closer, I realized the guy in each picture was . . . Tony.

Tony followed my gaze to the photos. "I took them myself," he said.

For the briefest second I thought it was a little weird to have multiple pictures of yourself hung over your bed. But then I remembered I was standing next to said bed belonging to a college guy who I knew wanted to have sex with me, so I said, "They're good." And they were, too. Tony was shirtless in a few, putting the bulge of his pecs and the slight ripple of his abs on display. I *had* to see those ripples in real life.

"Thanks." Tony lowered the blinds. "It's about the beauty of the male form."

Sure, that was narcissistic, but his form *was* beautiful, so he made a very good point.

Tony sat on his bed, his photo selves peering down at him with smoldering eyes. "So. What do you think?"

"Your room's nice."

"No," Tony said, smirking. "About us. I want to do this." He stroked the bed next to him. "Do you?"

Ohmigawd, YES!

I moved to his bed so fast that I tripped over my feet. When I plopped next to Tony, the mattress springs sent both of us bobbing up and down. I was like a little kid bouncing on the bed! I did not need Tony to look at me and think *clumsy toddler* just before he was about to swipe my V-card!

"Sorry, I—"

Tony took my face in his hands and kissed me, clearly unbothered by my clumsiness. He parted my mouth with his tongue, and I was instantly on fire. He used his tongue a *lot*, but in this way that wasn't slimy or wet, just controlled and purposeful. It made me imagine what his tongue would be like on every other part of my body.

PLACES WHERE TONY COULD PUT HIS TONGUE RIGHT NOW

1. My neck (And if it resulted in a hickey, so be it.)
2. My ear (I saw that on the internet once and it seemed to make the porn star go wild.)
3. My . . . ahem (You know what I mean.)

Without thinking, I moved my hands under Tony's shirt. His abs tightened as my fingers touched his stomach. I had to see what that picture-perfect torso looked like firsthand, so I grabbed the hem of Tony's shirt and pulled it over his head.

But of course, as I pulled his shirt up, it got caught under his armpits. I tugged and tugged, trying to get his arms to slide out of the sleeves and the shirt over his head.

It didn't work. All that happened was his tag popped out.

"Stop pulling!" Tony's voice was muffled under the 100 percent cotton.

I snatched my hands back. "Sorry."

Tony twisted his arms so they untangled from his sleeves, then seamlessly pulled his shirt off. How did he have such control over his body? "It's okay," he said.

It was more than okay. I was sitting on a bed with a shirtless boy.

Tony ran his fingers through his tousled hair, giving me time to take in every inch of his exposed skin. He looked perfect. Toned, tan, and with just the right amount of hair. It was on his chest, leading to the sexiest dip in between his pecs. He also had the smallest tuft of dark fuzz that trailed from just under his belly button to below the waist of his jeans. I wanted to kiss that tuft all. The. Way. Down.

Tony leaned back onto his pillows and swung his legs onto the bed. A plethora of positions flew through my mind. Should I straddle him? I really wanted to straddle him, wanted to know what it felt like to feel him beneath me.

Tony gave me that smirk. "Don't leave me hanging."

I swung my leg up, thinking it could go over his body and I could sit down on his crotch. But my knee landed hard on his left thigh, then slid down to the mattress just centimeters away from smashing the first penis I was ever going to see in real life!

"Shit!" Tony jolted up and rubbed the spot where my knee had jammed his leg.

"Ohmigawd, I'm so sorry! Are you hurt? Is there a bruise?" Why was my initial response to sound just like my mom when I tripped playing T-ball in the first grade?

I moved to put my hand on his leg, but Tony grabbed it. "No. It's fine." He took a deep breath. "You've never done this before, right?"

Max's advice echoed in my head. He'd told me not to let it spill that I was a virgin, but also to agree with whatever Tony said. This was way too much conflicting information in a very critical moment.

I was taking way too long to answer, so I finally said, "I guess it's pretty obvious." I couldn't make eye contact. I didn't want to see Tony's face fall or the pity in his eyes when he told me he didn't want the pressure of being someone's first.

"Hey." Tony gently took my chin in his hand and tilted my face toward his. "It's okay. We were all there once." He leaned forward and kissed me, using his tongue to caress my upper lip. "I can help. If you still want to do this."

I swallowed and nodded.

"Good," Tony said. "Let's try this again."

He kissed me once more, long and hard and scruff-filled, until the memory of nearly crushing his junk was washed away. Then he put both hands under my butt, lifted me up, leaned back on his pillows, and sat me down on top of him. It was like the hottest *Dancing with the Stars* move ever. I realized if I became famous for any reason and got on the show, I'd want to be the dance partner being led. It was so sexy when someone took the lead, when they showed you where they wanted you and did it all without a single hitch.

I was sitting down right over Tony's crotch. I could feel him beneath me, just as hard as I was. Knowing that I could make someone's body react like that sent a wave of pleasure washing over me. I felt powerful, I felt wanted, I felt unlocked. I had been waiting eighteen years for this moment, single and alone, and it was more than I'd ever imagined. I suddenly felt a connection to Tony that I had never felt before, a shared responsibility to bond our bodies and connect through every nerve ending inside them.

I leaned down and kissed Tony's neck. Gawd, he smelled so good. He didn't even wear any cologne, just the smell of his skin alone made me want to taste him. So I did. I ran my tongue against his neck. Tony moaned, and that thrill of knowing I was making him feel good surged through me again. It made me kiss him harder, deeper, I needed more, more, *more*. I moved down to see what it felt like for his chest hair to tickle my nose and chin.

It. Was. Everything.

Tony reached down, and before I knew it, my shirt was gone (of *course* he was able to take mine off in one fluid, sexy movement) and our bodies pressed together. We were both sweaty, but it wasn't gross like someone hugging you after working out. It was *so hot*.

A jingle caught my attention. I peeked down to see Tony removing his belt. Unbuttoning his jeans. Hooking his thumb under his pants and red boxer briefs at once so he could remove them both in one go. My heart raced and completely stopped all at the same time.

Tony tossed his clothes to the floor and he sprang up in the best millisecond of my life. Number seven was gone. Penis, IRL. Officially stricken from the Agenda forever as I stared at the best view I'd ever seen. He was beautiful.

I couldn't stop my hands from flying in between his legs.

"Unhh." Tony's moan was the sexiest sound I had ever heard.

He kissed me while I held on to him, but my whole body ached to put my mouth somewhere else. Tony ran his fingers through my hair, then gently took my face in his hands to pull our lips just centimeters apart. "Do whatever you want," he whispered. It was like he could read my mind.

I lifted my body, using the hand that was still on Tony's you-know-what a little too much to give myself a boost.

Tony shot forward. "Careful!"

"Sorry!" I let go, but with both my hands in the air unable to hold myself up, my head fell onto Tony's chest. He laughed softly, then moved my hands on either side of him so I could steady myself against the mattress.

"Try again," Tony said.

I braced myself against the bed, then kissed all the way down Tony's chest. I kissed through his chest hair, down to his belly button, and into that tuft at his waist. I looked up and Tony was watching me, smirking. He gave a slight nod.

I kissed all the way down until I was face-to-package. This was really about to go down. It was finally time to do all those fun things I'd imagined happening in item number seven.

I went for it.

At first, I wasn't sure what to do with my hands, so I

thought back to the kerbillion porn clips I'd seen on the internet (and yes, that's a technical number when talking porn viewing stats). No matter where I put my hands, it didn't feel natural. I probably looked like one of those car dealership air guys the way my hands kept moving back and forth into different positions.

Tony grabbed my head and pulled me up. "Stop, stop, stop!"

Oh gawd, I had completely messed up.

I launched myself forward, the mattress bouncing again when I landed next to him. "Is everything okay? Did I do something wrong?"

Tony gave one of his scratchy chuckles and reached over to rifle through a drawer in his desk. "Nothing is wrong." He lifted his hand, a condom between his fingers. "I just didn't want to finish yet."

I had almost made him *finish*. I felt a surge of pride again that was nearly as satisfying as everything else we were doing.

Tony took the corner of the condom wrapper between his teeth and tore it open. "There's something else we could try. If you wanted to take off your clothes."

He grabbed himself and rolled the condom on while I unzipped my jeans and tugged them off. I hooked my finger under the waist of my plaid boxers, took a deep breath, and off they went.

I was naked with another guy.

I WAS NAKED WITH ANOTHER GUY.

Tony's eyes roamed all over me. "Looks like you're

ready," he said, his gaze locked between my legs.

There were so many things going on inside my body: nervousness that this was actually happening, relief that I wasn't going to die a virgin, more nervousness, my heart soaring that a VSB actually wanted to do this with *me*, but most of all, one particular part of me was screaming, *YES! YES! YES! YES! YES!*

Outwardly, all I could do was nod.

Tony got on his knees. "Bend over."

Yeah, being led was definitely the sexiest thing ever. I rushed to all fours.

Tony reached back into his desk drawer and pulled out a bottle of lube. The *squirt* and *swish* as Tony rubbed it on himself sounded a lot like when you put condiments on a hamburger. I would never be able to eat one again without having a raging boner.

Tony put his slightly lube-y hand on my waist and pulled me toward him.

I once deep dove into virginity stats, and I saw this Reddit post that said four people lose their virginity every second. One second was all it took. One second I was a virgin, and in the very next, just the right amount of time for Tony to push into me, I wasn't. In the millisecond leading up to that moment, all those emotions I was feeling before raged inside me a thousand times heavier. Scared, nervous, excited, hard, but so fracking ready. Then, in that next moment, feeling pleasure, pain, so many things, one thought stood out the most: I was so happy to be one of those four people.

JAY'S GAY AGENDA

1. ~~Meet another gay kid. Somewhere, anywhere . . . please! in Seattle in, like, days!~~ ✓

1.5. ~~Get checked out by a very VSB!~~ ✓

2. ~~Go on any Digimals video game date with Albert a boy at the Space Needle and learn just how much game Albert's really got.~~ ✓

2.5. ~~Hold hands within the first ninety minutes a VSB after being pulled into my first-ever drag show by a queen named after a fish.~~ ✓

3. ~~Go to a d~~Dance with a boy and ~~have my first~~ kiss slow dancing to Shawn Mendes while getting caught in a surprise Seattle downpour.

4. Have a boyfriend, one who likes to wrap me up in his arms and let me be little spoon, and maybe ~~smells~~ tastes like ~~coffee from all the cafés he goes to~~ spearmint, and who ignites my soul and my sexuality.

5. Fall in love with a boy, but wait for him to say it first so I don't seem too desperate, and maybe he says it for the first time at Pike Place Market or in the first Starbucks.

6. ~~Make out with Albert, or Tony, or, you know, any guy who keeps himself in my personal bubble, with tongue, and hard enough that I'd get a little burn from his stubble. run my fingers along that perfect jawline. the hottest snowman this side of the North Pole.~~ ✓

7. See ~~another~~ Tony's penis ~~besides my own~~, IRL, and do fun things with it! ✓

8. Lose. My. Virginity! ✓

9. Become part of a super-queer, super-tight framily by impressing everybody with my epic costumier skills, erasing the "new kid" label, and becoming homecoming royalty.

10. Figure out a way to make my gay dreams come true and not destroy my bestie's life.

20.

✓ Be the Butt of the Joke

I rang Max's doorbell the next morning, bouncing on the balls of my feet. I had to tell *someone* about my night. I'd always pictured Lu being the one I told first about this, but since my sexcapade with Tony would reveal that Albert technically wasn't my boyfriend yet, it had to be Max. I'd texted him right when I woke up, and he'd invited me over for "breakfast and tea spilling."

Max answered the door in a dusty-pink silk robe. Wasting no time, he pulled me inside and pushed me down on his living room couch. "Lord and Taylor, tell me everything. Did you . . ." He paused, peering toward the kitchen where someone, presumably his parents, was making breakfast, based on the smell of bacon wafting through the house. He turned up the volume on CNN,

Fareed Zakaria blaring as Max sat next to me and leaned in. "Did you have sex?"

I nodded, completely unable to stop the smile that spread across my lips.

"OMFG!" Max squealed. "O. M. F. G!"

"I know," I said. "I just . . . I feel so different. But in a good way. In the best way."

Max did that excited little kid pose it seemed like every photographer put toddlers in for family pictures: elbows on knees with his face in his hands. "What was it like?"

His question caught me off guard. "Wait. Haven't you . . . ?" Fareed's voice filled my silence, his report on overdue volcanic eruptions surprisingly complementary to previously overdue eruptions of my own. "You've had sex before, right?" I'd just assumed. He was my Gay Guide and held himself with so much confidence that I figured he'd caught the train to SexTown long before I had.

Max tugged on one of his robe sleeves. "Not exactly. I mean, I've done *things*," he said, giving me a very pointed look, "but I haven't gone all the way. It's just confusing for me sometimes. I get into my head about what people expect of me if my body doesn't match my typically feminine presentation."

A flare of anger barreled into my chest. "Wait. Did Reese ever—"

"Oh no, it was never him," Max said. "He was actually always so understanding and patient when it came to sex. It's really more society at large. I know I'm this fashionable fierce femme entity, but I'd be lying if I said sometimes people's stares didn't get to me. Even if they don't say it, I can hear the word *freak* running through their minds. And that doesn't always make me feel so sexy. And, maybe this is an overshare, but sometimes I have serious questions about what's going on down there. Genitals-wise. Sometimes I relate to it, other times I don't. It's just never felt right to do *everything* yet, you know?"

I got it. I wouldn't feel so ecstatic if my whole body hadn't been super-duper clear that it was All Systems Go on Going All the Way. "Don't rush it," I said. "I mean, it's great. Really, really, *really* great, but only when you're ready. And for the record, you *are* fashionable, fierce, and femme, and any person you choose to share your body with is lucky to be with you."

"You're the sweetest." Max got back into his elbows-on-knees, hands-on-face, *tell me everything* pose. "*So,* what was it like?"

I never thought I'd be the one to tell somebody what it was like to have sex. It always felt like everyone else already knew. But there was some extra monumental-ness to this moment by describing gay sex to another gay person. Like we were in this weird, sex-crazed world together as people standing on the sidelines and figuring it out. It felt nice to reverse roles and be the Gay Guide for once.

"Well, it hurt," I said, then rushed to clarify. "At first. And like, then I got used to it and it felt good. Really good. But while still hurting a little bit. Like, it hurt a little but in an extremely pleasurable way. Does that make sense?"

Max chewed his cheek while tapping his finger against

his chin. "Mmm. Like those self-flagellating priests."

"Uh, what?" I'd watched a lot of porn, but that was one kink I hadn't heard of.

"The priests who whip themselves," Max explained. "They do it because it puts them into this spiritual euphoria. Pain turning into ecstasy."

That sounded so not sexy, while my night with Tony had been all sexy all the time. Pure, hot, sweaty sexiness. "I wouldn't say it's exactly like that," I said, "but sure. That's the general idea."

Max got up from the couch. "I bet after all that you've worked up quite the appetite. Come on, Jules and Dad made panca— WHAT THE FUCK IS THAT?"

Max screamed so loudly I sprang to my feet. His parents, Jules and Joseph, ran into the living room.

"What?" Joseph yelled. He was too worried to notice the glob of pancake batter oozing through his beard. "What is it?"

Jules rushed to inspect Max's arms, hands, face. "Are you hurt?"

Max didn't say a word. He simply pointed to the TV with a shaking finger.

We all turned. There, on the screen, was Reese. Reese taking an order from an All-American family eating at Red Robin, Home of the Gourmet Burger.

"Is that Reese?" Jules asked.

Max didn't move. He stared at the TV as a single tear fell down his cheek.

"Yeah," I said for him.

"He's in a commercial." Jules was very observant. "Good for him."

Max glared at her, and I swear the temperature in the room went up. Fortunately, Max's dad noticed and changed the subject before anyone got incinerated.

"Hey, Jay," Joseph said. He chuckled while scratching at the batter in his beard. "Ha! That rhymed."

Max rolled his eyes and snatched my hand when I moved to shake Joseph's.

"Bye," Max said flatly. He yanked me behind him and stomped up the stairs.

"Breakfast is almost ready," Jules called after us.

Max slammed his bedroom door. I guess that meant we weren't going to join them for pancakes.

"I'll never be able to eat at Red Robin again," Max said. "I'll never be able to eat again, period!" He made a path in his carpet as he paced back and forth. "I want to hear more about your night with Tony, I really do, but I need to vent. Can I? Just for a second? If I don't, I won't be able to focus."

"Totally." Max had shut off all his emotions to Damon and Cami and everyone in the QSA, and he shut down our convos pretty quickly when I ventured into talking about his breakup. I didn't want him to keep this bottled up anymore.

"Reese breaks up with me and now is booking *national commercials*?" Max threw his hands in the air, the angry whip of his robe punctuating his words. "That's a serious career move. Yet more proof that I was the one bringing him down, while Spencer is boosting him up. I want him to succeed, I do, but . . ." He looked lost, devastated, torn apart. "Why couldn't he succeed with me?"

"Oh, Max, I—"

But he wasn't looking for input. Not yet.

"I just know it's all we're going to be hearing about in Fashion Design this week." Max put on a fake British accent. "Did you see my commercial? Yes, yes, I was selected out of *thousands* who auditioned. It's running across the country, you know." I'm not exactly sure why Max chose an English accent since Reese isn't British, but it really didn't feel like the right time to nitpick.

"We have to make Reese eat it at the costume contest," Max continued. He rushed forward and shook my shoulders. "We have to. I want to wipe that smug, self-satisfied smirk right off his face, and let Spencer know I've still got one up on him."

I was more invigorated than ever to pay Max back. He was responsible for kicking off the chain of events that led to items seven and eight flying off the Gay Agenda.

"Honestly, there's no way Reese can beat me," I said. "I'm on a three-year costume-contest winning streak, remember?" Images of Lu and me dressing up together flashed through my mind. Some of that determined fire in my belly turned to guilt bubbles over ditching her and the hoedown.

Max dove through his bed curtains and plopped next to me. "All right, then, so let's finally pick a costume once and for all."

With so many items on my Homecoming in Hindsight list, I'd thought this part would be easy. But when we'd talked about them during our free periods, Max turned all my costume ideas down. According to him, Thor and Hulk encouraged too many tired tropes about what heroic men should look like; Jack and Rose on a waterlogged door together was funny, but lugging around a door for a dance would get old; and Bert and Ernie ventured too close to furry territory for his liking.

It was back to the drawing board.

"Okay," I said, "so Homecoming in Hindsight is the theme, right?"

Max gave me some serious side-eye. "Yeah, duh, you came up with it." He immediately grimaced and smacked himself with his robe sash. "Lord and Taylor, Max. Chill," he whispered, then turned back to me. "Sorry about that. Reese has put me in a mood. Your theme is totally brilliant."

"It's okay. I get it." And fortunately, this really was my jam. I was a bottomless well of couples ideas. "What about Abe Lincoln and the guy he was supposed to be shacking up with in that log cabin?"

Max stuck his finger down his throat. "Pass. I do not want to wear a massive beard that's going to be getting caught in my mouth all night. I don't like *my own* facial hair as it is. Besides, if you can't name the guy who was President Abe's one true love, then nobody will get it."

I nodded, my mind going down a White House rabbit hole. "Maybe we're thinking too romantically. You can have hindsight about all kinds of people. Like presidents. After all that time with You-Know-Who in office, I think we'd agree he was the *wrong* choice. What if we go as Hillary Clinton and Tim Kaine? In hindsight, she totally should have been Madame President."

"Hmmm." Max pursed his lips. "I see where you're going with that one, but who's Tim Kaine?"

"Her running mate!" I shouted. "The guy she put up for vice president."

"I don't know," Max said. "You might be the only person who still remembers what her VP's name was. People will get Hillary, but will they get Tim?"

"I could wear a Clinton-Kaine shirt," I said. "We have tons of them. Mom still sleeps in one every night. The grocery store union she's a part of was a big supporter of the Clinton-Kaine ticket."

Max sighed and flipped on his back. "This is a pretty liberal city. Politics are always on people's minds. I bet someone else is already planning on going as Hil and Timmy. We need something *unique*. What if we played off that saying, 'Hindsight is 20/20'? I could go as Barbara Walters! She used to host a show called *20/20*."

It was my turn to give some serious side-eye. "Barbara who?"

"Barbara Walters!" Max whacked me with a lilac quilted pillow. "Journalist extraordinaire, first woman to co-anchor a national evening news program, creator of *The View*."

"Yeah, if you're worried about people no one at school

knows about, Barbara's definitely that," I said, although I bet Lu knew who she was. "So presidents and obscure news anchors are out. Maybe we're thinking too literally. We don't have to be people. Most outfits will consist of humans, so if we do something abstract, we'll stand out."

"Okay," Max said. "How can we fit the theme and not be people?"

I got up from the bed, following Max's lead and pacing in front of Naomi Campbell and Cara Delevingne. "Two years ago, the hoedown theme was Perfect Pairs. Lu and I went as Netflix and Chill." More guilt bubbled in my gut. "I was a Netflix homepage."

"So, like, go as a pair of glasses or something?" Max suggested. He threw on a pair of gold butterfly sunglasses from his nightstand. "Because we're talking about sight?"

I snapped my fingers. "Yes, you're on the right track." I paced some more, repeating, "Hindsight, hindsight, hindsight." The word was too close to "behind," which of course made me think of seeing Tony's perfect ass the night before. Then it hit me. "Behindsight."

Max coughed. "Come again?"

"Behindsight is 20/20. Homecoming in Behindsight." I couldn't believe the words that were about to come out of my mouth. "We dress as a giant butt in glasses. We each go as one cheek." I face-palmed. I couldn't help it. It sounded so stupid saying it out loud.

Max whipped off his sunglasses, a look of total bewilderment on his face. "That's ridiculous," he mumbled.

"I know, I know, but they say to just blurt out any idea that enters your head when brainstorming."

"No." Max was wild-eyed. "It's so ridiculous, it's genius. *No one* is going to dress like a giant butt. Behindsight is 20/20. It's brilliant! And if the state of American entertainment these days has taught me anything, it's that people love fart jokes." He looked consolingly at his wall of runway models. "Sorry, ladies."

To be honest, I was surprised Max was embracing the butt. He'd seemed so particular when we were coming up with outfit ideas for the Lambda Chi party, and with all other ideas I'd thrown his way for the dance, so I hadn't thought he'd sign up for this. But he leaped from the bed and grabbed me in a hug, solidifying our costume decision. "This is so good, Jay. Like, totally stupid, but that's the beauty of it. Nobody at CHHS is going to think that fashion star Max would ever dress as a butt." He laughed, his giggles getting louder and louder. "This is so ironic!"

"What is?" I asked.

Max wiped at the tears that started pouring down his face. "That I'd have to dress like an ass to get back at that ass, Reese."

I laughed, but nothing compared to how hard Max cackled. He clearly needed to let off some steam. "You're ass-cracking up," I said. Which, of course, only made us laugh harder.

We brainstormed ideas for how to pull the outfit off, and I peppered the conversation with details about Tony's glorious body. The costume was going to be epic. And I had Tony's beautiful butt to thank for the idea. Hooking up with him clearly gave me great inspiration. If I had to keep hooking up with him to figure out the best way to implement our plan, so be it.

21.

✓ Have the Best of Both Worlds

There really wasn't a word to describe the feeling that came over me when I opened my phone after the QSA meeting the next day. There, in glorious iPhone HD, was a picture of Tony, his real-life eggplant emoji front and center.

Round 2? 😌

I couldn't stop my grin or my boner.

How about toni

"What's got you so happy this afternoon?"

I looked up and nearly collapsed against Ms. Okeke's bookshelf of Nigerian literature. "Albert, hi!" I fumbled with my phone and shoved it in my pocket. My heart fluttered on overdrive. One, because Albert was in front of me and he always made me twitterpated, and two, because I didn't think he'd feel so great with me looking at a picture of some other guy's junk. "It was just some stupid cat meme." I let loose a very awkward laugh. "What's up?"

"I had an idea for something we could do tonight," he said. "If you're free, that is."

He leaned forward and gave me the most gentle kiss. It was nothing at all like the kisses Tony scratched against my face with scruff, but it made me flush just as much. Any thoughts of Tony's eggplant emoji were instantly deleted. "What did you have in mind?" I asked.

"I remember you saying that you liked drag," Albert said. "There's this drag queen photo exhibit that just opened here on the Hill. I thought you might like it."

"I'd love that."

Albert's date sounded a *million* times better than watching that stupid red balloon drift around. Honestly, I'd totally picked the best person to pursue as my first boyfriend. Even if Tony was the current wiener—I mean winner—in the sex department. One guy had my heart, the other guy had my . . . well, you know.

"Great," Albert said. "I've got to meet Shruti and Regina quick for a Digimals battle, but I'll pick you up at seven." He leaned forward and kissed me goodbye. As his teeth grazed my bottom lip, I wondered how long it would be until we did more than just kiss. After this weekend, I'd added a perpetual item to the Gay Agenda that would never be crossed off: *More penis.*

But in the meantime—with those soul-sharing kisses

and elbow Morse code and mesmerizing Digihips—Albert was totally worth the wait.

Dad walked into the bathroom while I put on a finishing spray of cologne.

"So," Dad said. "It's *Monday Night Football*, and I thought I'd order Thai for dinner."

My phone pinged with a text from Albert.

Here ☺

"Sorry, Dad, can't. I've got a date tonight."

I moved past Dad to grab my jacket from my bedroom.

"Whoa, big man over here. Another date. Who's it with this time? Tony, Albert, or some other fella?"

I rolled my eyes. "I'm not a *big man*. I'm just actually getting to date for the first time ever after you and Mom decided to keep me in gay purgatory all my life."

"Just don't go being a heartbreaker or anything," Dad said. "You're excited, and that's great, but don't crush any suitor's dreams by being in a rush."

"Nobody says *suitor*, Dad. And don't worry, I got this covered." I'd put everything exactly in its place: Tony and I were just hooking up, and Albert and I were headed on the path to boyfriend-dom.

Dad walked into the living room and grabbed the remote as I moved toward the front door. He turned on the TV, football players running across the screen. They made me think of Damon and Max icing him and Cami out. Maybe if we won homecoming royalty, Max would finally be over his no-talking-about-Reese rule and speak to his former friends again.

"Well, me and the guys are here waiting for you if your plans end early," Dad said.

"Great, thanks!" I called. "See you later." I flung the door open. Albert stood there, a Mario umbrella open above his head. The character's big eyes and mustached nose stared down at me.

"So it's just going to be the three of us," I said, pointing to the umbrella.

Albert guffawed, his laugh reverberating through my heart. "It was the only one I could find. It's my little brother's."

"I think it's adorable." I stepped under Mario, and Albert leaned forward to give me a soft kiss. It was like my mouth was being caressed by his, and there was more emotion behind his slightly parted lips than Tony ever had. I felt like if he stayed there with his lips against mine long enough, we'd become one person and share our souls and thoughts forever. It made me light-headed as blood rushed to my chest, my heart beating with something entirely different from lust.

Albert pulled away. "I missed you," he breathed. He had that smolder to his eyes again, which were beautifully framed by his glasses.

"It's only been three hours."

Albert nodded. "I know. But that's three hours too long. Don't you think?"

"Yeah," I whispered. "I do."

Albert locked the fingers of his free hand with mine. They fit as perfectly together as his lips had against my mouth. He smiled and said, "Glad we're agreed."

—*ᴍᴍ*—

"Ohmigawd, these queens are stunning. And their names are epic: Sissy Spankit, Nita Razor, Tampa Bae. Have you ever thought about what your drag name would be?"

Albert just smiled and shook his head. He'd been so great at letting me geek out over the exhibit. If Lu had been there, she would have been dying. Her appreciation for drag was just as strong as mine. The photo series showed the queens glamming themselves up from man to woman. Some of the images were super blurry, so you couldn't always tell what stage of the process they were in. A description on the gallery wall said it was to show that there's really not much difference between men and women, highlighting the arbitrary nature of gender rules. Max would have loved it here, too.

Once we'd spent an hour among the queens, I pulled Albert toward the exit. "Want to get out of here?" I asked. "We could grab something to eat." As much as I loved getting to take in all these gorgeous ladies, the proximity of other exhibit attendees was making it way too difficult to try to make out.

Albert nodded just as two men looked our way, pointing at us in front of a massive portrait of Sissy Spankit. "Oh, that's so cute!" one of them said. "Little gays in love. They're so itty!"

The other one waved. "You two probably don't even know if you're tops or bottoms yet," he said. "Remember those days, Markus?" He put his arm over Markus's shoulders. Meanwhile, I face-palmed and Albert's cheeks bypassed pink and went straight to cherry red.

With the loudest awkward laugh ever, I rushed to the door and pulled Albert behind me. I didn't want to be asked any more questions about our sex lives. The farther I was from a conversation where I might let slip I'd just had sex, the better.

We stepped out into the rain, and Albert opened his Mario umbrella with way more force than necessary. "Why do gay guys have to be like that all the time?" he asked. "It seems like we always have to talk about sex. Why should they get to know whether I'm a"—he looked over his shoulder—"a top or a bottom?"

"You're right," I said. "It's nobody's business."

Although I did have to admit, it was a question that had crossed my mind too. After being with Tony, my body wanted more nakey-time fun. And if Albert could make me feel so special and bonded with a kiss, what would it be like when we had sex? But that was for us to figure out together, not for some random strangers to force upon us before we were ready.

"I just feel like it's everywhere in gay culture," Albert said. He pointed back at the photo gallery, glittery drag queens staring at us from the window display. "I have a hard time getting into all the sex jokes and dick references in drag. Less is more sometimes, right?"

"It's not all bad," I said. "It's also about bending the arbitrary rules society puts on gender and showing how it's all just an act. Like, why do guys have to only wear pants, but girls get pants and skirts and dresses and jumpsuits and makeup? Not that I want to wear any of that personally, but what's the big deal about a guy wearing a dress? I mean, look at Max. He always looks so great: skirts, leggings, jeans, blouses, whatever."

"I get that," Albert said, "and I one hundred percent always want people to be who they are. I just don't get why we've got to specifically call out genitals so much in the gay community to do it. Why is it all packaged with penis puns?" He rolled his eyes and groaned. "Like me pairing *package* and *penis*. I swear I wasn't trying to be funny."

I laughed and nudged his shoulder. "I totally get what you're trying to say. I think it's just different levels of comfort for different people. You're totally allowed to not be into it."

"Thanks." Albert linked his fingers in mine again. "And you're allowed *to* be into it." He thrust his hips from side to side. "I mean, you let me be me. You fully embraced the Digihips, after all." He grinned sheepishly. That dimple of his could totally rival Tony's smirk. "Metaphorically, of course. Unless, you know, you ever wanted to embrace them. Literally."

"Yes," I said, making Albert laugh. "Metaphorically, literally, the answer is always yes."

We had made it to Cal Anderson Park. It was dark by that point, and with the steadily increasing downpour chasing away any nighttime joggers, the whole space was empty. It was kind of like being back on our property in Riverton: open sky, nature in my peripheral vision, no other people in our vicinity. It made me feel a lot closer to Albert, like we were the only two people in the city. I would never have said this when I felt stuck and alone on the other side of the state, but it was nice to have this moment, totally away from the hustle of Seattle while still technically being right in the middle of it. Standing there in the park with no one around and the open sky above made me feel for just a bit like I could breathe easier.

So much had been knocked off the Gay Agenda so fast. I'd met gays, kissed a couple of them, had sex with one, was quickly falling for another, and while I wanted everything to happen that had happened, I needed a moment to take it all in. To process how quickly my life was changing, and all the feelings I had about Lu and the hoedown. She still hadn't called me. I'd tried calling her Sunday when I got home from Max's, but she texted that she was taking an extra shift at the diner and insisted she'd call me when she was free. It felt wrong that it had been two days since I lost my virginity and I wouldn't be able to tell her about it. But she thought I was going to homecoming with Albert because we were boyfriends, so I couldn't very well tell her about my time with Tony. Lu and I told each other everything, but now I was telling half-truths and she was avoiding me. With time to stop and think about it, I was getting mad at her. I'd gone our whole lives hearing about the relationship milestones she'd had, but when I'd started to have firsts of my own, she couldn't be bothered to be there for me. Instead, I had to protect her feelings about everything, so much so that I'd declared Albert my boyfriend before he'd officially asked.

Albert squeezed my hand, snapping me out of my thoughts. "Can I be totally honest?"

I nodded. He had such a serious expression on his face that he must have been grappling with drama of his own. It made me nervous. My first thought was that he'd found out about Tony and was mad at me for seeing other people. But we'd never had the DTR, so I should be allowed to hook up without him getting upset, right? Max had said those were the rules.

"I'm sure I sounded like such a prude back there," Albert said, "but I'm not a virgin."

That was the last thing I expected him to say. Honestly, I wanted to shout, *Great! Let's get it on!,* but he looked like he had more that he wanted to get out, so I kept my mouth shut.

"I've had sex, and I want to have sex again," Albert continued, "with the right person." He brought my hand up to his lips and kissed it, all but outright saying I was that guy. "I mean, I like you, Jay. You seem like such a great guy, and you're someone I can just be myself around. I might not want to talk about my sex life with strangers, but I can talk about it with you, and just so you know, I want to get to that place with you. I can feel myself getting closer to that every time we hang out."

"Me too," I whispered. My crotch was swelling, but so

was my heart. The feeling was totally different from the one I had with Tony, who made it clear we were just doing things for fun. Albert made sex sound so much more special, like it wasn't just a mashing of parts, but a bonding of bodies and souls. I wanted to feel that with him.

"But I'm not quite there yet," Albert went on, and the swelling in my heart and other parts deflated. "My ex wasn't so patient with me. It seemed like overnight he was all about sex, and I felt pressured to go all the way before I was ready. I just kept thinking about all those stupid stereotypes again, that Asian men are only comical or somehow have no sex drive, so I did it to prove the labels wrong. And I felt terrible after."

Albert's confession made me realize just how dangerous stereotypes could be. Ever since I'd come out, I'd been hyper-aware of gay tropes, trying to dispel them, letting my classmates know that just because I was into certain stereotypically gay things didn't make them some law of nature of what it meant to be gay. It was frustrating and annoying, but Albert was sharing how stereotypes can affect a person's body. How they can dehumanize someone so much that they make choices that feel completely wrong just to prove they are human. It wasn't right.

"After we had sex, I told Kyler we needed to slow down," Albert said. "He dumped me. He wasn't willing to wait. I decided after he left that I'm just going to be myself, no matter what. I won't compromise like that again. So what I'm trying to say is: this has been amazing. And, kissing you is—*peeeeoooww!*" He perfectly mimicked the mind-blown emoji. "If things keep going this direction, I'll be ready. But we've only really known each other for a couple weeks. I'm not ready yet. I just wanted to be up-front before this goes any further. I don't want to be hurt again. If you can't wait, you are more than free to go."

Albert baring his soul only made me fall for him further. I hadn't known when I'd created the Gay Agenda that vulnerability and honesty were totally the qualities that would lead to number five, falling in love. But after a couple weeks with Albert, it was obvious. And I wanted to return the favor.

"I am ready," I admitted. "For sex." Gawd, I sounded like such a caveman. "I—" Something tugged at the corner of my mind, stopping me before I mentioned Tony. I'd admitted to Albert on our first date that I was a virgin, so if I let him know I wasn't one now, he'd know that I'd been hooking up with someone recently. Would that totally blow our chances of getting to boyfriend status?

TO TELL OR NOT TELL THE TONY TRUTH

1. Tell him I'd had sex. (But then he might think I'm a sex-crazed addict like his ex.)

2. Tell him I hadn't had sex. (It might make him feel better, but it's an outright lie.)

3. Let him just keep thinking I was a virgin. (Since what he didn't know wouldn't hurt him, right?)

The third option seemed the safest. I loved our dates, whether Albert wanted to have sex yet or not. When the time was right for him, the time would totally be right for me, and me having already had sex with Tony wouldn't change that. In fact, me having sex with Tony might actually make me better at it so that I wasn't so fumbling and awkward like when I nearly kneed Tony's dick to death. All telling Albert about Tony could do was hurt him or make him worry when he literally had nothing to worry about. Then we could continue on our trajectory to become boyfriends, and when Albert said he wanted to be in a relationship, I'd say yes instantly. I could just tell him I wanted to be official myself, but if I told him right then, I worried he'd think I was trying to speed him along in the process of hooking up. So in the meantime, Albert and I could keep falling for each other at our own pace, while Tony and I could continue fooling around because we both knew that what we were doing was just for fun. No strings attached; nobody would get hurt.

I decided to tell Albert something that was 100 percent true.

"I can wait for you."

When we finally had the DTR, I'd gladly become a one-man guy. It was something I could hardly wait for. And when it did, I was ready to replace the Gay Agenda with a whole new list. It would be full of experiences I wanted to have with one boy in particular.

And I'd call it the Albert Agenda.

By the time our date was done, it was only nine o'clock. The Mexican restaurant we'd eaten at was just a couple blocks away from Albert's place, so I walked him home before heading back to mine. Our kiss good night was just as tender and spirit-shaking as the one at the beginning of our date, if not more so after Albert had bared his soul to me in the park. It left such a buzz in my body that I decided I'd have to jog home to get the energy out.

I picked up the pace, but my phone vibrated with a text before I was even at the end of the street. I couldn't stop smiling thinking about Albert being just as eager to talk to me as I was to him.

But when I pulled my phone out of my pocket, Albert's name wasn't the one scrolling across the screen. It was Tony's.

Don't leave me hangin.

The eggplant emojis following his words sent all the blood out of my twitterpated heart and into my crotch. It was alarming how quickly my body could switch from love to lust at the drop of a text.

I hadn't responded to Tony's message that afternoon. He still wanted a repeat of what had gone down over the weekend, and I wouldn't have minded one either. Albert still hadn't broached the DTR and wanted to wait to see where everything between us was going. So it wouldn't be breaking any rules if I hooked up with Tony again. I could have a date full of heart and a hookup full of head. It was the best of both worlds.

And I still had two hours before my curfew to do it.

What are you up to now? I texted.

His response was immediate.

Cum over 😉

It was the hottest text I'd ever received in my life.

22.

✓ Get Caught in the Act

The week went by in a complete blur. Albert and I finally went up to the Space Needle and kissed with the city blooming below us. I immediately wanted more heartfelt kisses, so I locked him down for a date over the weekend. Tony and I hooked up two more times, and Tony supplied his own condoms so Mom wouldn't be able to snoop and see that any were missing from the box she left under the sink. Tuna Turner sent in her homecoming track list to get the songs preapproved by the principal so no dirty lyrics could corrupt our impressionable young minds. Lu texted, which was good because we'd finished our tote bags in Fashion Design and I could actually send it to her since she was talking to me again. She even asked what costume I'd come up with for homecoming.

She didn't like to admit when she was wrong, but I would gladly take her reaching out and asking about my boy-filled life as an apology.

"I cannot believe that my award-winning costume abilities are being used to make a huge butt," I said while I showed Max a sketch of my vision. It was Saturday, and Max had come over with a ton of beige fabric. We would create two huge round masses out of the material and stuff them with cotton. Then we'd hang the masses around our necks. We'd also make long skirts of the same fabric to drape over our legs. When we came together, the two cheeks would press close, obviously making the butt, and then our skirts right next to each other would look like the legs the Great Behind was attached to.

"Oh, it's not that bad," Max said. "It's not like you're making an ass of yourself." He didn't even wait to see my reaction before bursting into laughter. "This is never going to get old."

My phone buzzed with a call from Lu. Relief washed through me that we really were getting back to normal. This was how things were supposed to be: me and my two best friends hanging together—even if one was over the phone—while I forged ahead with the Gay Agenda.

"Hi, Lu," I said. "I've got you on speaker. Max is here."

"Hey, girl!" Max called. He waved even though she couldn't see him, his ponytail swishing back and forth.

"Take me off," Lu said. She didn't seem right. Her nose sounded stuffed and the words came out like she was forcing them through a lump in her throat.

I instantly jerked the phone to my ear. "What's wrong?"

"Headline news: We've been evicted. We couldn't pay rent on our trailer."

"No, Lu." The breath was knocked out of me. My gut twisted. "What can I do?"

She let out a sob. This was bad. So, so bad. Lu did not cry.

"Nothing," she choked out. "We've been saving all the money we have from my job and the very few clients Carol gets at our trailer. But it wasn't enough."

"But like . . ." I couldn't believe the question I was about to ask, or that Lu would actually have to worry about this. "Where are you going to sleep?"

"Leslie said we can stay in the salon office until her lease runs out at the end of the month." Lu drummed her nails faster than I'd ever heard before. "This is so pathetic."

"Stop," I said. "Don't say that."

"But it is!" Lu wailed. "I need you, Jay. This is the exact reason Chip en—" Her voice hitched. "Chip ended our relationship. Why stay with a broke high school girl who can barely afford her phone? Who doesn't even have a home?"

"Lu, I . . ."

I didn't know what to say. How do you make somebody feel better when their entire world is crashing around them? When you're suddenly living the life you've dreamed of, and there's nothing either of you can do to stop the train that's barreling down the tracks, ready to flatten your best friend while you cruise on by?

"This was not supposed to be senior year," Lu said, angry now. "I should be applying for college and I should be able to afford it and I shouldn't be sleeping on the same air mattress as my aunt—who I shouldn't even be living with, by the way, because both of my parents shouldn't have died—and I shouldn't have to be hundreds of miles away from my best friend."

I felt a knife through my heart. Planning dates with VSBs or hooking up with them in dorms all seemed so ridiculous now. Lu was what mattered. I needed to be with her, not focusing on frivolous crap.

Max typed into the Notes app on his phone. **Is she okay?**

I grabbed his cell and typed back, **No. I don't know what to do.**

Max snapped his fingers. "Tell her we're going as a butt to homecoming. Invite her to come, she won't be able to help but *crack up* at our costume." He moved his mouth so it was as close to the speaker as possible. "Come to homecoming and witness Albert ask Jay to be his boyfriend."

I swear the air got sucked out of the room.

"What did Max say?" Lu whispered.

"Lu—"

"Albert is going to *ask* you to be his boyfriend? I thought he already was. You said you couldn't come to the hoedown because you needed to spend time with your *boyfriend*. And then you guilted me for all the time I spent with Chip. That was you who said all those things, wasn't it, or am I making this up?"

I would kill Max.

"It's just that I'm starting to make a life here, Lu, and I couldn't just up and leave when things have been going so well. I mean, I do want Albert to be my boyfriend, and I've been hooking up with this guy and lost my virginity and—"

"You lost your WHAT?" Lu screamed. "When were you going to tell me?"

"Well, I tried, but you've been so busy." I knew it was a weak excuse. "And everything seemed like it was kind of crashing down around you. I didn't want to make it worse by rubbing it in your face how awesome things were going for me."

"Excuse me if my life is such a *downer* for you, Jay."

I wanted to hear Lu clacking her nails again. If she clicked her nails, it meant she was more sad or nervous than angry. When Lu got angry, it was nearly impossible for her to snap out of it. But the clacking never came. Lu was pissed, and when that happened, she clenched her hands in fists.

"No, that's not what I meant," I said. "Why don't you just fly here and come to homecoming with us?" I was grasping at straws, but I'd try anything to make Lu less angry with me.

"I can't miss a whole weekend's worth of shifts, Jay. Haven't you been listening to me, or are you too busy coming up with whatever lie you're going to tell me next?"

"Come on, Lu, you know I've been—"

She cut me off before I could give her another pathetic

excuse. "It's fine. You know what? Enjoy homecoming. Enjoy your new life. Because I don't want you in mine."

Click.

I called back, but Lu just sent me straight to voice mail. I tried again, and she did the same thing. The third time I called, she picked up, screamed, "FUCK YOU!" and that was that.

Max fidgeted nervously with his ponytail. "Did I just mess up?"

A wave of heat washed over me. If Max had just kept his fracking mouth shut, none of this would have been an issue.

"That is the *biggest* understatement. I'd come up with the perfect reason I couldn't go back to Riverton, but you—"

Something in my gut stopped me from stabbing an accusatory finger in Max's chest. This really wasn't Max's fault, was it? If I had just been up front with Lu from the start, I wouldn't be in this mess.

Max looked like Damon back on the second day of school. Like if he spoke too loudly or said the wrong thing, I might bite his head off. "Hey, Jay, I'm really sorry," Max mumbled. "I totally didn't mean—"

"You don't have to apologize." I meant it, I really did, but I still couldn't stop replaying Max letting it slip that Albert wasn't my boyfriend. He told Lu in so many words that I'd lied to her. If he'd just kept quiet, I could be comforting Lu about getting evicted. Instead, she'd evicted me from her life.

Max picked at nonexistent fluff on his track pants. "Should we get back to the Great Behind?"

I looked to the mass of beige fabric and bags of cotton balls. My mind couldn't focus on how to put the items together. Instead, I kept replaying Lu's *FUCK YOU!* on repeat with images of her clenched fists squeezing my heart into a pulp.

"S-sorry," I stuttered. I couldn't even speak straight. "I just need some time alone. To figure this out."

Max rushed forward like he wanted to give me a hug. "Jay, I promise—"

I put my hand out, stopping him before he could reach me. "Please." My breath was coming hot and fast now. I knew my anger at Max wasn't justified, but I couldn't stop thinking about how different this afternoon would be if he hadn't said a word.

"Okay." Max sulked as he made his way out of my room.

My breathing didn't slow, not even when I heard Max shut the front door, giving me the space that I demanded. I was panicking.

I thought it was against all odds that I was the only gay person back at Riverton. It seemed even more unlikely that I would meet a boy who wanted to date me, and another who would want to hook up with me at the drop of a text. But the thing that I thought would never happen, *could* never happen, not in a million trillion years, was losing my tried-and-true BFF in a matter of minutes.

But against all odds, I did.

I was so pent up with anger that there was only one thing I could think of to get it out: Tony. When I made it to his dorm, he was waiting for me, naked on his bed. One look at him made the worries clouding my mind drift away. At least temporarily.

I felt like a ravenous beast, devouring every inch of Tony to distract myself from the hurt and frustration. It probably wasn't the healthiest way to let off steam, but in that moment, it really helped.

Even Tony noticed. "That was . . wow." His panting gave me that now-familiar surge of pride. "Where did that come from?"

"I just had something on my mi—" The door rattled, the harsh shaking of the metal knob cutting me off. Someone was trying to get in. "Who's that?"

A sharp voice called through the door. "Tony?"

"Shit!" Tony hopped out of bed and pulled on his pants.

The doorknob-rattling was replaced by pounding. Angry, belligerent, rage-filled pounding. "Tony! I can hear you in there! Open this door!"

A sinking feeling entered the pit of my stomach. "What's going on?" I asked.

"Put your clothes on!" Tony frantically whispered. He grabbed my jeans and shirt and threw them at me. He wasn't looking where he was throwing, though, and the button on my jeans smacked me right in the eye.

"Ow!"

More brutal pounding. "Tony, I swear to fucking gawd if there's a guy in there with you, I'm going to kill him! Then I'm going to cut off his flaccid dick, wrap it around your neck, and strangle you with it!"

I sat there, stunned by the threat of castration and my dismembered member being used as a murder weapon.

"Move!" Tony was hysterical. "He's not kidding! He is going to kill you!"

I pulled my jeans over my legs, forced to go commando because Tony rushed me too fast to find my underwear. "Why is this guy going to kill us?"

"That's Dylan." Tony threw a shirt on over his head, his mouth popping out just in time to pile on the bad news. "My boyfriend."

"Your WHAT?!" I screamed.

The pounding turned to kicking. "I knew it!" Dylan shrieked. "I knew someone was in there with you!"

I couldn't believe this was happening. Max said Tony wasn't the relationship type. *Tony* said he wasn't the relationship type. He had never once talked about Dylan. We were just hooking up, and nobody was supposed to get hurt. He was supposed to be the no-strings-attached kind of guy, but apparently he had all kinds of strings attached to Dylan.

"You couldn't have told me about him?" I demanded. "Before we had sex? Before *any* of the times we had sex? What the hell is wrong with you?"

"He goes to Portland State," Tony said, as if that explained everything. "I didn't know he was coming."

"Your excuse is you didn't think you'd get caught? You've got to be joking." I snatched my shoes off the floor and flew out of Tony's room. "He's all yours," I said to Dylan, whose look made me truly understand the meaning of the phrase *murderous rage.*

I ran down the stairs as fast as I could. Dylan's shouts while he laid into Tony followed me all the way to the front door. I threw it open, ready to storm out into the street, but someone was blocking the way.

"Jay?"

There, on the doorstep, were two guys, one of whom was the absolute last person I thought I'd see at Lambda Chi Alpha.

"Reese? What are you doing here?"

Reese pointed at the guy next to him. It was Spencer, Reese's new boyfriend and costar in all his Instagram pictures.

"Spencer's thinking of rushing the fraternity," Reese explained. "The guys invited us over to check the place out." He and Spencer stepped inside.

Pounding footsteps echoed throughout the foyer. "Get back here, you stupid slut!"

Dylan rushed down the stairs, ready to beat me to a pulp. Tony followed right behind.

"Dylan, don't!" Tony pleaded. "You're causing a scene!"

Reese looked at Tony, then at Dylan, then back at Tony, then at me. I could see all the wheels turning in his mind. Then his eyebrows shot up.

He'd figured it out. He knew what I was doing there.

Reese frowned. Not the reaction I was expecting. If anything, I thought he would be grinning maniacally like he'd caught me in the act. "What are *you* doing here?" he asked, even though we both knew he had the answer.

"I, uh . . ."

"He's about to get the shit kicked out of him, that's what he's doing here," Dylan said. "For thinking he could fuck my boyfriend!"

Dylan was within lunging distance now. I had to duck when his fists came swinging.

"I didn't know Tony had a boyfriend," I said, my hands up defensively. "There are tallies of the people he's slept with on his door. He never even mentioned you."

Dylan's fists stopped flying as he slowly turned to Tony. "You said those marked how many beer-pong games you and Victor won."

Any trace of the smooth sexiness I'd come to expect from Tony was washed from his face. "Dylan, I . . ." He hesitated, searching for the right thing to say that could get him out of this. "It honestly didn't mean anything. Jay just had this list of sex things he wanted to do. There was no emotion behind it, right, Jay? You just needed to try things out. What did you call it, your Gay Agenda?"

I became the human personification of that blue-in-the-face screaming emoji. I had never mentioned the Gay Agenda to Tony. There was only one person in this entire city I'd shared it with.

"Max told you?" I was going to throw up.

Tony nodded. "At the drag brunch. He thought I could

help you out. And I did, right, but everything's over now."

I couldn't believe Max would do that. Telling Tony was such a stab in the back. He was supposed to be my Gay Guide, but he'd totally corrupted the Gay Agenda. Everything on that list was supposed to happen organically because of a connection or attraction I'd waited eighteen years to form with someone. Not because Max told Tony, "Hey, hook up with my horny, desperate friend." I didn't ask for that kind of handout. I felt dirty. Betrayed.

Used.

Tony looked anxiously at Dylan while he tried to save face. "Yeah, it's over, Jay." He said it defiantly, like I was trying to force him to be with me. "Totally over. I couldn't do that to Dylan." He put his hand on Dylan's shoulder, which was immediately shrugged off and followed by a glare that could almost rival Reese's.

Almost.

"This is just the cherry on top of a *really great day*," I said. "I'm leaving." I moved to walk past Reese, but he grabbed my arm.

"Aren't you and Albert dating?" He seemed really fracking pissed.

"Y-yes." I cleared my throat. "Albert and I have gone on some dates. But we're not exclusive."

"Is he an item on your Gay Agenda too?"

I couldn't say anything. Albert starred in all my favorite items. The ones about slow dancing, about becoming my first boyfriend, about falling in love. But I couldn't say that out loud. It would sound like I was using Albert, just like Tony was using me for an easy lay. I wasn't like Tony. I wasn't.

Reese nodded slowly, my silence all the answer he needed. "Right." He pushed my arm away from him. I was too dirty to touch anymore. It was clear he was done talking, but I had an awful feeling the conversation wasn't over.

Dylan was sobbing now, and Tony lamely patted his back. Spencer looked around awkwardly, completely unprepared for his first look at the fraternity to be so full of drama. "Maybe this isn't a good time," he mumbled.

I walked out the door and slammed it behind me. I swear I could have breathed fire. I felt so gross. Who the hell did Tony think he was, having me come over so many nights and never once mentioning Dylan? There weren't even any pictures of Dylan in Tony's bedroom. Or on his Instagram. But there were certainly all kinds of pictures of himself. What kind of heartless boyfriend was he?

And *Max* telling Tony about the Gay Agenda! I might not have had a great reason to be mad at Max before, but now I sure did.

I opened my phone to call Max, and the churning in my stomach increased by about a million. I had seven texts from Albert, and my heart sank further and further as I read each one.

Hey, I'm outside your place.

Hello? Are you there?

Maybe my texts aren't going through.

I just knocked and your dad says you're not home.

Did I get the day wrong? Are we supposed to meet tomorrow?

Just reread our texts. It was definitely today.

See you around, I guess.

I had blown Albert off. I'd gotten so caught up in Max telling Lu that Albert and I weren't boyfriends yet that I'd completely forgotten about the date that *I* planned.

I needed to text Albert back, but how could I explain what happened? I couldn't just say, *Hey, sorry I forgot about you so I could have angry sex with some other boy who happens to already have a boyfriend.* Telling the truth would crush him. I let him think I wasn't some guy only out for sex, but I ditched him specifically *to have sex.* If he found out, we'd be over before we even started, but I had to tell him before Reese did. They had the Digigang bond, and I bet Reese had texted Albert the second I stormed out onto the street.

I'm so sorry, Albert. Can we talk? We need to talk.

I waited for the ellipses that meant Albert was typing back, hoping he'd respond. I'd had the best idea for a date too. I had found this adorable place called the Seattle Pinball Museum that had all these ancient types of arcade games from as far back as the '60s. I thought Albert's gamer-heart would love it.

With no ellipses, I tried calling Albert myself. He sent me straight to voice mail, but I couldn't get all the words right in my head to leave a meaningful message. I needed him to know that I cared about the things he liked, that I cared about him and his feelings, that I wasn't a heartless liar like Tony.

"Oh, frack," I moaned.

I had one of those horribly clichéd movie moments when a realization smacks the main character right in the face. That's exactly what I was: a heartless liar.

The average eighteen- to forty-four-year-old lies twice every day. I used to think that I was above that. I was a totally honest, rule-following stats lover who couldn't hurt anybody with his lists. But I was lying to myself all along.

Ten minutes went by with no response from Albert.

Twenty minutes.

Nothing.

Thirty.

Not a word.

I still hadn't heard anything by the time I got home and collapsed on my bed. The guilt bubbling in my stomach was at full throttle. I had lost every relationship that meant anything to me in a matter of one day. No Lu (because I let her down when she needed me the most), no Max (because he'd stabbed me in the back by sharing the Gay Agenda), no Tony (because he was a lying bastard), and no Albert (because *I* was a lying bastard).

It was a good thing I'd crossed off so many items on the Gay Agenda over the past few weeks. The odds of anyone helping me out with the rest were slim to none.

23.

✓ Dig Your Grave Deeper

Sunday came and went without a single word from Albert or Lu. I got a few calls from Max after I texted **YOU TOLD TONY?!**, and I ignored him every time. But the satisfaction of blocking him out wasn't enough to get rid of my guilt over Albert. I paced through the house, trying to get my nerves to settle. Mom was away again for the weekend, and Dad knew something was up. After repeated attempts to try to get me to talk, he finally gave up and went on some Uber rides. As he put it, he'd rather deal with the gloom outside than the gloom I was bringing into our place.

I walked to school Monday morning focused on what I was going to say to Albert. I would find him before his robotics class and try to explain what had happened over the weekend. I knew I couldn't lie to him and had to come up with the right way to word why I was with Tony.

JAY'S A FLAKE FACTS

1. We weren't exclusive so I was hooking up with another guy. (True, but harsh)
2. You said you wanted to wait, so I was just trying things out with Tony. (Also true, but heartless)
3. Everything I did with Tony paled in comparison to the time spent with you. (Weak)
4. He had my dick, you have my heart. But I really want you to have both my dick _and_ my heart. (Too crass)

There was no way to word the reality of the Tony situation without it sounding bad.

When I made it to the science and math building, everything I wanted to say flew out the window. Albert was standing in the hallway, his back turned to me while he talked to Reese. My heart sank. There was no way Reese hadn't already told him about the fraternity run-in.

Reese immediately started shooing me away when he saw me over Albert's shoulder. "Leave Albert alone," he said. "Don't you think you've done enough damage already?"

I was right. Reese had spilled everything, and it looked even worse that he'd told Albert before I had.

I walked up slowly, mimicking the _don't run away_ stance I'd seen Damon give Max, Max give me, and Tony give

Dylan. "Can we talk?" Reese stepped in front of Albert like he needed a shield, but I was certain that if Reese would just get out of the way and leave, I could make this better. "Alone?"

Reese widened his stance. He wasn't going anywhere.

"I'm so sorry for missing our date," I began. "It was a total jerk move."

Albert's eyes met mine, and I lost my breath. I could see just how hurt he was, and I was entirely the cause of his pain. He had been so vulnerable with me, telling me about how he was tired of being treated like a stereotype, about his hesitations about sex, about how he wanted to get to know me more before taking it to the next level. He said I was someone he could just be himself around. I had completely destroyed that. I would give up every single moment with Tony to have his trust back.

My mouth flapped open, trying once again to find the magic words that would make this all better. But of course, there were none. "Albert, I—"

Albert's perfect jaw clenched before he snapped, "Is it true?"

"I'm not sure what Reese told you," I said. Although my gut told me he had spilled everything.

"You have a Gay Agenda?"

That was not what I'd expected him to say. I thought he would ask about Tony first. About how I went behind his back. "Yes," I said.

"And I'm on it." It was a statement, not a question.

I nodded. He'd been added to it after I'd already

created it, but the look on Albert's face told me the *when* of his appearance on the Gay Agenda didn't really matter.

"So that's all I am," Albert said. "A notch on your belt. Somebody to cross off and be done with."

Nothing could have been further from the truth. Yes, I wanted to experience some firsts with him, but I didn't want to throw him aside after. He needed to know about my plans for an Albert Agenda, about all the things I wanted to do together, about all the romance and love. "Albert, that's not it at all."

"How am I supposed to trust anything you say?" Albert pushed Reese aside so he could face me head-on. "You kept me in the dark about Tony. You told me you were a virgin. You said you could wait. What the fuck, Jay? Why didn't you just tell me the truth?"

"Because I didn't want to scare you away," I said. "I didn't want you to think I was like your ex."

Reese laughed with disdain. "Oh, that is *rich*, Jay. You're saying this is Albert's fault?"

I'd never felt as furious as I did in that moment. All I could comprehend was a deep, consuming rage that made my anger over the weekend look like mild irritation.

"Why don't you just shut your fucking face for once, Reese?" Everyone in the hallway turned to witness my tirade. "Why are you even here? You are such a drama queen. Max was right about every single thing he said about you: you're a conceited, self-centered asshole. He's so much better off without you in his life."

My whole body pulsed, and my breaths came in heaving, ragged gulps.

Right before I came out, I'd looked up the stats on getting into a fight. About one in four high school kids come to blows. I thought if I was ever going to be one of them, it would be sticking up for myself as the only gay kid at RHS. I never thought I'd be the cause of a fight. That I'd scream at and insult somebody so much that I wouldn't be surprised if they wanted to punch me.

But Reese didn't fling his fists or get in my face. He didn't move a muscle. Instead, his icy glare blurred over with tears. "He said that?"

I was so worked up I couldn't keep my thoughts in order. "Who?"

"Max," Reese choked. "He said I was conceited? And self-centered?"

"Yeah, he did," I said, anger flaring up again. "Why else would you dump him at the drop of a hat? He supported you. He wanted to help you along in your acting. He loved you, you know that? No. You wouldn't. You're too self-absorbed to notice anything but yourself."

"Of course I knew that," Reese whispered, and he lost all control of his tears. For the first time, he seemed surprisingly . . . human. Reese's chest was the one that heaved now as he struggled to speak. "I wanted to be with Max more than anything." His words were warped and distorted as he spoke through his tears. "I had to leave him. I knew if we stayed together, I wouldn't focus. I *couldn't* focus. My whole world was him, so much that I missed three auditions and my agent threatened to drop me. I couldn't find the balance. I had to leave but I didn't . . ." Reese stopped. His shoulders shook with sobs.

I actually felt sorry for him. No wonder he was so standoffish when I first met him. I was with Max all the time. He must have thought I was helping Max leave any thoughts of Reese behind. If only he'd known how many times I'd seen Max look longingly at Reese's Instagram and tear up any time he saw a picture of Spencer.

Wait a minute.

"Oh please, this is all an act," I said. "If you were this torn up about Max, why are you dating Spencer?"

Albert put Reese's glare to shame. "Are you serious? Spencer is in Reese's acting class. They're just friends. Reese hated being alone after he broke up with Max. He even thought *you two* were dating until he found out that we were. Reese spent so much time with Spencer because he had no ties to Max. The connection you and I have. No, *had*"—the change in tense sent a knife through my heart—"and your closeness to Max was too much for him to handle; he told me after Pike Place. But this whole time I told Reese he had nothing to worry about. I told him you were a great guy. But we really don't know each other that well, do we, Jay?" Albert scoffed, shaking his head. He said so much with the movement: he was disgusted with me, disgusted with himself, probably reliving everything his ex had put him through. "Guess I was wrong."

A glint of light caught my eye as Reese moved to wipe snot from his lip. Two matching gold bracelets slid down his wrist, just like Max's. They'd been hidden all along in the folds of the NYU sweatshirt he always wore.

That's how I knew that Reese was telling the truth. He really missed Max.

The bell rang, but nobody moved. Everyone kept staring at me—Albert, Reese, the whole student body— waiting for an explanation. I knew no matter how long we stood there, I wouldn't be able to come up with something that could justify my actions.

"I should get going," I finally mumbled. "I'm gonna be late."

I whipped around, the backpack Albert gave me slapping my side with each hurried step.

So much for making things better.

I'd only made them worse.

The hurt in Albert's eyes haunted me for the rest of the day. No matter where I looked, Albert's face materialized, going through the pained emotions of the morning: his betrayed stare when he mentioned Tony, his disgusted glare when I yelled at Reese, his gut-wrenching pain when I confirmed he was a part of the Gay Agenda.

As I should have expected, word traveled quickly about the fight. People pointed and talked in hushed whispers as I walked past. By the end of the day, I was exhausted from trying to avoid Albert's eyes in my thoughts and the judgmental stares in the hallways. But I still had the QSA meeting to go to. Every ounce of me wanted Albert to be there so I could try to explain myself one more time. Simultaneously, every ounce of me wanted to bail on the meeting. But if I didn't show, I would just look like a coward. I couldn't avoid things any longer.

The push and pull of seeing Albert or not left my mind when I walked into Ms. Okeke's room. I'd run on autopilot, arriving early so I could help Max get the meeting schedule in order. Max was there, alone, nervously twiddling his thumbs at a desk in the front row. He was mumbling to himself like he was practicing a speech, and didn't notice me walk in.

Seeing Max sent a wave of fury over me again. I was so focused on Albert that I didn't think about what it would be like to see Max face-to-face after he spilled about my Gay Agenda.

"I never meant to tell Tony," Max mumbled to himself, still not seeing me in the doorway.

"Then why did you?" I demanded.

Max whipped his head toward me, blond hair flying. Dark circles were under his eyes, and his normally perfectly smooth hair had flyaways and frizz. He looked like he hadn't slept all weekend.

"Jay, it was a total accident."

But then a mass of students piled in, ready to create clock decorations and paint the giant Homecoming in Hindsight banner that we'd be putting up in the gym the next week. They immediately fell into an awkward silence, giving me looks that ranged from *Oh gawd, I wonder how he's doing after that fight* to *Jay's a piece of shit for stomping on Albert's heart like that.*

"I, uh, I think I'll go make copies of the Best Costume ballots," I said. It was still on the dance to-do list I'd made on the whiteboard, giving me the perfect excuse to get out of there. I avoided everyone's eyes as I grabbed the finished ballot from Ms. Okeke's desk and shouldered my way through the throng of staring QSA members. I guess I'd accomplished one more item on the Gay Agenda. I wouldn't be known as the new kid anymore. Instead, I'd go down as the asshole who didn't care how many broken hearts he left in his wake.

I made it to the office and hit Print on the copier with so much force I thought I might have jammed the button. The last thing I needed was for Mr. Hammond to be pissed at me too. But the printer started shooting out copies just fine, and I thanked the homecoming gods for sending me to a school with so many students. With 1,800 of us, I'd be standing at the copier for a long time and wouldn't have to worry about seeing Max.

"Jay?"

Or not. Max had followed me.

"Can we talk?" he asked.

I motioned toward the printer. "I'm pretty busy."

I turned back around, the copier effortlessly shooting out ballots while I searched for anything that could make it look like I wasn't just standing there. But of course, there was nothing.

"Fine." I whipped back around. "What?"

"I swear to gawd I didn't mean to tell Tony about the Gay Agenda," Max said. He bit his bottom lip, and his eyes darted to his feet. "Okay, I might have meant to a little. You were instantly crushing on Albert, who's friends with Reese over that dumb Digimals thing, and I wanted to have a friend who had no connection to Reese this year. So when I saw Tony checking you out at the drag brunch, I let it slip. I thought he might distract you away from Albert. I made Tony promise not to say anything because I didn't want you to be embarrassed. And I . . ." Max hesitated, nervously twirling his hair around his finger so hard I thought he might rip it from his scalp. "I may have encouraged you not to bring up your virginity so Tony wouldn't tell you he knew about the Gay Agenda. I know it sounds bad, but honestly, Tony didn't care if you had a list of all the things you wanted to do. I actually think he was kind of turned on by it."

Max's excuses showed that he didn't get it at all. "I don't think you understand what you really did," I said. "This isn't about being embarrassed. The Gay Agenda wasn't about accomplishing some checklist that I could insert just anybody into. It was about bonding with gay guys for the very first time. It was about feeling wanted, and someone being attracted to me, not taking my virginity in some sort of weird pity handout. I wanted to cross those things off when the connection was real." I never thought I'd be backing up such flimsy science, but Gay Agenda items were meant to be accomplished when the universe brought the right person my way. "You took that from me, Max. You made me just a . . . a tally on somebody's list of conquests."

Ohmigawd, the tallies on Tony's door. That's all I was, another notch on Tony's belt, and it didn't matter to him who he hurt to gain that notch. Which was exactly what Albert had said that morning. I'd made him think he was replaceable, that anybody's name could be inserted into the Gay Agenda and I'd be happy, when that was the furthest thing from the truth. I imagined Albert in all those items about dating and love because my connection with him was real. It was natural and organic. It had to be Albert.

Honest, thoughtful, sexy, beautiful, goofball, uninhibited Albert.

"Jay." The dark circles under Max's eyes were magnified by his tears. "I don't know what to do. How can I make it up to you?"

I didn't want to talk to him anymore. Max's loose lips sank ships, and my life was the *Titanic*. He blabbed to Lu that I didn't have a boyfriend, and blabbed to Tony about the Gay Agenda, setting off a whole chain reaction that ensured I wouldn't have a social or romantic life ever again.

"Think of this like you and Cami and Damon," I said. "I just need some space. *From you.*"

I turned my back on him, grabbing the dozens of ballots that had already printed out.

"Ow!"

I snatched my hand back. A bright red streak marred my palm. A paper cut. It was actually a welcome distraction. The throbbing lessened the pain of the knife Max had stabbed in my back.

24.

✔ Out with the Old and Start Something New

The rest of the week was just as shitty. There wasn't a statistical formula or some epic theory or an agenda that could salvage the situation. But one thing was completely certain, and I didn't need a theory to prove it: I was such a dick.

How could I have done that to Albert? How could I have gotten so caught up with a jerk like Tony? How could I not have seen that Reese actually did have a heart? How could I have kept everything from Lu for so long? How could I get out of this spiral of asking myself nonstop questions?

Albert didn't show up for either of the QSA meetings that week, and he was such a noticeable absence. I didn't think I was making it up that people kept glancing toward the door, then sneering at me, rightfully blaming me for the sweetest, most caring, most loveable, hottest goofball of the whole group not showing up. Everyone looked at me like *I* was a VSB: a Very Shitty Boy.

And they weren't wrong.

It looked like I wouldn't ever get to cross off the framily item on the Gay Agenda. Nobody wanted to hang around me anymore. I couldn't call Lu and ask for her advice, because she had officially blocked my number. The only thing I had to keep me company was the steady Seattle rain, which had been pouring ever since my hallway showdown with Albert.

Max did try to talk to me in Fashion Design. But each time he opened his mouth to say sorry, I slammed down on my sewing machine pedal so hard that I'm pretty sure I left an indent in the floor. It felt surprisingly good to see his face fall when the pounding of the needle drowned out his words.

I wasn't ready to talk to him yet. If Max had never told Tony about the Gay Agenda, I wouldn't have gotten caught up in this love and lust triangle. But because he had, I'd be spending the rest of my senior year as an outcast.

"Someone sure thinks this assignment is the *tops!*" Mr. Bogosian said, this week's dad jokes focusing on the T-shirts he'd assigned. "I appreciate the enthusiasm, Jay."

"I'm just thrilled," I said, and slammed the pedal down while glaring at Max.

Max sighed and flipped his hair over his shoulder, blocking me from his peripheral vision.

When class was finally out, I lingered at my table so Max could get sufficiently ahead of me. I didn't need him trying to strike up another conversation in the hall.

"You know, you should really give him a chance."

Damon stepped into view. The angry thunderbolt on his jersey looked as chaotically mad as I felt.

"Why do you give him such a break?" I asked, my anger at Max seething over into how dismissive he'd been of Damon. "He's shut you and Cami out for the past six weeks. Take it as a gift from the universe and move on before he can shit all over your life, too."

"I can't drop him like that." Damon pulled out his phone, showing me his screen saver. It was the same picture Max had on his nightstand with Damon laughing and trying to squirm out of Max and Cami's hug. "He's part of the family. Cami was always the ringleader of our group, and whenever she got her mind set on something—like becoming my cheerleaders—Max was always on board. That's how Max is: he wants to help whenever he can." Damon stared at the three of them beaming from his phone. "I just wish he'd take some help for his own problems from time to time."

It seemed like they had a lot of history, and I wouldn't take that away from Max, Damon, or Cami. But the good Max did in someone else's life didn't wipe away the bad he'd brought into mine.

"Yeah, well, that's not the Max I know," I said. "His *help* led to a whole lot of hurt."

Damon's worried stare turned into wide-eyed disbelief. "You don't really think this is his fault, do you? All that went down between you and Albert has nothing to do with Max."

The past few weeks with Tony and Albert blew through my mind: me choosing to hook up with Tony, me deciding not to tell Albert about it when all he asked for was honesty, me forgetting about our date over the weekend so I could have sex and discover I was somebody's dirty little secret all this time.

Max didn't make me do any of that. That was 100 percent Jay.

I couldn't meet Damon's eyes. "I guess you have a point."

"If Max is actually trying to talk about this problem between the two of you, you should take him up on it. He's trying to make it right." Damon sighed with his whole body. He really missed Max. "Which is new, since he usually avoids conflict or anything that might make him feel bad."

Damon was right. Max was putting in the effort to make it better between us. Meanwhile I was just making it worse by pushing him further away. Kind of like Max was doing to Cami and Damon. I guess I'd learned a lesson from my Gay Guide after all:

How to blow up relationships that matter.

I ripped off my rain boots the next afternoon and threw them to the apartment floor. The resulting splatter looked just as disgusting as I felt. I'd spent the whole day trying to come up with a way to fix everything, but no inspiration had struck.

"Something wrong?"

Dad leaned against the wall, as stoic and collected as ever.

"That's an understatement."

He frowned, then motioned for me to follow him. "Step into my office."

We walked into the living room. *SportsCenter* played on the TV, and a Bud Light in a beer cozy sat on one of the side tables. The sofa already had the beginnings of a solitary indent in it. It was the spot where Dad sat each night, alone. He made sure he was home every day for dinner, but I'd been so caught up in boys and Gay Agendas that I hadn't made any time for him. And I'd blown him off on the weekend when he'd tried over and over to get me out of the house. With Mom gone for work the majority of the time since we moved, Dad had been waiting for anyone in the family to spend time with him.

Yet another person I'd let down.

"Gawd, Dad, I'm so sorry." I dropped onto the couch and put my head in my hands.

"Sorry for what?" he asked.

"For leaving you here with no one to talk to. For running

out to spend time with guys. For holing myself up in my room when I'm home. For making you feel as alone as I feel right now." All this time I'd focused on the Gay Agenda to bring me closer to people, but it ended up just pushing me further away from the relationships I already had.

Dad sat next to me, put his hand over my shoulders, and pulled me into him. He still smelled like motor oil and pine trees, despite the fact he hadn't worked in a car shop or lived in the woods for over a month now. "At this stage in your life, you're supposed to be finding out who you are," he said. "I don't feel abandoned at all. You're becoming a young man, and that means leaving the nest."

After four days' worth of being avoided, it was a little jarring to hear someone sound so understanding. I didn't feel like I deserved it. "You're not mad?"

Dad shrugged. "You haven't done anything to me to be mad at. You're just becoming Jay, and you should be proud of that."

"I really don't think I've done much to be proud of lately."

"We all make mistakes as we develop into the person we're meant to be. It's how you make up for those mistakes that matters."

I scoffed, head still in my hands. "Easier said than done. I really screwed up, Dad. And now Lu and Albert won't even talk to me. How am I supposed to apologize if they just keep shutting me out? And I've totally taken out my anger on Max." He'd finally had enough of my being a dick to him, and steered clear of me in the halls that day too. The weird irony was that when I had been the only gay kid at school, friendships were easier. They were way less complicated than when romance and feelings and hormones and horniness became a part of everything.

"You just got to keep at it," Dad said. "Don't take no for an answer. Let them know how truly sorry you are." He squeezed my shoulders. "You know what always cheers me up?"

"What?"

"*Monday Night Football*. I DVR'd this week's game."

I laughed. If only it were that easy.

"Want to watch together?" Dad asked. "Like old times?"

He grabbed the remote and started the game. The camera panned to a coach beside his team, the players lined up in a row of muscular butts in tight pants.

"I guess my timing is perfect," Dad said, pointing to the TV. "It's your favorite view."

I smiled weakly. "Ha. I do feel like an ass, that's for sure." Dad must have really been trying to make me feel better because he didn't scold me for cussing. "If only I felt like one that looked that goo—"

I stood straight up. Everything clicked.

I was an *ass*. I had to give everyone an apology that let them know I felt like one.

I slapped Dad on the back. "You're brilliant!"

"About time you figured that out," Dad said. He took a satisfied swig from his beer. "Now if you could just tell your mother."

I grabbed my backpack, pangs hitting my heart when

I thought about Albert giving it to me with PrinterBot. I pulled out my notebook, the pangs increasing by about a million when I saw the Gay Agenda and all my horny hopes and dreams that had warped me into this person who wrecked people I cared about. I took the paper in my fist and ripped out the Agenda with everything in me, letting loose the anger and frustration at myself for everyone I'd hurt. I tore the list into piece after piece, first dates gone, IRL penises torn in two. My soul felt like it could stitch itself back together as the items I got so caught up in were tossed away.

Dad stared at me in shock. "Do you . . . still need to talk?"

"No," I said, and snatched a pen. "I've done enough talking." It was time to *show* people how sorry I really was. A new agenda was in the works.

JAY'S APOLOGY AGENDA

1. Give Max a chance to redeem himself.
2. Show Reese I actually have a heart.
3. Let Albert know he's more than a list.
4. Have Lu's back again.

I was about to set the new plan in motion, but stopped when one of my Gay Agenda shreds crinkled beneath my heel.

9. Become part of a super-queer, super-tight framily

Of all the items I had left on the Gay Agenda, that was one I wanted to keep. But I'd never be able to accomplish it if I didn't start saying sorry.

I raced to my room and opened my closet. A cascade of unused fabric and cotton pooled around my feet. I took a picture of the mess and sent it with two identical texts.

I need your help.

The Apology Agenda was a go.

25.

✓ Make an Ass of Yourself

"Jay, I'm so glad you texted. Let's just move on from here, right? How can I help?"

Max barreled through the front door, a relieved smile plastered across his face. But when he saw what I hoped was being read as my tough-but-tender pose, his smile drooped instantly.

"You're not going to just let this one go, are you?" He massaged his temple. "Lord and Taylor."

"You need to face your problems head-on," I said.

Max sneered. "Oh, please. That's the Louboutins calling the Choos designer."

"Um . . . what?"

"It means you're a hypocrite," Max said. "Weren't you the one who purposely avoided telling Lu the truth? I didn't mean to tell Lu that you didn't have a boyfriend. And while I did let the Gay Agenda slip, I didn't think anybody would get hurt. I thought I'd help you have fun, and is that so bad? I didn't mess up your life. *You* did."

He no longer had the don't-scare-the-puppy pose he'd been giving me all week. Instead, Max looked like he was going to poke the angry rottweiler and didn't care what came next. Actually, he looked like the rottweiler.

"You're completely right," I said.

Max's expression changed to curious dachshund as his head cocked to the side. "I am?"

"Yeah. You didn't cause these problems, Max." I put my hands on his shoulders so I could look him straight in the eye. "I did. I should have been up-front with everybody about what I was going through. I should have told Lu I couldn't go to the hoedown. I should have told Albert I was also seeing Tony and let Albert decide what was best for him. And I should tell you now that I'm sorry for blowing up at you. I'm sorry, Max."

"Wow." He looked stunned, completely still other than the moon charm on his earring swinging back and forth. "So this is what sharing your feelings is like."

"Mmm, not quite." I spun him around so I could lead him down the hallway and into my room. I had definitely had visions of a football player on my bed before, but they'd never looked like this. Damon was perched at the edge of my mattress, the stitching technique we'd learned in Fashion Design coming in handy while he helped me create a costume out of beige fabric and cotton balls.

"Oh. Hi," Max said, taking in the mountainous mass in Damon's lap. "What are you doing here?"

"*This* is what sharing your feelings looks like," I said, steering Max toward my bed. "And I think there's someone you've shut out who really needs to hear from you."

Max scuffed a pink sneaker against the floor. "Is this an episode of *Intervention*?"

"It's actually going to be more like an episode of *Project Runway*," I said. I knew my obsession with reality TV would come in handy someday. I grabbed the fabric from Damon so I could give him and Max room to talk while I continued the costume. "And you two need to get to the confessional before you hit the fashion show."

"I'm FaceTiming Cami," Damon said. "She deserves to be here for this too."

He pulled out his phone and dialed, positioning the screen so that it faced Max. Cami answered on the second ring. She was surrounded by sand, lying on a towel, her braids framing her face. A spot of sunscreen she'd missed stood out on her dark brown shoulder, and sounds of waves crashing in the background came through the speaker. But despite her picture-perfect surroundings, Cami scowled when she saw Max. Their eyes met, and Max looked down at the floor.

"Yeah, you know what you did," Cami said. "Do you know how many times I've called you?"

"A lot?" Max's voice was barely more than a whisper.

"*One hundred fourteen*," Cami said. "Are you serious, Max? After everything we've been through, you're going to throw that away because you're upset about a man?"

Cami's words had so many parallels to what I'd done to Lu. I'd blown up our relationship over boys despite years of friendship.

Max lifted his head, and his forehead furrowed into a scowl of his own. "That's just it. I was trying to get over Reese, and you and Damon kept bringing him up. Everybody kept bringing him up. How was I supposed to move on if I was forced to keep thinking about him?"

"We were trying to be there for you," Cami said. "You know that. It's not fair for you to just act like you and Reese were never together. You made him a part of my life when you started dating, and I got used to that. I made memories with Reese, too, and you don't get to pretend like that didn't happen. You have to let me get used to the fact he left you, too."

"I never thought of it like that," Max said.

"Well, you would have if you had answered one of my damn calls." Cami sat up, positioning the camera so we could see bright blue skies and the ocean behind her. "LA is everything I wanted, Max, and I thought it was what you wanted too. You're supposed to join me here at FIDM so we can change the fashion industry together. You said we were inseparable. Are you really going to let me go like that?"

Max was silent, then, "At first I was just so mad at everybody. I was mad at Reese for leaving me, I was mad at you and Damon for wanting to talk about him, I was mad at Dad and Jules for making it seem like it wasn't that big a deal to break up from a high school relationship.

But then I started to move past that anger and really miss you, but it just felt like the universe's worst joke that you weren't around anymore and off in college. I thought it would hurt too much to see you over the phone when I couldn't actually *see* you in all this. So I just blocked you out. And Damon too, because he made me think of all the things we did together."

"You know that's really shitty reasoning, right?" Cami said. "Missing me so much that you shut me out altogether?"

Max laughed as her words sunk in. "It really is, isn't it? I'm so sorry, Cami. You're more than just my best friend, you're my soul mate, and I really messed this up. I lost my mind."

"I'll give you this one, but I deserve better than that. You can't do that to me again. I know you did the same thing to your mom, so this is what you do, but honestly, we need to work on your coping mechanisms. They're not healthy."

"Your therapist mother is showing," Max said with a grin.

"That's right, she is, and this is free therapy coming your way, so you should recognize it as the privilege it is." Cami set the phone down and pretended like she was leaning in to give the camera a hug. "Now get in here. And grab Damon, too."

But Damon was one step ahead of his sister, swooping in to wrap Max in his arms. "I'm sorry to you too," Max said.

"I'm with Cami; you'll get this one. But you've got to promise to come back to our games and be my cheerleader. The team's missed your pom-poms."

"My pom-poms do bring all the boys to the yard."

"That's a fact!" Damon said, and playfully punched Max on the shoulder. "They need to be brought out of retirement. I've missed my friend. Senior year would've sucked without you."

"And as Kelly says, my *life* would suck without you." The Apology Agenda was turning into a sappy after-school special, and I loved everything about it.

Max introduced me to Cami, and we talked for the rest of the night. The way the two of them and Damon dropped into a rhythm together gave me hope that I could fix things with Albert and Lu and Reese. I couldn't give them excuses anymore. Just like Max, I had screwed-up logic of my own that I needed to fess up to.

And I knew just the way to do it.

—〰〰—

"Left, right, left, right, left, right."

When I'd come up with the Great Behind, I'd had no idea how hard it would be to walk in. Coordinating our steps so that Max and I stayed next to each other turned me into a drill sergeant until we could finally get in sync. There were a few times when I'd wondered what it would be like to get butt implants, but if this was any indication of how hard it would be to walk with an enlarged derriere, an enhanced behind was coming off any future to-do lists.

But maybe "become a costume designer" could go on that list instead. Max, Damon, and I worked into the early hours of the morning putting everything together. Our butt cheeks were perfectly round, the "leg" skirts were even, and the crack was tasteful without a hint of garishness. And if the handful of catcalls Max and I got walking down the Capitol Hill streets meant anything, it was fairly realistic too.

Slowly but surely, we finally made it to the SIF building. There was barely enough room for the two of us to walk side by side down the decrepit hallway, but we made it to the workroom doors just in time for class.

I turned to Max, cotton swishing with the movement. "You ready for this?" I asked.

"This will go down in history as the most ass-tentatious outfit I've ever worn," Max said. He didn't laugh at the butt pun like he usually did. Instead, he took a fortifying breath like on the first day of Fashion Design. This was his moment of truth. "Let's do this."

We burst through the workroom doors and everyone went silent. Well, except for one quick, clipped command that came from Damon, grinning from ear to ear at his worktable in the back of the room. "Heart, heart, hike!"

In expert precision, the football team formed a heart shape around the worktables, leaving a clear space at the tip for Max and me to waddle into. There was just one person left sitting at a sewing machine, looking suspiciously at the football players surrounding him.

"What's going on?" Reese asked. He turned his icy

glare to me and Max. "Here to humiliate the 'self-centered asshole' again?"

I deserved Reese's anger; I really did. But hopefully we could melt that cold exterior with the right apology.

"You weren't the ass, Reese," I said, motioning to the huge butt cheeks around our necks. "I was. For yelling at you for something you didn't deserve. For not being honest with Albert, and for assuming you weren't hurting after breaking up with Max." Reese's glare didn't budge, so I tried my hand at cracking a joke. "You know what they say when you assume."

"You make an ass of Jay and me," Max said, then frowned. "Wait. That's not right, is it?"

"No, actually it is," Reese said. "You and Jay are total asses."

Max stepped forward, breaking the illusion of the giant ass as he walked toward Reese alone. On his own he looked more like a huge, nipple-less boob. Which, based on our behavior, was fitting too.

"I miss you so much," Max said. He had made it to Reese's workstation, his protruding fabric smooshing against the edge of the table as he tried to get as close to Reese as possible. "I wish we could have a do-over. I'd remind you of your auditions, I'd make sure we stopped making out enough so we could run lines, I'd make sure you always knew how much I wanted you to succeed, because what makes you happy makes me happy. *You* make me happy, so when you broke up with me I became . . ." He stopped, searching for the right word. And it was right in front of him, butting up against Reese's sewing machine.

"I became an ass," Max finished. "I'm so sorry."

"I tried to explain things to you," Reese said.

"I know."

"But you were so dramatic, you didn't give me time to talk it out. There's an entire GIF to prove it."

"That's why we're so good together," Max said. "We're both drama queens."

Julian laughed out loud, and Damon elbowed him in the ribs.

"You shut me out before I could explain what I needed," Reese continued.

"It's something I tend to do to the people I care about most." Max looked apologetically at Damon. "And it's not right. I'm working on that."

Reese nodded, quiet and serious, while the rest of us waited. I swear the football team kept inching closer, then pulling back, like the heart they'd formed was beating while we waited for Reese to say something. And then . . .

"I'm sorry too," Reese said. "I blamed you for getting in the way of my goals. It wasn't your fault."

Max reached forward and put his hand in front of Reese. His twin gold bracelets slid down his wrist and jingled against each other. "I want us to always be by each other's side."

"Max," Reese breathed. "I want that too." He placed his hand on top of Max's and pulled back his sweatshirt sleeve. His own gold bracelets gently clinked against the ones Max wore. "I almost threw these away," Reese said. "After Jay screamed at me. But I couldn't bring myself to do it."

Max intertwined their fingers. "I'm glad you didn't."

"Me too." I'd never seen a look as tender as the one Reese gave Max. He got up from his stool, leaned forward, and gently kissed Max on the lips. It was short and soft but said so much. Reese really was good at showcasing emotions with the tiniest nuanced movements: a glare, a kiss. I bet he was a stellar actor.

The football team let loose an avalanche of hoots and whistles, making Reese chuckle as he pulled away from Max. "I think we just starred in our own romantic comedy."

"Maybe you could try your hand at directing one too. We've got one more rom-com that needs its happy ending." Max moved back beside me, and the Great Behind formed again as he stood with me in solidarity.

Reese's icy glare was back as he eyed me skeptically. "I'm listening."

"Sorry I'm late." We all jumped and Julian yelped as the workroom doors burst open. "I-5 was backed up all the way to Tacoma." Mr. Bogosian stopped, taking in the football heart formation, Reese looking lovestruck and annoyed at the same time, and Max and me making up the Great Behind. "I can't say I see it walking down the runways of Paris, kids, but I appreciate the originality."

"Mr. Bogosian, do you mind if Reese and I talk outside for a moment?" I asked. I wanted to explain the whole plan I'd made the night before. I'd need him and the Digigang to help me out or this next part of the Apology Agenda would be over before it started.

"Sure, but be quick about it. I don't want the two of you getting"—Mr. Bogosian wiggled his eyebrows—"*behind.*"

—*mm*—

I had no idea an office chair could move so fast. They were, like, supersonic.

"Wait!" I shouted at Shruti. "I need to catch my balance!"

I was sitting on my knees on top of a roller chair. Shruti had attached a motor to it for her own entry in the Make the Robotics Teacher's Life Easier contest. I probably wasn't going faster than five miles per hour, but when you're precariously perched on a skinny roller chair with a huge fake ass trying to tip you forward, it feels like you're going at hyper speed. Which was exactly what I needed, because if Max and I had to waddle through the halls in these cumbersome outfits, we'd never get to Albert before class ended.

"Keep it down!" Regina whisper-shouted. "Or you're going to get us caught before you can apologize to Al."

She was armed with an iPad that steered Max in another roller chair next to me.

"I don't know that I care so much about being caught as I do making it out of this thing alive," Max said, and his hair billowed behind him as his chair picked up speed.

"Got that right." I made a mental note to check the stats on roller chair–related deaths.

The world suddenly tilted as we careened around a corner. Shruti steered me toward the Civics classroom through her own iPad app. If the zombie apocalypse ever happened, I wanted to be holed up with the Capitol Hill High robotics team. They would have technology up and running in no time.

"Ohmigawd, ohmigawd, ohmigawd!" I prayed to every deity imaginable that Shruti wouldn't kill me. It had seemed like she might when Reese first brought me over to her and Regina to explain the Albert apology plan.

"I don't expect you or him to forgive me at the drop of a hat," I said. "But please let me try."

Shruti pursed her lips. I wasn't sure if she was mulling over what I'd said or if she was considering punching me in the face. I wouldn't blame her if it was the latter. She finally said, "I guess not every attempt at something can succeed from the get-go. Look at the Apollo missions. But if you fuck with him again, I'm going to go supernova on your ass."

"Yeah, and I'll, like . . ." Regina hesitated. Even though she rocked the goth look, it was clearly hard for her to come up with something doom-and-gloomy to say. "Hope you get really painful wisdom teeth or something."

"Understood." Honestly, if I ever hurt Albert again, I'd deserve to be sent into the biggest of black holes or have a wisdom tooth removal with no Novocain.

Our chairs finally slowed as we neared the Civics room. My padded butt gently bumped against the door while Max smacked into me. Apparently Regina wasn't as practiced a driver as Shruti. Thankfully with all the material around us, Max bounced off me like we were two Michelin men playing bumper cars.

I could hear Mrs. Gakstetter's muffled talking on the other side of the door.

"You ready?" I whispered.

Max nodded. "This will probably get us detention."

"Albert's worth a teacher or two thinking I'm a delinquent."

"Then let's do it." Max grabbed hold of the door handle and pulled. As soon as it opened, our chairs zoomed forward. I grabbed the edge of Max's seat so that we'd be side by side, the Great Behind taking the spotlight from Mrs. Gakstetter's lesson on huge asses in politics.

The class burst into laughter as Mrs. G hollered, "What is this? What's going on?"

Albert sat in the second row back, two from the left, like he did in every class. I had to yell over the laughter to make sure he heard me. "I was a giant ass, Albert. You were never just an item to mark off my checklist."

Albert's jaw clenched as all eyes in the room zeroed in on him. Then he opened his mouth wordlessly over and over, still a VSB even when he looked like a fish.

Mrs. Gakstetter stomped in my direction. "You have a really bad habit of disrupting my class, Jay."

Shruti steered me closer to Albert, my big butt cheek knocking into the desks as I wheeled in between rows. I motioned toward Mrs. G. "I don't have much time," I said. "If you can't forgive me, I totally understand. And you can make me the butt of every joke from here on out. I just wanted you to know I was sorry."

I placed a note on Albert's desk. I wasn't the best with words; I never had been. That was Lu, in her newspaper articles, or Max, always able to entertain an audience. For me, the only place that I could ever fully express my thoughts was in my lists. I'd ripped my favorite one out of my journal soon after decimating the Gay Agenda. I hoped that Albert saw in each item not a quality that I wanted to check off and move on from, but a list of things I wanted to be around each and every day.

"I made this over the past few weeks," I told him. "The most important list I've made to date. You're unlike anybody else I've ever met, Albert, and I made this because I couldn't stop thinking about how singular and amazing you are."

ALBERT ADJECTIVES

1. Sexy (I mean he is a V, V, V VSB.)
2. Sweet (Who else would help pick up all my crap even though I had gum on my face and my hand was soaked in blood?)
3. Adorable (I'm talking puppy-dog-eyes adorable.)
4. Smart (Where do you even get started on building a robot?)
5. Unabashedly Albert (As evidenced by the prevalence of Digihips with no mind for who's watching.)

6. Accepting (Nobody else made me feel this safe to be me, exactly as I am.)

7. Honest and Accountable (Okay, I know that's two, but these get linked because they're the two things I can learn from the most. I'm so sorry I hurt you, Albert. I got carried away in my excitement to be around other gay guys for the first time, and I should have just been open with you about where I was at. I was worried I'd look like an idiot, or scare you away with my inexperience with other guys, or come on too strong once I started getting experience. These aren't excuses. I know I messed up, and the worst part is that my epic screw-ups hurt you. Know that I don't expect you to just forgive me. You don't ever have to see me again if you don't want to. But I hope we can move forward. There are still so many firsts I'd like to have with you. And seconds. And thirds. And four—well, you get the idea.)

I wanted to give Albert space to read the list and process everything I was throwing at him, so I started scooting out of the classroom. But I was stopped before I could reach the door.

"Not so fast, Jay," Mrs. Gakstetter said. She pulled a pink pad of detention slips from her desk and scribbled out two notes: one for me and one for Max. "You can't just barge into my class whenever you feel like it."

The material in our butts rustled as we reached for the pink paper. "Sorry for the interruption," I said.

Mrs. G frowned at our costumes. "I have to ask you to take those off. It's a distraction to the learning environment."

"Sorry, Mrs. G, but I can't," I said. "I've been a real ass, and I'm not going to take this thing off until I deserve to be forgiven."

"No cussing," Mrs. Gakstetter said through gritted teeth, waving the detention slip pad. "Or you're getting another one of these."

"You can give me another one if you want." I looked at Albert. "He's totally worth it."

Mrs. Gakstetter started writing my name on another slip, giving me a *tsk-tsk* before she said, "Suit yourself."

But Albert shot up from his desk, grabbing everyone's attention. "Wait." Our eyes locked, and I felt a tiny glimmer of hope.

"I forgive you," he said. "You still have a lot of explaining to do, but—" The tiniest smile played at the corners of his lips. "If you don't take that off, Mrs. G might . . . crack."

I laughed, then quickly face-palmed as Max started chanting, "Kiss him. Kiss him. Kiss him."

"Max," I moaned.

"What?" he said with a shrug. "It was really great kissing Reese after my apology. I thought you might want that rom-com moment. I'm your Gay Guide, remember? I'm supposed to help these things along."

"That's enough of that," Mrs. Gakstetter said, pointing at Max. "We are not turning Civics into a make-out session. Now, I think it's time to get out of this classroom and take off that outfit before I call the principal's office." She motioned to our robot chairs. "And *walk* those things out of here before you run somebody over."

I stood up from my chair, and it took off on its own. Apparently Shruti didn't have audio to hear Mrs. G's instruction to walk it away. I had to hustle out of there or the Apology Agenda would need to be renamed "Steps for Suspension."

"I'll call you after detention," I said to Albert just before Mrs. Gakstetter shut the door in my face.

Guilt bubbles took over my stomach. The last time I told Albert I'd do something, I'd completely blown him off. But I would never let that happen again, and he had to know that. I decided to risk Mrs. G coming at me with her detention pad and yelled one last thing through the door.

"I promise."

26.
✓ Kiss and Make Up

My stomach was full of flutters during detention. Not because my parents might be mad (they wouldn't, when I explained this was for love. Well, Dad might have something to say about it, but I knew he was a softie at the core). I was nervous about seeing Albert. Or rather, not seeing Albert. He'd said he forgave me, but that didn't mean he'd want to see me anymore. This could be an *I forgive you so I can move on* kind of thing, with a nice flourish of *But get the frack away from me*. And I wouldn't blame him if that was the case.

"He'll pick up when you call him," Max said. "I know it in my soul. He's a Pisces."

"What does that mean?"

"Pisces are very forgiving."

"No talking," Mr. Henderson barked.

It was just silent, anxious anticipation from there.

But when the two hours were up and we were allowed to leave, Albert didn't answer my call. He did me one better. He was already waiting outside, ready to face this problem head-on like I should have done from the start.

"You didn't have to wait for me," I said.

Albert shrugged. "Yeah, I know, but at the rate you're getting detentions, I didn't think I'd have another chance to talk to you before you got expelled."

"Are you sure you want to be seen talking with such a troubled youth?" I asked.

"I don't care how troubled you get at school. I just don't want you to ditch me ever again." *Assertive* needed to be added to the list of Albert Adjectives too.

"I'm so sorry, I—"

"I need to say this," Albert said. "Let me finish."

I pressed my lips tight and my heart clenched with nerves. I needed to let him vent, but gawd, it was never fun to hear about what a piece of shit you are.

"You lied to me, Jay. By omission. You never shared with me that you were having sex. Or *are* having sex, if there's anyone else out there you're hooking up with. And I would never have known that if Reese hadn't told me. Were you ever going to mention anything about Tony, or were you just going to lie to me forever?"

My stomach turned with those ever-present guilt bubbles. "To be totally honest, there's nobody else, but I wasn't going to say anything about Tony."

Albert deflated. His glasses even slipped down his nose a bit. It wasn't the answer he'd wanted to hear.

"But only because I didn't want to hurt your feelings," I blurted. "Whenever you said you were ready to have sex with me, I was going to say I was ready too. I didn't want you to feel rushed or forced into anything you didn't want to do."

Albert scowled. "I'm a big boy. I can handle hard stuff." He face-palmed—like, actual Jay-Collier-move face-palmed. "What is it with me and making unintentional penis puns when I'm upset? *I can handle hard stuff?*"

"And you also dropped that you're a big boy," I said, looking up at him sheepishly.

Albert rolled his eyes.

"What? I'm just trying to be honest with you!" I said.

Albert's chuckle faded into thoughtful silence. I could only imagine what shitty things he was thinking of me. And he had every right to think them. But then, against all odds—and giving me much more than I deserved—he slowly reached forward and held my fingers in his.

"What I'm trying to say is, you should have been honest from the start," Albert said. "I mean, it's not like you had to tell me every single thing you wanted to do. And I appreciate you not wanting to rush me into anything. But you should have told me about Tony. It's not the fact that you had sex; we were never exclusive. But when Reese told me about Tony and the Gay Agenda, and how you never mentioned either of those things, it made me feel used. Like a means to an end, but not the end goal. If we're going to see where this goes"—he motioned between us—"you've got to be honest with me about where you're at. Where we're at. Where you're at with other people. Just be you, Jay. I like you." He used his free hand to punch my shoulder, hard enough to just barely classify as playful. "Well, I'm still a bit pissed at you right now, but I liked who you were before all this went down."

"I'm still that same guy. I messed up *big*-time"—I squeezed his hand for emphasis—"and I don't want you to think I'm making excuses for that. I was being who I thought other people wanted me to be, instead of just being true to myself. And honest with you."

Albert looked at our hands. They were back in that linked position we'd had on our dates that felt like second nature. "Honestly, I wasn't ready to lose you to another guy. Learning I had competition all of a sudden really hurt."

His pained expression sent knives into my gut. "I'm so sorry for that, Albert. Really, I am. It's always been you." From that first moment when he bashed into me with PrinterBot. Albert was the person who was always in my heart. But I stopped thinking with my heart when faced with a guy who was so up-front about wanting to have sex. "I got too carried away by the Gay Agenda. You can't imagine how lonely it's been my whole life. I was the only gay guy, not a single person to even kiss while all my straight friends were hooking up and pairing off. I didn't think about how having those physical milestones while we were dating might affect you. And that wasn't right."

"Okay," Albert said. He unconsciously licked his lips, drawing my attention to his mouth.

"In the spirit of honesty, can I tell you what I'm thinking right now?" I asked.

Albert nodded.

I took a step closer, leaving only an inch between us. "I really want to kiss you." Not in a weird *let's hook up* way, but in that way Reese and Max did. Kissing to say sorry, kissing to share how hurt they were, kissing to take the first step toward making it better.

Albert looked down at my lips. He nodded again.

I closed the distance, tingles shooting up and down my spine as our lips touched. His were perfectly wet from licking them. It made me want to lick his lips, too, my tongue moving forward to gently brush against his bottom lip. Albert sucked in a breath, and I could feel the tension in his shoulders relax.

"Was that okay?" I asked.

"Honestly," Albert said. "I liked that."

"Me too."

Albert squeezed my fingers as I smiled into his lips. I moved to pull away, but he tugged me closer. Albert was saying everything with his mouth without uttering a word. I could feel his hurt, his relief, his uncertainty, his hope. It was so much more personal, so much more special than any kiss we'd had yet.

Albert slowly pulled away. "You're gonna owe me quite a few of those to make up for being a dick." Albert's eyes went wide. "I did it again! To make up for being a *jerk*."

I shook my head and looked as solemn as I could. "Punishment is the worst."

Albert laughed and started walking down the hall, pulling me along with him. "And you still owe me a few dances at homecoming. You better get ready for these Digihips."

I stopped. Albert turned around, concern covering him like those ever-present Seattle clouds. "What is it?"

"I can't," I said, sending a prayer to every Gay God that he would understand. "I'm not going."

"But I thought you were going with Max."

"I was. But you're not the only person I've hurt." The hope I'd felt from Albert's kiss was washed away thinking of Lu, alone, living in the salon office until that roof was ripped away from her too. "I was an ass to just about everyone I care about, and there's still one more person I have to apologize to. Please don't think this means I don't want to be with you, or make it up to you for being such a douche. It's just if I don't do this, I think I'll lose my best friend forever."

JAY'S APOLOGY AGENDA

1. ~~Give Max a chance to redeem himself.~~ ✓
2. ~~Show Reese I actually have a heart.~~ ✓
3. ~~Let Albert know he's more than a list.~~ ✓
4. Have Lu's back again.

Albert stood there, that worried look still on his face.

"Albert, I'm so sorry, I—"

He stepped forward and grabbed my face in his hands, kissing me deeper than before, the heart behind it even more present. Despite all the things Tony and I had done together, he'd never touched me like this. Loving and safe and like I was the only thing that mattered.

Albert pulled away, but still held my cheeks, and his expression changed to that smoldering look I loved so much. "That's the best reason for having to bail."

"It is?"

"Yeah," Albert said. He laced his fingers in mine again and pulled me outside. "Owning up to your mistakes is a big turn-on."

27.

✓ Come Home

I'd barely been gone for a month, but driving back through Spokane and into Riverton felt like going to a different country. Everything seemed so small and isolated compared to the hustle and bustle of Seattle that had become my new normal. I was surprised that I didn't feel anything as I drove past Riverton High and the gas station / garage where Dad used to work. I didn't miss it here, this physical space, despite it being all I had ever known up until very recently.

Pulling up to Tough as Nails, however, was a different story. My stomach tightened and my heart clenched seeing movement behind the glammed Rosie the Riveter window decal. It was Lu. The physical space of evergreen trees and lonely run-down strip mall might not feel like home, but Lu absolutely did. I had forgotten that in all the distraction and drama of being around boys who like boys for the first time in my life. But one glimpse of Lu doing her nails at the sad manicure table, and I knew how much I needed her.

I hopped out of Dad's pickup and shut the door. The noise made Lu look up. When she saw me, the nail polish in her hand fell to the floor.

I gave her a weak wave, causing the massive boob I wore from my solo portion of the Great Behind to wobble back and forth.

"Hi, Lu," I called through the window.

She didn't respond. Instead, she whipped around and marched right into the back office. I could hear her slam the door, even from outside.

"Lu!" I yelled. "I'm so sorry!"

Someone stepped out into the hallway. At first, I thought it had worked and Lu was going to come back out, but it was Aunt Carol. She came to the front door and swung it open, bells tinkling as it moved. Hearing them *ting* sent another stab of homesickness through my heart. Lu and I had spent so much time in that salon. We belonged together. This couldn't be the end of our friendship.

Aunt Carol frowned at the beige fabric bulging from my torso. "What in the hell are you wearing?"

I laughed at the look on her face: her eyes all bugged out, her focus so drawn to the padding that she didn't notice her blond-streaked red hair sticking to her lip gloss.

"I've been a total boob, Aunt Carol. I came to apologize."

"You came all this way from Seattle?"

I nodded, and Aunt Carol smiled, her eyes welling up.

"I don't know that Lu wants to talk," she said, looking over her shoulder to the closed office. She sighed, and I knew we were both thinking about how stubborn Lu could be when she was upset. Even though Lu was rightfully angry, I needed her to hear me out. "But you might as well give it a try."

I walked into the salon and was instantly enveloped by the smells of disinfectant and nail polish and peppermint foot scrub. They were the smells of Tough as Nails, the smells of home. One whiff of that mix of chemicals and floral scents, and image after image of laughing my head off with Lu in the pedicure chairs washed over me. Even if the salon was closing, we had to make more memories wherever life was going to take us. We had to.

I ran to the office, ready to get Lu back, the giant boob bouncing with each hasty step. I gently knocked on the door and asked, "Can we talk?"

No response.

"Lu?" I knocked a tad louder.

Still nothing.

"Lu!" I yelled, slamming my fist on the door, extremely reminiscent of Dylan freaking out at Lambda Chi. "You are not going to let it end like this. You're my best friend and I'm not going to let you go!"

The door flung open. Lu's chest heaved up and down, and her hair blew wild from the fan that whirred on the desk. She looked ready to kill.

"I'm the one who let this end?" she yelled. "This is on *you*, Jay." She jammed her finger into the padding covering my chest. "*You* dumped *me* for the hoedown. For a boyfriend who didn't even exist! What is wrong with you?"

I swallowed the shame that threatened to clog my throat. If we were ever going to get past this, I needed to own up to what a colossal dick I had been. "I got so caught up in the possibility of having boys in my life for the first time, Lu. I should have just told you up front that I didn't want to go to the dance."

"This isn't about the stupid fucking dance!" Lu's face was as red as her hair. "This is about you thinking I'm some fragile female who needs protection. I'm not a helpless girl, Jay. Yes, our world may be cr—"

Her voice caught, and suddenly it became impossible for me to swallow the lump in my throat anymore. She fought so hard to keep her head above water when she'd lost her phone, her boyfriend, her house, her parents, and she never quit. Lu was the strongest person I knew.

"Our world may be crashing down around us, but you lying to me doesn't help. I can handle harsh truths, Jay. I've been dealing with them my whole life. I can even handle losing all of this." She motioned around at the salon, then stuttered again, this time unable to stop tears from pouring down her face. "But I never thought I'd lose you."

That's when I lost all control. I wailed, complete with a spit bubble flying out of my mouth, and lunged forward to wrap Lu in my arms. It wasn't as tight a hug as I wanted thanks to the boob bulge, but I got her as close to me as I could. "I'm so sorry." The words sounded warped as I pushed them past my throat lump.

"You should be," Lu said, her face smooshed against my shoulder.

"I am, Lu. I was completely wrong. I was—" I leaned back and pointed to the mass of fabric covering my torso. "A gigantic boob."

Lu looked down and laughed, wiping sadness snot on her sleeve. "That's not quite big enough," she said. "You were way more of a boob than that."

"I was." I scooped her into another hug. "And I'll do whatever it takes to make it up to you."

A sob came from behind us. I turned to see Aunt Carol in one of the pedicure chairs clutching a box of Kleenex.

"Carol?" Lu pushed past me to kneel next to her aunt.

"Oh, don't pay any attention to me." She waved her tissue in the air. "I just couldn't imagine the two of you not being friends anymore. It's been breaking my heart."

I knelt on the other side of the chair and grabbed Lu's hand over Aunt Carol's lap, our tiny framily together again. "Mine too."

Lu looked at our hands, her black nails chipped, and gave a weak smile. "I'm sorry about Chip. I left you hanging there a few times over the summer, didn't I?"

"Yeah, but at least you were honest about it." I thought of all the times I spent alone in my room, bingeing reality TV on my bed while Lu was crossing off relationship milestones of her own. She deserved to have those. Just like I did. But the difference was Lu was honest about needing them. Meanwhile, I tried to make everyone happy by keeping what I needed to myself. I guess the one thing everyone kept from me while they were hooking up was the extra steps it would take to maintain friendships while balancing romance and love and sex. "I can't promise that I'll be available for everything from here on out," I said, "but I can promise I'll never lie to you again."

"Agreed." Lu shook my hand, sealing the deal. She glanced behind me, her gaze directed toward the shirtless firemen calendar Aunt Carol always kept hanging on the wall. That day, October 9, was circled, the word *Hoedown* written in Lu's cursive, but with an angry red gash crossing it out.

"You missed your homecoming," Lu said.

I looked around the salon, the second-most-familiar place in my life other than our log cabin: there were nail polish bottles piled high in boxes, a few pairs of those disposable pedicure sandals in the trash, and empty Diet Coke cans on the manicure station. Lu and Aunt Carol had been slowly packing up the salon, having to stomach that this chapter in their lives was closing. It had to have been an epically shitty past few weeks for Lu: betrayed by her boyfriend, by her best friend, by life. I could never let her down like that again. From here on out, Lu would always be a part of any list I ever made about what I wanted to do and who I wanted around me.

"No, I didn't," I finally said, meeting Lu's eyes. "I came home."

28.
✔ Start a Jay Agenda

The dirt parking lot was full as I pulled Dad's pickup into Blue Bluff Orchards. The huge Blue Bluff Blue Barn sat before us, row upon row of apple trees spreading out behind it. I always liked the order of this place, how clean and neat the trees all looked in perfect lines. It was one of the only places in Riverton that felt right to me, not just in how thoughtfully it was put together, but because it was the setting for all those great memories between me and Lu as we took home so many Best Costume awards. Hopefully I hadn't messed everything up so badly that we couldn't take home the trophy one more time.

"You ready for this?" I asked, turning to my best friend.

Lu slipped her half of the costume over her head, the red, round bulge smooshing against the dashboard. "Ready."

The greatest thing about the Great Behind was that it was versatile. When the two halves were spray-painted and pressed together, it looked just like an apple. Sure, the costume didn't really fit the *Roses Are Red, Violets Are Blue* theme, but I hoped we might be able to get some sympathy points dressing as an apple at an apple orchard.

We hopped out of the car to Lil Nas X and Billy Ray Cyrus's "Old Town Road" thumping out of the open doors of the barn. Hearing the crowd go wild for a favorite country song and the sounds of their feet pounding against the wooden floorboards made my heart clench. Maybe Riverton had a bigger place in my soul than I'd initially thought. I might have fallen back on a stereotype of my own, thinking the country and gay guys don't mix. It might not have been where I wanted to spend the rest of my life, but it was a part of me, the place I grew up, and the setting of so many memorable moments. In all the excitement about the Gay Agenda, I'd decided I could just forget Riverton entirely. But I realized then, that wasn't what I wanted. If my first few weeks in my new life taught me anything, it was that sometimes you'll make the wrong assumptions before you finally learn what's right.

I grabbed my half of the costume from the truck bed and threw it on. "Let's do this."

Lu grabbed my hand, the familiar feel of her pointy

nails pressing gently against my skin. Having her next to me after weeks apart put me at ease. We walked hand in hand toward the barn, the two halves of our costume seamlessly coming together to create a perfect apple. I was sure we still had a chance at the cash prize.

We walked through the blue barn doors and the music stopped, Mayor Wilkins sashaying up to the stage in a rose-patterned dress. "Y'all look so great tonight," she said. It was a funny thing how people who lived in the Inland Northwest country all their life had subtle Southern accents despite never having set foot in the South. "And I'm so excited to announce the winner of this year's Hoedown Costume Contest. Congratulations, Bob and Jackie Andrews! Come get your cash!"

We were too late. Bob and Jackie, the owners of the Andrews Green Nursery in Deer Park, took to the stage. Bob had on a suit covered in violets, and Jackie had on a skirt decked out with real rose petals. Their interpretation of the theme was pretty literal, but it probably took hours for them to glue each individual flower and petal.

My heart sank as the Andrewses grabbed their envelope full of cash. Lu could have really used that right now.

"Our winning streak is over," I mumbled. "Gawd, Lu, I'm so sorry."

"I'm not." Lu marched over to a table loaded with cider, a surprising spring in her step.

"But what about the prize money?" I asked.

Lu grabbed two cups and shoved one into my hands.

"Do you seriously think that would have solved our problems?"

"You could have used it for phone bills or paid part of the rent to get your trailer back or—"

Lu cut me off by nudging my cider to my lips. "Jay, like I said before, I'm not a helpless female. I don't need you to feel sorry for me. I just need you to be there by my side when things get tough." She held her cup toward me, waiting for a cheers. "Deal?"

It all seemed too easy. Like we could just brush the hard things aside, or power through life even if those things weren't resolved yet. But over the past month, my initial instinct had been to fix everything for Lu and to decide what was best for Albert, and look where that got me. Sometimes the best solution for a tough situation was just to name it, to say how much things sucked or were weird or difficult, and to figure out how to move forward together. Even if that meant the suckiness and weirdness and difficulty wouldn't change.

So I decided to accept that our life was new, that it had difficulties we hadn't expected before I moved away, and clicked my cup against Lu's. "Deal."

"Besides," Lu said, "Ruth Mortimer is going to let us stay in her RV. She may have antiquated ideas about how women should behave, but at least she has a heart for people going through rough times. Next year, things will be better."

She had a glint in her eye, something she hadn't had

for a while when talking about the future.

"Why is that?" I asked.

"Because you're looking at the most recent winner of the Washington State College Journalism Association scholarship. My piece on the bus-driver gender pay gap won! I didn't even know it'd been submitted, but the *Riverton Reporter* crew had my back. My first year of college is paid for as long as I stay in state and declare journalism as my major."

"Lu!" I lunged forward and pulled her as close as our apple would allow. "Why didn't you tell me?"

Lu rolled her eyes. "Because someone made it our MO to keep things from each other this year, remember?"

"I deserved that."

"You did." Lu chugged her drink and tossed the cup into the trash. "Now let's hoedown!"

We danced our asses off. Or I should say, we danced our apples off. We grapevined, we do-si-doed, we line danced. I might have become a city boy, but I was more than happy to get a little bit country from time to time.

Between the dances and more cups of cider than you can count, we talked about everything. I told Lu about Albert and Max and Reese and how my boobery extended to them too. I told her about Tony and losing my virginity and how I had become this horny unleashed beast. I told her about Albert being able to share his soul with a kiss and how epic it would be when we had sex, but I definitely could and would wait for him. I told her about Mom and Dad and our new life and not missing Eastern Washington one bit, but missing Lu with every bit I was made of.

Lu told me about how hard things had been, about sleeping in the back office with Aunt Carol, about just barely being able to keep themselves afloat. She told me with Ruth Mortimer's help they'd have some space to get back on their feet. She told me how Aunt Carol was thinking she'd wait until Lu graduated, then move to Spokane and get a salon job there. And with her new scholarship, Lu was certain the year would turn out way better than it had started. I promised I would be there for her whenever she needed me. Always.

We laughed until we were in tears, and we cried some real tears too, but thankfully people just thought our faces were dripping with sweat from dancing so hard. You could have made the sappiest montage of us holding one another, throwing honey sticks at each other, and laughing hysterically. Essentially, we were just like one of those cheesy movies where two estranged friends become besties again. I didn't want it to end. But we eventually drove back to the salon, where neither of us could keep our eyes open. I woke up curled in a sleeping bag next to Lu in the back office.

That feeling of contentment and ease from the night before wobbled. I knew I had to get back to Seattle. It'd be a nearly six-hour drive, and I still had some homework due the next day that I had to finish. If my grades dropped on top of the detention I'd received the past week, Dad would totally kill me. But what shook me hardest was having to be so far apart from Lu when we were heading into the rest of the most monumental year of our lives. It had already been a shaky start, and I wanted to get us on solid ground. If there was one thing I knew could do that, it was a list:

LU LOVE LIST

1. Digital Saturday sleepovers are reinstated immediately (with make-up days if something comes up).

2. Instant updates on any new milestones (<u>actual</u> first boyfriends; major kissing moments; texts in ALL CAPS if anyone ever hears the L-word or says it to someone else).

3. Apply to the same colleges together (allowing for this year to be just a small hiatus apart if we both get into the same school).

It wasn't as good as being face-to-face, but it was a start.

"I think there's now a permanent track of my snot on your shoulder," I said to Lu as I pulled out of our final hug. The driver's-side door to Dad's pickup was open, but no part of me wanted to climb in and leave Lu again.

"It almost matches my favorite color," Lu said. She'd redone her manicure before we left for the hoedown, and she held her neon-green nails next to the streak. Yes, it was gross, but I'd have taken any and all snot talk to make the moment last longer.

"Speaking of your favorite color . . ." I reached into the truck and pulled out the tote I'd made in Fashion Design. "I made you something."

Lu squeezed the bag to her chest. "I love it!"

"There's something inside," I said.

Lu pulled out the envelope and looked questioningly at the airline gift card inside. "What is this for?"

"I know it won't fix what's been going on lately, but come visit me whenever you can take a weekend off from the diner. You deserve a break."

Lu leaped at me and flung her arms around my neck. We stood there in each other's arms, and I realized it felt just as good as Albert's kiss. Just as loving, just as tender, but in its own special way.

Aunt Carol's nose blowing practically sounded like an airhorn, bringing us back to reality. She watched us through the window with tears in her eyes, that box of Kleenex clutched in her hands again.

"You can always depend on Carol to lighten the mood, can't you?" Lu laughed softly and pointed toward the truck. "Okay. Get in there already. It's not like this is goodbye." She tapped the envelope with the gift card against my nose. "Boop."

"Seriously, come whenever you want," I said. "Any time is a good time."

"Headline news: I love you, Jay."

I smiled. "Love you too, Lu."

JAY'S APOLOGY AGENDA

1. ~~Give Max a chance to redeem himself.~~ ✓
2. ~~Show Reese I actually have a heart.~~ ✓
3. ~~Let Albert know he's more than a list.~~ ✓
4. ~~Have Lu's back again.~~ ✓

The rain started as soon as I got over Snoqualmie Pass. It gushed the entire rest of the drive, an hour and a half in a torrential downpour. During the past week, the Seattle rain had really been reflecting my mood: dark and dreary. But that day, it felt different. Cleansing. Like the lying ass I had been was washed away so that I could just be Jay again. I'd been through a lot, grown a lot, done a lot that I had been fantasizing about for years as the statistical anomaly of the only out queer kid at RHS. But like my homecoming theme said, everything was so much clearer in hindsight. Turned out, I didn't need a Gay Agenda, I just needed a *Jay* Agenda. Being gay was a part of me, and I deserved to experience and enjoy all those firsts. But being gay wasn't the only part of me that mattered. I had old friends and new ones, parents who cared for me, a guy who I really liked and liked me back, a whole new city that still needed exploring, college applications—the list went on and on. And as the epic crash and burn of the Gay Agenda proved, life doesn't always go as planned, even with a list. No matter what the universe threw my way, I just needed to remember to be me.

"Jay and proud," I said, and immediately cracked up. That was a Digimals name Albert would love.

The rain still hadn't let up when I finally made it back to Seattle. The neighborhood was packed, so I had to park a couple blocks away from our duplex, and *of course* I didn't have an umbrella. I ran to the house as fast as I could, but when I turned into the walkway leading up to our doorstep, I stopped right in the middle of a puddle.

A VSB was waiting under the awning at the front door, his back to me.

"Albert."

He turned. "You're soaking wet. Haven't you learned yet you always need an umbrella in this city?" He grabbed a handle poking out of his jacket pocket and pulled out his brother's Mario umbrella. Albert snapped it open and jogged toward me, bursts of water splashing around his feet with each step.

"Mario always saves the day," I said when Albert moved the umbrella over my head. The light coming through the red material tinged us both in a pink glow.

"The hero is really the guy at the controller," Albert said. He motioned toward his fingers clutching the handle. "So, I guess that would be me."

"My plumber in shining armor."

Albert laughed, that dimple lighting up my soul. He stepped closer. Our noses nearly touched. "We missed you last night."

"Sorry I couldn't be there," I said. "How was homecoming?"

Albert shrugged. "Eh. Actually, it isn't over yet."

"What do you mean?"

Albert threw the umbrella to the side, rain drenching us as he wrapped his arms around my waist. "There's still one more dance."

We stood there swaying, sopping wet, kissing softly, slowly, deeply, dancing to nothing but the sound of the rain.

I realized then that there was one other thing on the Gay Agenda I didn't want to let go. It would make a great addition to my new and improved list.

JAY AGENDA

1. Become part of a super-queer, super-tight framily.
2. Make sure I get my daily dose of Lu.
3. Fall in love with a boy.

Fifty-five percent of all people fall in love for the first time between the ages of fifteen and eighteen. That day, kissing in the rain, was I ready to cross first love off my agenda?

Not quite.

But I didn't think it would take too long.

Acknowledgments

In true Jay fashion, these acknowledgments wouldn't be right unless we put them in a list.

JASON JUNE'S THANK-YOU AGENDA

1. Tear-soaked, ugly cry thank you to the people who made my novel dreams a reality

This book might just have my name on it, but it wouldn't be here without the passion and guidance of so many people. To Brent Taylor, you are the dream hustler agent that I can always feel pushing me forward with love and ambition. Thank you for all the calls to chat about the little things (like our favorite reality shows and Coach bags to buy next) and the big (how that reality dating show can inspire my next work, and how we'll accomplish every single item I have on my career agenda). To my brilliant editor, Megan Ilnitzki, for getting what I was trying to do with Jay's story from the start. Every single note you gave rang in my soul, answering without question that editor soul mates are for sure a thing. To Ricardo Bessa, for this epic cover that made me gasp and cry and remember what it was like to fall in love for the first time simply through the look between Jay and Albert. To Ivan Leung, for making this a better story with your thoughtful feedback. To David DeWitt, Sabrina Abballe, Katie Dutton, Sam Benson, and to the whole Harper team for making *Jay's Gay Agenda* a reality, from marketing to design to publicity to sales. I heart you all so much. Special shout-out to senior production editor Laura Harshberger for making sure the layout of this whole book filled with lists looked perfect, and to the fracking amazing Maya Myers and Lana Barnes for copy editing a whole treasure trove of mistakes.

2. Extra-long hugs to my loving and supportive framily

I don't know how I ever could have gotten to this moment without the multitude of friends to talk me through the odd mood swings that come from grappling with people who only live in my head. To all my writer friends who have written with me, read my work, cheered me on, or given me the best critiques that I can put in nifty to-do lists: Shruti Saran, Cate Berry, Aimee Thomas, Christina Soontornvat, Gene Brenek, Andrew Thomas, Sean Petrie, Debbi Michiko Florence, Kim Turrisi, Mackenzi Lee, Carrie Jones, Cynthia Leitich Smith, all the AAWs, Lori Snyder, Kat Shepherd, Peter McCleery, Anthony Piraino, Deb Beauchamp, Laura Gehl, Lori Richmond (ohmigawd *Porcupine!*), Camille Andros, Tara Luebbe, and all the

21ders (we're really doing it!). To the framily that's been with me through the most transformative decade of my life, sharing in my successes and helping me grow after my failures: Andrew Gruver, Michael Calabro, Nic Marlin, Todd Williamson, Mike Belyea, Travis Sablas, Enrique Sapene, Danny Garcia, Candis Cayne, Katey O'Regan, Hannah Blaylock, Justin Wakefield, Benjamin Dougharty, Bayne Gibby, and Sara Sargent.

3. All kinds of gratitude to those who've shown me the way

I am so lucky to know a multitude of amazing women who saw something in me when I was trying to get my start as a writer. My whole trajectory into children's literature wouldn't have started unless the stars aligned and introduced me to Jen Rofé. Jen, you are my mentor, sister, and friend, and I look up to you more than you know. To Stacy McAnulty and Jill Esbaum for making me believe I could be published someday. To Erin Murphy and Tricia Lawrence for giving me that first chance and writer framily. To Annie Nybo for getting my humor and saying yes. To Bethany Hegedus for boosting me up and giving me the tools to become a better writer. To Tina Love and Jackie Stallcup for cheering me on not only through my master's program, but to this very day.

4. Extra love to the booksellers and authors who inspire me

To Joy Preble for being such a vocal cheerleader and having

my back. To the amazing booksellers at Brazos Bookstore, BookPeople, and Auntie's Bookstore for making me feel like I was a part of your teams and welcoming me into your communities. To all the authors who took the time to read Jay's story, blurb it, and share your soul-boosting feedback with me: Becky Albertalli, Kalynn Bayron, Ronni Davis, Mason Deaver, Emma Lord, L. C. Rosen, Phil Stamper, Aiden Thomas, and Julian Winters. I can't thank you enough for making me feel so seen and supported. To all the queer writers out there, thank you for paving the way and welcoming me with open arms. It is an act of love and bravery to write openly about sexuality and gender identity, and I appreciate every word you've put to the page to make this a better world.

5. Don't forget where you came from

I wouldn't be where I am today if it wasn't for my amazing family who has been by my side since day one. To Ali, Andie, Cam, and Nina, for always being there, I still get that little-kid thrill when I get to see my cousins. To Krystal, Luke, Scott, and Sherra, for embracing our crew and becoming such important parts of it. To all the aunts and uncles, who are really just other versions of my parents, there is a bit of each of you in me, and I love being a puzzle of your zaniness. To Gramps, for being the ever-watching, always thoughtful, zinger-and-love-filled originator of our family. To Grandma Joan, I can still see you setting up that typewriter for me when I was eight. Zach, I'm so lucky to have you as a big brother. I know I didn't say it a lot growing up when I screamed my head off at you or tried and failed to make you the victim of payback pranks, but I look up to you so much. At least half of the things I've accomplished so far are because of your example. To all the Murrays, who have made me a part of your family from day one, I love y'all so much and I'm so proud to be a part of your ranks. To my nieces and nephews, who make me so happy to be your Auntie Uncle. Dad, I will never forget the hours you spent reading *Dinotopia* to me. Those nights left me so amazed by made-up worlds and set me on the track to becoming a writer. Mom, I hope you can see that the badass that is Tami Collier is entirely inspired by you. Your determination to achieve everything you wanted in life, and your ability to bring as many people as possible along with you, set such a far-reaching example that influences every decision I make. Mom, you've had this innate ability to see my heart in every stage of life. When I told you I was gay, when I told you I was genderqueer, you only ever responded with love and instantly acknowledged how I was just being me. That understanding and knowing I could work through the messy stages of figuring myself out in front of you gave me the strength I needed to actually do it.

6. Shout-out to the amazing readers who picked up this book

I'm looking at you. Yes you, the one holding Jay and his world and these words in your hand. I am so unbelievably grateful to you for taking time out of your life to read what I wrote. When I was a lonely gay kid growing up in Eastern Washington, I never thought that it would be possible to write this story and share it. Know that no matter where you are on the planet, no matter what boxes or stereotypes society wants to force you into, no matter whether you're certain about your sexuality and gender or still figuring it out, your life is worthy of a story (or two or three or as many as your heart can contain). I see you, I'm so thankful for you picking up this book, and I can't wait to read your stories someday too.

7. Realize there are no words to truly express how I feel about the love of my life

Jerry, this section is dedicated entirely to you. You have never once wavered in your support of my career and have always pushed me to make the decisions that are best for achieving my dreams. There is no doubt in my mind that I would not be here making real-life books if I didn't have you by my side. In any and every agenda I make, you will always be on it. I love you.